BLACK BOX

www.transworldbooks.co.uk

New York Times and *USA Today* bestselling author Cassia Leo loves her coffee, chocolate, and margaritas with salt. When she's not writing, she spends way too much time watching old reruns of *Friends* and *Sex and the City*. When she's not watching re-runs, she's usually enjoying the California sunshine or reading – sometimes both. She is the author of the ***Shattered Hearts*** series (*Relentless*, *Pieces of You*, *Bring Me Home*). She is also the author of the hugely popular *Luke* and *Chase* series.

Chat with her on Facebook:
www.facebook.com/authorcassialeo or
Twitter: www.twitter.com/AuthorCassiaLeo

Or you can follow her blog at www.cassialeo.com to stay up to date on new releases and giveaways.

Thanks for reading!

By Cassia Leo

ABANDON
BLACK BOX

The Shattered Hearts series

RELENTLESS
PIECES OF YOU
BRING ME HOME

BLACK BOX

Cassia Leo

CORGI BOOKS

TRANSWORLD PUBLISHERS
61–63 Uxbridge Road, London W5 5SA
A Random House Group Company
www.transworldbooks.co.uk

BLACK BOX
A CORGI BOOK: 9780552171120

First published in Great Britain
in 2014 by Transworld Digital
an imprint of Transworld Publishers
Corgi edition published 2014

A CIP catalogue record for this book
is available from the British Library.

Addresses for Random House Group Ltd companies outside the UK
can be found at: www.randomhouse.co.uk
The Random House Group Ltd Reg. No. 954009

Penguin Random House is committed to a sustainable future for our business, our readers and our planet. This book is made from Forest Stewardship Council® certified paper.

Printed and bound in Great Britain by Clays Ltd, Elcograf S.p.A.

Typeset in 12/15pt Adobe Caslon by
Kestrel Data, Exeter, Devon.

2 4 6 8 10 9 7 5 3 1

For anyone who has ever felt like Mikki

Chapter One

January 8th
Mikki

The moment you realize you're going to die is nothing like I imagined it would be. I imagined a deep internal struggle coupled with a visceral, physical response – fight or flight. But there's no fighting this. I'm going to die.

It's possible that everyone on this plane is going to die. I wonder if they feel this overwhelming sense of peace, or if the squeal of the plane engine has drowned out all their thoughts.

He grabs the oxygen mask as it drops from the compartment and he's yelling something as he puts the elastic band over my head. He pulls his own mask over his head then he grabs my hand and looks me in the eye. There's no panic in his eyes. Maybe he feels this same calm I'm feeling. Or maybe he just wants me to know that he loves me.

He loves me.

Or maybe the look in his eyes is his way of telling me he trusts that whatever happens to us in the next few seconds was meant to be.

Fate.

I used to think fate was for religious nuts and people who were too afraid to take their fate into their own hands. Now I know the truth.

Chapter Two

January 3rd
Mikki

Rina,
Please don't look for me. You probably won't find me. This shouldn't come as a surprise to anyone, and please don't blame yourselves. I'm just tired. Trying to cope . . . trying to forget . . . It's not enough any more. I just want to close my eyes and know that it will all be over soon. There's nothing anyone could have done. You've all done more than enough. I hope you all find peace knowing I am no longer suffering. I love you guys. Tell Meaghan I leave her my black box.
Mikki

I used to write long suicide letters, but I don't see the point in it any more. If I'm going to leave this world a better place, I don't want to leave behind a ten-page letter detailing all my emotional baggage. Besides, most of the people who know me, the ones close enough to read the letter, already know how screwed up I am.

I tuck the note inside a plastic baggie and seal it tightly, then I lift my bedroom window an inch and lay the bagged note on the window sill. I shut the window tight to trap the note there.

Taking one last look around the bedroom, I smile as I think of how much I won't miss this house. The pink tulip-shaped knit cap my best friend Rina bought for me in Holland sits on top of my dresser. I've only worn it once, the day she brought it back for me from her family vacation last summer. I was in High Point Treatment Center at the time, in the dual diagnosis unit because I'm one of the special cases that needed treatment for attempted suicide *and* drug detox.

'You look awfully cheerful for someone who's traveling alone.' Meaghan's green eyes follow my suitcase as I drag it behind me, violently bumping along the stairs.

My sister is seventeen, but she's not stupid. She knows the signs, which is why I'm trying my hardest not to exhibit the typical suicidal behavior. I didn't give away all my belongings. I'm not traveling light. I have tried not to appear too chipper over the last couple of days. Yes, it feels amazing to have a plan. It feels like a ten-ton slab of cement has been lifted off my chest. I can breathe. I can think about the future without the crippling anxiety and depression that comes with not knowing if the pain will ever end.

But I can't let Meaghan or my parents see how ridiculously relieved I'm feeling. They've seen that behavior too many times. The last time I made plans to die, three months ago, my mom saw the signs and followed me to the hotel room where I was going to hang myself. The time before that, I swallowed a bottle of pills in my uncle's bathroom. It was my cousin Gertie who noticed I was acting too happy. She told my Uncle Cort, 'Mikki is smiling again.' Uncle Cort broke down the bathroom door and that's when I ended up in High Point. That's also when I swore I wouldn't commit suicide anywhere that someone could find me.

'Cheerful?' I repeat Meaghan's adjective as I pull up the telescoping handle on the suitcase and roll it across the tiled foyer toward the front door. 'More like nervous as hell. I've never flown without Mom.'

Meaghan yanks her green parka out of the coat closet and pulls it on over her hoodie. 'I'll take that.' She pulls the hood of the parka over her long, brown hair and grabs my carry-on bag.

I open the door and we both suck in a sharp breath when we're blasted with a flurry of freezing winter air. The snow sticks to my face and I quickly close the front door so it doesn't get inside the house.

'Jesus fucking Christ. It's colder than a witch's tit out here. They're going to cancel the flights if this shit keeps up,' Meaghan says as we carefully descend the front steps. My dad covered the steps in his special mixture of salt and sand, but it's not foolproof.

'I have to at least show up. I saved up three months' paychecks for this fucking ticket.'

Meaghan opens the wooden front gate and the cab driver scurries out of the car to help us with the bags. As he stuffs the bags into the trunk, I turn to Meaghan and she's crying. Something tells me she knows. But she would stop me if she knew – wouldn't she?

'Why are you crying? It's just a job interview. I'm coming back in four days.'

'I know.' She wraps her arms around my waist and squeezes me so tight it hurts. I wish I could make myself cry. 'I'll miss you. Bring me back a hot actor.'

'I will.'

We hug like this for far longer than normal. It takes every bit of self-control in me not to tell her that everything will finally be okay when I'm gone.

At last she pulls away and punches my arm. 'Get the fuck out of here.'

'I love you, too,' I say, sliding into the backseat of the cab. My heart stutters as I look at the house I grew up in for the last time.

The driver slams my door shut then scrambles around the front of the car and gets into the driver's seat. 'Logan?' he asks as he turns up the heater.

'Yeah, Terminal B.' I watch Meaghan scurry into the house to escape the cold. Her heart will heal. She'll be okay.

I reach into my handbag and pull out my gloves, then I spot the bottle of pills. I lay the pink gloves on my lap and reach into my purse for the bottle. On the outside, this is just a normal bottle of anti-psychotic meds. On the inside, this is my self-prescribed emergency meth stash. Each capsule is carefully filled with one dose.

I quit meth last week. Something about booking a plane ticket to Los Angeles to end my life gave me the fortitude to face the world without drugs. Besides, I was never really addicted. I just didn't want to quit because it made me feel as if I were in control. But, even though I'm technically no longer a meth-head, I brought my emergency stash in case I lose my nerve to get on that plane.

I'm going to Los Angeles, specifically to the Pacific Ocean, to down this bottle of pills then swim out into the open ocean until I can't swim any more. The water is so cold this time of year, my body will be numb and exhausted by the time I reach the point of no return. I won't be able to fight it when the water enters my lungs. Plus, I'll be so far out in the ocean, the odds of my body being found will be slim. My parents won't have to identify me.

The cab driver turns the volume up on the radio and 'Take You Higher' is playing. The dance beat buoys my mood and I allow myself to smile for the first time in days. I set the bottle of pills back inside my purse and pull my gloves on as I sit back.

Fifty minutes of horrendous traffic later, the cab pulls up in front of Terminal B and one of the two guys working at curbside check-in rushes over to help us.

The cab driver gently places my suitcase on the curb and the skycap waits patiently to help me inside. I pay the driver and he mutters a quick thank-you before he hurries back inside the warm cab.

'Holy shit,' I whisper, yanking my faux-fur-lined hood over my head.

'I ain't seen it like this in years. I bet they're already canceling flights,' the skycap says as he takes my carry-on bag and we race toward the automatic sliding doors. He leaves my bags and me just inside the doors then he jogs back to his station outside in the freezing cold. What a terrible day to have an outdoor job.

I push my hood back and begin peeling off my pink knit gloves. The line at the check-in counter snakes across the floor as everyone watches the TV monitors for updated flight information.

'Canceled,' a voice says behind me.

I whip my head around and find a guy with messy brown hair sticking out the front of his knit cap. He's sitting on a gray suitcase with his phone in his hand and a guitar case propped up against the wall behind him. Something about him looks familiar, though I'm pretty certain he's the kind of guy I would not forget if we'd met before.

'You can probably still catch a cab if you leave now,' he continues as he thumb-types on his phone.

'Then why aren't you running outside to catch a cab?'

'I'm in no hurry to go back.'

I stare at the curb outside just as another cab pulls

up to drop off another unknowing passenger. I told Meaghan I'd go home if they canceled the flight, but that's the last place I want to go right now.

'Yeah, me neither.'

The guy looks up from his phone and smiles. 'Yeah, you also have to check in to get your flight rescheduled.'

'Yeah, that too.' I try not to blush. Something about his smile makes me feel naked.

Chapter Three

January 3rd
Crush

The flattened penny gets warm as I rub it between my thumb and index finger. I've memorized every dip and rise in the design: Hillman's Diner, established 1923. My grandfather bought me this flattened penny from a vending machine at Hillman's Diner when I was ten years old, a couple of months before he died. The crushed penny is one of three gifts from my grandfather that I've carried with me everywhere since his death. Well, actually, the third gift, his only copy of *Black Box*, has been missing for nearly four years. I guess the book is technically not missing if I willingly gave it to a stranger, but it's definitely gone for ever.

The flattened penny now serves as a guitar pick – my lucky pick – and it looks as if I'm going to be spending a lot of time with it over the next few days since my flight to Los Angeles was just canceled. Staring at the monitor above the airline check-in counter, I try to imagine what my grandfather would say in a situation like this; flight canceled right when I've finally decided to take this music gig to the next level. Grandpa Hugh would probably say something like, 'You can't choose the road you take; you can only hope to avoid the pot-holes.'

As much as I loved Grandpa Hugh, that's a ten-ton load of bullshit. I don't believe my life is already planned out. I refuse to believe that I don't have control over my worthless fate. I'm not a brilliant man like my grandfather, but I am a pragmatic man. And life has shown me all too often that there is no rhyme or reason to the cruelty inflicted upon humanity.

The glass doors slide open and a girl rushes in with a skycap, bringing with them a swirl of freezing air. The skycap leaves her luggage just inside the entrance doors to the terminal then he rushes outside to his curbside post. She's tall and thin, and when she pushes back her hood I get a strange feeling in my belly. Something about her looks familiar. Maybe we shared a class at Harvard. No, I would definitely remember if she were in one of my classes.

She continues to stare at the monitors above the check-in counter in a daze. I feel the need to help her. 'Canceled,' I say, pulling my phone out of my back pocket to type a response to Harlow's text message.

My older sister Harlow is the quintessential over-achiever. She graduated from MIT four years ago and now works on the West Coast as a social media advisor to the CEO of one of the largest tech companies in Silicon Valley. I'm not supposed to disclose the name of the company to anyone. She almost made *me* sign a non-disclosure agreement, that's how serious she is about her job.

But, as serious as she is about her job, she's even more serious about staying in touch. She's a social media addict. She sends me at least ten messages, tweets, or comments per day. She's able to multitask better than anyone I've ever known. She's married to a geek she met at MIT and they have their first baby on the way in less than three months, which hasn't slowed her down one bit. She's been trying to convince me to go to Los Angeles to record this demo for years. She found out my flight was canceled before I did, so now she's texting me to make sure I don't allow this to stop me from going to L.A.

Harlow: I swear to fucking God, if you back out on this I'll plant naked pics of Mom on your phone.
Me: Lol. I'm not backing out. And if you do that, I'll gouge my eyes out. Do you want to be responsible for blinding me?

I glance up and the girl is looking at me strangely. And now, seeing her face straight on, she looks even more familiar. 'You can probably still catch a cab if you leave now,' I add because she looks confused about what she's supposed to do now that her flight is canceled.

'Then why aren't you running outside to catch a cab?'

Her voice has a hard edge to it, but it's wrapped in soft uncertainty. She doesn't *sound* familiar, but something about her lightly freckled skin makes my chest ache. 'I'm in no hurry to go back.'

No need to elaborate. She doesn't need to know that I'm leaving Massachusetts because I'm tired of screaming into a void. I'm exhausted from all the talking I've done that hasn't done a damn thing to make anyone understand me better. Not my shrink, my family, or my friends; no one understands what I've seen. I'm almost glad for that.

I'm not going to record this demo for fame and fortune. I've got plenty of fortune and I have no interest in fame. I'm going because I don't know what else to do at this point. And a small part of me thinks that maybe if I get a record deal, I'll never have to speak to anyone again.

I look down at my phone to read Harlow's newest text:

Harlow: Geez. Do you really have to make it so easy for me to dish out meaningless platitudes?

'Yeah, me neither,' the girl replies.

I look up from my phone screen and smile, trying not to chuckle. 'You also have to check in to get your flight rescheduled.'

She smiles and her cheeks blush crimson. 'Yeah, that too.'

She covers her face with both her hands as she shakes her head. She's probably embarrassed that she's blushing in front of a stranger. I can tell by the obviously dyed black hair that hangs above her emerald eyes and the tattoos on her fingers that she's not the type of girl who blushes often.

'Go away,' I say and she uncovers her face.

'What?'

'The tattoos on your fingers.' I point at her hands as they drop to her side.

She glances at her fingers. 'Oh, yeah, I got those when I was young and stupid. You know how that is.'

My eyebrows knit together in confusion. 'How old are you?'

She swallows hard as she turns away to look at the flight monitors again. 'Older than . . . Nineteen.'

'Nineteen? So you think you're past the young and stupid phase already?'

She doesn't look at me. She continues to stare at the monitors for a moment before she grabs the handle on her rolling suitcase. 'I have to check in.'

She gets in line behind thirty-some other bodies with suitcases, but she's not a body. She's a soul. That much is plainly obvious by the way she stands in line with her eyes closed, thinking. Maybe she's silently screaming into the void.

I text Harlow back:

Me: Your meaningless platitudes are the bread that feeds my soul. Never give up. Keep on trucking. It's not about the destination, it's about the journey. Always separate your whites. And so on. See ya soon.

I tuck my phone into my back pocket and stare, unabashedly, as the soul makes her way through the snaking line and half-heartedly argues with the check-in clerk about something. She tries to hold her head high as she lugs her suitcase and carry-on bag toward me.

'Did they give you a hotel voucher?' she asks me.

I shake my head. 'Nope. I'm only thirty minutes away. They're only offering vouchers to layover customers.'

She sighs heavily. 'Shit.' She turns to stare at the monitors again and I can feel the desperation pulsing off her.

She doesn't want to go home. Neither do I.

'Hey, how about we go get a cup of coffee while we figure out what the fuck we're going to do?' She turns to me and I see a glimmer of fear in her eyes. 'I'm not trying to hit on you. I'm just not ready to go home yet.'

She doesn't look convinced, but she must really not want to go home because she holds out her hand to me. 'I'm Mikki.'

I stand up from my suitcase and grab her hand. I'm six-foot-one and this girl is almost as tall as me in flats. For some reason, I find this extremely attractive.

I take her hand in mine and give it a gentle shake. 'Crush.'

'Crush?' she repeats. 'That's your name?'

'Not my birth name, but it is my legal name. I had it changed a few years ago.'

'Crush.' She tilts her head as she stares at me. 'Cool name.'

'Now it's my turn to blush.'

She lets go of my hand and her smile disappears. 'I don't have money for a cab.'

'I'll take care of it.'

The uncertainty returns to her features and I can't fight the feeling that I know this girl from somewhere. If I tell her she looks familiar, she'll think this is just a creepy come-on from a stranger.

'We'd better hurry up and get a cab before this mob beats us to it.'

She nods as she pulls her pink gloves back on over her tattooed fingers. She follows me as I grab my suitcase and guitar case. We head outside and walk around the curved sidewalk until we find an empty cab pulling away from the terminal. I flag it down and the driver helps us load our luggage into the trunk. We rush into the backseat and my nose and ears are already frozen from the few minutes we spent outside. I look at Mikki and her nose and lips are so red they're almost purple.

'Render Coffee on Columbus,' I instruct the cab driver and he immediately drives away from the terminal.

'What's that?' she asks, settling back into the seat as she begins removing her gloves.

I grab her hands to stop her and she flinches at my touch. 'Sorry, but you'll want to keep those on. Render is just a few miles from here. They have the best coffee in Boston. Have you ever been to Boston?'

She crosses her arms, tucking her gloved hands under her arms as she gazes out the window. 'Only twice, when I was young.'

There she goes again. She's only nineteen, but she doesn't think she's young. What the hell has this girl gone through?

'Well, I'm going to get you the best fucking coffee in all of Boston. And maybe you can give me something in return?'

She turns to me, her face livid as if I've asked her to give me a blowjob.

'No, nothing like that,' I insist. 'I was thinking maybe you could . . . Oh, forget it.'

What the fuck is wrong with me? Why was I going to ask her to listen to my song?

She pulls her feet up onto the seat and hugs her knees. 'I just want to go to L.A. I'm so tired of this fucking place.'

'What's in L.A.?' I ask as she rests her chin on her knees.

She takes a deep breath and smiles. 'The rest of my life.'

Chapter Four

January 3rd
Mikki

The warm air circulating in the cab is stifling. My face is burning up and my hands instantly begin to sweat inside my pink gloves with the cutoff fingers. I want to take my gloves off, but this guy insists I keep them on. Why did I listen to him?

I lower my feet onto the floor of the cab and begin peeling off my gloves, trying not to glance at Crush to see if he's watching. I lay my hands flat on top of the gloves in my lap and smile as I remember the day I got the words 'GO AWAY' tattooed on my fingers. It was a few months after *the night of the party*. My shrink told me I need to stop referring to it as the night of the party, as if nothing of significance happened that night other than the party. As far as I'm concerned, nothing happened.

People want you to confront your past, stare down

your demons, and all that other bullshit. Most of them don't have the kind of demons I have breathing down my neck, so it's easy for them to dish out banal clichés on facing the past. I don't want to remember. I don't want to think about the night of the party. The more I think about it, the more control I surrender; the more I remember, the more pieces of myself I submit to them. I will remember only in the moments when I choose to remember, not when someone else snaps their fingers and tells me it's time to talk.

Talking is overrated.

And I'll be damned if I listen to some stranger about where and when to wear my gloves. I don't care how good-looking he is or how cute his name is. And if this asshole asks me any more awkward questions, I'm out of here. I can find a cheap motel to stay in near the airport.

I glance at Crush and he's staring out the window. I get a weird pang of guilt in my stomach as I realize he's not going to pressure me to keep the gloves on. I'm trying to make a point when there's no point to be made.

Fine.

I pull my gloves back on just as the cab begins to slow down in front of a café with a cute little sign hanging out front: Render Coffee. The name sounds vaguely familiar. I'm sure Rina may have talked about it before. She's probably even invited me to come here. She is ridiculously persistent in her attempts to get me out of the house.

Crush hands the cab driver a fifty-dollar bill for a twenty-four-dollar cab ride then tells him to keep the change. I roll my eyes as I scoot out of the backseat and my boots land in some fresh snow on the curb. Crush taps my hip for me to move out of his way and he steps out after me. The driver sets our bags and the guitar case on the curb and nods before he gets back inside the cab and drives off.

I should pull my hood up, but I'm frozen. Something about this whole situation feels weird.

'Why do you look confused?' Crush asks as he slides the handle of my carry-on bag over the telescoping handle of his suitcase.

How do you tell someone that going to a coffee shop feels weird because it feels too normal? I'm not used to normal.

'I don't get out much.'

My phone vibrates in my coat pocket and I curse myself for forgetting to turn off the vibrating ringtone. Crush looks confused by my response as I pull my phone out of my pocket and stare at it. The snow immediately melts on the screen and blurs the letters flashing in front of me.

'I should probably check it inside.'

He nods and I follow him up the eight concrete steps to the entrance of Render, amazed at how he makes hauling two pieces of luggage and a guitar case up a flight of stairs, and also holding the door open for me, look so fucking easy. He could probably carry the weight of the world on those shoulders. He flashes me a charming half-smile, as if he knows what I'm thinking. I brush past him, close enough to get a whiff of the warm scent wafting off his gray twill coat. He smells like a summer breeze in the middle of winter, and the scent stops me cold.

I blink furiously against the memory; *the tangy, metallic scent of blood . . . I can't see through the blood, but I can feel. I'm broken in every sense of the word.* I squeeze my eyes tightly and take another deep breath. I smell coffee now. Opening my eyes, I grit my teeth and blink a few more times, to completely clear the memory.

'Got some snow in my eyes,' I mutter when I notice the concerned look on his face.

The café is almost empty; just a couple of girls in hipster glasses hanging out at the bar counter overlooking the sidewalk, watching the snowfall. Looks like no one wanted to brave the storm for a cup of the best coffee in Boston. At least we have plenty of room to sit down with our luggage.

The glass pastry case is filled with untouched croissants, muffins, scones, and quiches. I don't eat this stuff unless Rina brings me something shitty from the local donut shop. People think it's weird that I'm nineteen and I don't drive. I don't understand what's so weird about that. I don't trust myself with a car.

Crush clears his throat and I tear my gaze away from the pastries. 'You hungry?'

'Are you buying?'

He purses his lips and shrugs adorably, and I finally notice his eyes. They looked dark in the terminal, but they're actually as green as mine. I've never seen anyone with eyes as green as mine, except for Meaghan.

'I did ask you to come here, so I guess I'm buying,' he replies.

I turn back to the pastry case and point my finger at a huge muffin with some kind of crumble topping. 'I'll take that and an iced mocha with extra caramel sauce,' I say to the guy behind the counter.

'Somehow, I am not at all surprised by that order,' Crush says, shaking his head as he peers over my shoulder into the pastry case. 'I'll take a breakfast bagel and a non-fat cappuccino.'

'Wow. You're way more boring than I thought you would be.'

He laughs as he pulls his wallet out of the back pocket of his jeans. 'Just wait until we sit down and I entertain you with the topic of my senior thesis.'

'That sounds like a threat.'

He shakes his head as he hands the barista his credit card. 'I guess that depends on how much you enjoy discussing the cross-cultural significance and dimensionality of emotion in music.'

He doesn't look at me as he waits for the guy to give him back his card. I get a strange feeling like he's waiting for me to judge him. 'I'm just a sophomore, so I haven't chosen my senior thesis.' *And I never will.* 'But I think the study of emotion in music is probably one of the coolest thesis topics I could ever imagine.'

He takes his credit card back from the barista then uses his finger to sign the white computer screen. 'Maybe I'm as interesting as you thought I'd be.'

Suddenly, my stomach feels jittery and my mouth goes dry. I want to reach into my purse and take a pill from my emergency stash, but something tells me this guy would know they're not medication. Then it hits me.

What if my parents sent this guy to keep an eye on me?

No, that's crazy. That's the kind of thought that will get me locked up again. But why else would he be this nice to me? He's way out of my league. He's 50 per cent rock star and 50 per cent Harvard.

'Are you okay?' he asks and I nod as I grab the handle of my suitcase and pull it toward the tables in the back of the café.

If I thought I had any chance of keeping up this charade for another two or three days, or however long it will take for this storm to pass, then I'd go home. But I've put too much work into this. I've been speaking with academic counselors and psychologists for weeks, building this elaborate lie of transferring from Massasoit to Santa Monica College. The purpose of this trip is for a job interview at a local youth center. It would have been easier to do the Federal Work Study program, but I thought they'd think I was more serious about putting the night of the party behind me if I told them I wanted to work with at-risk youth.

I take a seat at a table and it's a bit dreary in here with the glass ceiling of the patio enclosure covered in snow. Crush sets his guitar against the wall and moves both of our suitcases next to the case so they're out of our way. He takes a seat across from me and I quickly pull off my gloves and tuck them inside my purse. He removes his gray twill coat, but he keeps his green hoodie on.

He hangs his coat on the back of the chair and sits across from me. He stares at my hands for a few seconds before he looks up. 'Do we know each other?'

Chapter Five

January 3rd
Crush

Mikki sits back in the wooden chair and nothing about the tattoos on her fingers or the color of her eyes, or hair, are familiar. I can't grasp what it is about her, but I keep feeling as if I recognize something about her that no one would ever notice; like the curve of her neck or the sound of her breath. That's insane.

She chuckles softly as she crosses her arms over her chest. 'Is that your best pickup line?'

I smile back at her and shrug. I knew she would think this was a come-on. 'It doesn't matter if we know each other. We have plenty of time to rectify that. So what do you do? Do you work, go to school, raise hell?'

'All of the above. I work in the admin office of the community college where I also go to school.'

'You didn't tell me where you raise hell.'

Her eyes fall to the floor as she gently shakes her head. 'Why don't you tell me what *you* do? I mean, it's pretty obvious that you're a music major, but is that it?'

'Actually . . .'

The barista with the shaggy brown hair shows up with our food and coffee. He flashes us a tight smile as he sets everything down on the table.

'Cream and sugar are over there,' he says, pointing behind him, then he walks away.

Mikki grabs her iced mocha and takes a long draw from her cold beverage.

'I guess this is where I ask you why you're drinking an iced coffee during a blizzard, but I'd rather steer clear of clichés.'

She looks at me as she crudely tears her muffin in half then breaks a piece off the bottom and pops it into her mouth. 'You still haven't told me what you do besides school,' she says through a mouthful of muffin.

I push my bagel and cappuccino aside so I can lean forward and watch her up close as she devours her pastry. 'I told you, I'd rather steer clear of clichés.'

She takes a long sip of her mocha then sits back to put some more space between us. 'Are you calling yourself a cliché? What do you do, play guitar at local bars?' She leaves the top of the muffin untouched then pushes the plate away.

'You don't eat the muffin top?'

'Everybody loves the top of the muffin.' She casts a scathing glare in the direction of the muffin top.

'No one ever stops to think about the poor, neglected bottom.'

'Somehow, I have a feeling you're not being purposely contradictory.' Her hands are trembling as she reaches for her drink. 'Are you cold?'

The café is stiflingly hot, but I don't bother mentioning this. Something tells me she's not shaking with cold. She pushes her coffee aside without taking another sip then she eyes the muffin top as if she's considering compromising her principles to satisfy her hunger.

'No,' she replies, tucking her hands under the table.

I'm overcome with an intense urge to reach underneath the wooden surface and grab her hand.

'Why are you going to L.A.?' I ask, hoping the change of subject will help her relax. 'You said the rest of your life is waiting there. Does that mean you're moving there?'

I say a mental prayer that she's not going there to meet a guy. Not sure why I should care. I've known the girl for thirty seconds.

She stares at the table, a faint smile pulling at the corners of her mouth. 'A job interview.'

Her smile is hiding something and, truthfully, it looks a bit sinister. When she looks up from the table, she sees my unease and quickly casts her gaze downward as if she's ashamed. *What are you running from?* I want to ask.

'So why are *you* going to L.A.?' she asks, still staring at the table.

'To record a song.'

'For your thesis or to get rich and famous?'

'Both and neither.'

Finally, she looks up and in that one second I feel it again. This intense déjà vu.

'Don't tell me you're doing it for artistic purposes?'

I chuckle as I reach for my cappuccino. 'Do I look like the kind of guy who would do something for artistic purposes?'

'Are you deliberately trying to confuse me?'

'Excuse me?'

She shakes her head and looks away from me, toward the snow-covered foliage behind the café. Resting her hands on the table again, she closes her eyes and takes a slow breath.

There it is.

That's how I know her.

No fucking way. I have to be imagining this.

My chest constricts with the anger I've been unable to shake free of for the past three years. Gritting my teeth against the force of the memories, I try to keep myself from wishing it's her. If this is her, it doesn't look like she's coping well.

It can't be her. That would be way too much of a coincidence.

She opens her eyes and reaches for the purse she hung on the back of her chair. She plunges her delicate, tattooed hand inside and comes up with a prescription bottle of pills. Her hands are still trembling as she opens the bottle and shakes out one blue capsule.

She holds the capsule between her thumb and forefinger and holds it up for me to see. 'I'm bipolar. Is that sexy?' She pops the pill into her mouth and guzzles it down with some iced coffee. 'Why do you look like you just saw a ghost? Have you never heard someone admit to being mentally ill?'

'You remind me of someone I once knew . . . very briefly.'

I push my cappuccino aside and I can't even imagine eating the bagel now. I know this girl isn't her, but I've lost my appetite. That's the way these things go. Once you dredge up the memories you've spent years trying to bury, suddenly they're everywhere. There are two people I've been trying to put out of my mind for years: the first is Jordan and the second is her. Though I've failed miserably on both counts. Sometimes I wish I never listened to Harlow about going to L.A.

I began writing this song three years ago and worked on it every day for two years, until I gave up on it last year. It will never be perfect. There's something missing; something I'll probably never find, which is why I allowed Harlow to set up the meeting with Kane Bentley in L.A. to listen to the demo. It's time to put this song, and the memories, and the *longing* to rest – if that's even possible.

Harlow met Kane at a charity event. Without my consent, she used her irresistible charm and wit – and maybe the promise of some social media seminars – to get me what may be the most important meeting of my career. Kane is a producer who's worked with everyone from Michael Jackson to Lady Gaga. I have exactly four days to record and edit the demo before my meeting with Kane on Saturday. Every day the flights are delayed is one less day I have to record.

So after one year of avoiding certain streets, certain songs, certain people, last week I dug up the song from the archives of my laptop. I dusted off the acoustic-electric guitar that I put in storage because it reminded me too much of her. Then I warmed up my flattened penny and I haven't slept much since then. That's the way these things go.

'You don't remind me of anyone,' she says, standing from her chair. She begins scratching her head as she looks around the café. 'Where's the restroom?'

She scoops up her purse then disappears through a marked door in the corridor at the bottom of the steps leading to the patio enclosure. I pull my phone out of my pocket and see I have another text from Harlow and one from Bethany: a girl I slept with a couple of days ago, after Aidan's New Year's Eve party. I hardly know Aidan, though we shared a dorm last year before I moved off campus. Harlow is the only person who really knows me and not even she knows everything about me. A consequence of losing someone close to you is that you also lose a piece of yourself. And you never really know when it's safe to give away another piece.

I wait at least fifteen minutes, while carrying on a text conversation with Harlow, before I decide to check on Mikki. I make my way to the restroom door and listen for a few seconds. Hearing nothing, I knock three times.

Chapter Six

January 3rd
Mikki

The knocking on the door doesn't startle me. I sit on the toilet with my panties chained around my ankles, staring at the cream-colored walls. I've been in here a while, and the meth is finally kicking in; my heart is racing and my fingertips are starting to get a little cold and numb. I'm not breathing fast enough to keep up with my heart. That's okay. I like the numbness.

Grabbing my purse off the sink, I pull a large, sharpened safety pin out of an inner pocket. I gave this safety pin a name because he's my trusty little friend who I knew I could count onto make it through airport security. I call him Casper. I unclasp the safety pin and stare at the sharp point, the way it glimmers in the awful bathroom lighting. I press the point against the fair skin at the top of my thigh, almost where it meets my hip, then I drag it lightly across my skin. It stings a little, leaving a thin pink line that fills me with relief and revulsion. I dig the pin deeper into my skin and drag it across again, over the same pink line, applying more pressure this time. My stomach clenches inside me until I pull the pin away from my skin and let out a deep breath. Tiny red droplets of fresh blood bubble up from the scratch. I close my eyes as I cross my arms over my belly and double over.

The knocking has stopped. Hopefully, Crush has realized that he should just grab his fucking bagel and leave me, and my craziness, far behind.

Another knock. 'Miss, are you all right in there?'

Fuck. Crush has enlisted the help of the nerd behind the counter. I quickly get dressed and stuff the open safety pin into the pocket of my skinny jeans. Maybe it will prick me while I'm walking around looking for a place to sleep tonight. *Stupid storm.* What kind of cheap motel room am I going to get with $70 in my bank account?

I had to buy two plane tickets for this trip and both of those were canceled today. One of those flights has an overnight layover in Chicago and the other – the flight I was really going to take – was a direct flight that was supposed to land at LAX in five hours. The flight with the layover isn't supposed to land until 2:00 p.m. tomorrow. But now that all flights are canceled, my parents and Meaghan and Rina are going to start looking for me. Rina will find my letter. I can't wander the streets of Boston. It won't take long for the cops to spot a girl with black hair, tattoos on her fingers, and a scar running from the corner of her mouth to the point of her chin. I have to hole up somewhere until this storm passes.

A key slides into the lock and the bathroom door opens just as I'm drying my hands on a paper towel. 'Can't a girl take a piss in private?' I say, pushing past the nerd.

I walk right past Crush, ignoring him when he calls out to me. 'Where are you going?'

I want to shout back, *I need a cigarette before I become homicidal!* Pushing through the door, a flurry of icy wind blasts me in the face. I gasp and curse at the same time. 'Fucking shit!'

Crush appears behind me at the threshold looking a bit pissed off. 'What the fuck are you doing?'

'What does it look like I'm doing?' I reach for the pack of cigarettes in my coat pocket, but my pocket is missing and my wool coat doesn't feel like wool.

I'm not wearing my coat.

'Get in here before you freeze to death.'

My hands tremble as I stuff them into my jeans pockets in an attempt to cover up my moment of meth-induced mania. I step back inside, making sure not to touch him as he stands like a fucking stone column in the middle of the threshold. I can feel the embarrassment curling my shoulders as I attempt to retreat into myself. Why am I here with a complete stranger? And why is this stranger so fucking concerned with my safety? Offering me a cab ride and some breakfast, knocking on bathroom doors, chasing me out of coffee shops.

'What are you, some fucking superhero for freaks?' I mutter as he takes the seat across from me at the table.

'Super-freak?'

I smile reluctantly at this joke, but the moment he smiles back I feel sick to my stomach. I take a deep breath as a wave of regret overcomes me and the guilt comes. Whenever I'm high around friends or family, there's always a measure of guilt for not being totally present. But I don't know this guy. Why should I even care if he thinks I'm a bit weird or spacey?

Because, for some weird reason, he seems to care about me.

'That will be your nickname.' I reach for the discarded muffin top and break off a piece. 'Super-freak.'

He smiles, probably thinking I'm going to put the muffin in my mouth. 'Ah, hypocrisy flourishes in the face of hunger.'

I break up the muffin and watch it crumble from my fingertips onto the plate. 'I'm not eating it. I'm merely destroying it and everything it stands for.'

'What does the muffin stand for?'

'Conformity and exclusion. If you're not the best or the prettiest – or the tastiest – then you're worthless. That's what the muffin top stands for.'

'God,' he whispers. 'Can you be any more charming?'

'Maybe if I had a drink or two in me.'

'It's ten o'clock in the morning.'

'Yeah, and it's really fucking cold. So cold we may all be frozen to death by tomorrow morning. Do you want to spend the last day of your life worrying about the appropriate time to start drinking? Cause I'm pretty sure the appropriate time was about one hour ago when they canceled all the flights.'

He nods as he stands from the chair and begins to put on his coat. 'You make a good case. I will not be filing an appeal this time.'

I pull on my black wool coat and he leaves some cash on the table, then we grab our luggage and head for the door. Yanking the drawstrings on my hoodie as tight as I can, I brace myself for the inevitable blast of cold air. Crush exits ahead of me, presumably to absorb the brunt of the blast.

'I know a place just around the corner from here on Mass,' he shouts over the whoosh of the wind. 'You think you can make it? Looks to be at least four inches of snow on this pavement.'

'I'll let you know if I feel a bout of death coming on.'

We keep our heads down as we drag our suitcases down Columbus Avenue through the snow; or, at least, I attempt to. It takes about fifteen seconds of this for me to regret every single piece of clothing I packed in this suitcase in my grand scheme to appear normal. We're halfway down the block when the chest pains begin.

'Wait,' I wheeze, clutching my chest as I try to catch my breath.

'Do you have asthma?'

'No.' *Just meth-induced heart palpitations.*

He waits a couple of minutes for me to catch my breath, then, without a single word spoken, he grabs the handle of my suitcase and begins to drag it toward Massachusetts Avenue. I keep my head down and press my lips together to keep them warm – and to hide my smile.

We cross Mass Ave, passing a pizza place, and continue half a block before we turn right into a small side street that looks more like an alley. My heart is racing again. I shake my head, taking quick, shallow breaths to try to stave off a panic attack.

'Where are you taking me?' My voice is muffled by the fear flooding every vessel in my body.

'What?' he says, looking over his shoulder as he continues down the tiny street toward an empty parking lot.

'Where are we?' I shriek.

He stops and stares at me. 'Are you all right? I'm just taking you to this jazz club.' He points at the brick-faced building where a sign reads: Wally's Café. 'See?'

I draw in a long breath of freezing cold air, then I nod my head and continue after him. 'Isn't it a bit early to go to a jazz club?'

'I know the owner. If he's not there, the manager will be there. They don't officially open for another eight hours, but there's pretty much always someone here. They'll let us hang out and keep warm as long as we want.'

'How do you know the owner? Are you related to him or something?'

'No, Wally's is sort of a training ground for local musicians – particularly music students. It's one of the oldest and best jazz clubs in Boston and, if we stick around till six, you'll hear some of the best live music you've ever heard; guaranteed. Tonight is blues night.'

As he approaches the door to Wally's, I don't bother telling him I've never actually heard live music before.

He has to knock a few times before someone finally shouts through the door, 'Who is it?'

'It's Crush!' he shouts back. 'And it's colder than a Yankee's heart out here. Open up!'

The door swings open, revealing a tall, thin black man in a blue and white plaid dress shirt and gray chinos. 'Get your butt in here, boy. You're letting the snow in.'

Crush quickly pulls the suitcases and the guitar case into the club and I smile at the man as he holds the door for me to enter. Crush rolls the luggage into a corner near the entrance of the dark club, dusting off the snow before he turns to me.

'Leroy, this is my friend Mikki. Mikki, this is Leroy. He manages the club.'

I nod at Leroy and he scrunches up his eyebrows. 'Nice to meet you too, young lady.'

I hate talking to strangers. I'm not sure how Crush

has been able to break through that social anxiety, but Leroy is making me nervous. I feel as if he's expecting me to say something clever or funny, just because I walked in with Crush.

'Sorry. I . . . it's nice to meet you.' I hold out my hand to him.

He pauses for a moment as he looks at the tattoos on my fingers, then he smiles as he shakes my hand. 'Y'all can go hang out at the bar. Jimmy's coming in about an hour. He'll fix y'all a drink. I'm going to get this damn schedule worked out. Third Monday in a month I got a cancellation.'

The club is tiny and very dark, but it's warm; and not just because the heat is working. Something about this place feels . . . safe.

We sit down on some stools at the bar, which runs almost the entire length of the narrow room. I take off my coat and lay it across the stool next to me and Crush does the same.

'When Jimmy gets here, he'll make you the best damn martini you've ever had.'

'This place has the best music *and* the best martinis? Sounds like heaven.'

'It is,' he replies proudly. 'And he won't even card you.'

We sit in silence for a moment; just long enough for the dark anxiety to start building inside me again. I begin thinking of how I almost freaked out in the alley a few minutes ago and wondering when my craziness is going to be too much for him to handle.

The alley.

Don't think about it, the voice inside my head shouts. But, on any given day, my thoughts vary between a leaky faucet and a fire-hose of negativity, drowning me or just annoying the hell out of me until I'm forced to do something to make them stop.

'What are you thinking?' Crush asks, and suddenly I notice that he's holding a crushed penny in his hand; actually, he's rubbing the penny between his thumb and forefinger.

'Do you think saving someone's life cancels out taking another person's life?'

He looks horrified by this question. 'What? What do you mean?'

'I mean exactly what I said. If you kill someone, can you erase that sin by saving someone else's life?'

He drops the penny onto the bar. 'Why would you ask me that?' I wait for him to pick up the penny before I reply.

'Look, it's just a question. No need to freak out. I didn't kill anyone.'

'That's not what I was implying.' He shakes his head. 'Just excuse the minor spaz-out. The answer to your question is *no*. I don't think saving someone's life cancels out killing someone else.'

He casts his eyes downward after he says this; a sure sign that he's lying or he's hiding something. 'Have you ever killed anyone?'

Chapter Seven

Eleven years ago
Crush

The book in Grandpa Hugh's hands is so old it looks like it could be from dinosaur times. When he told me he had a surprise for me in his study, I thought he was gonna give me a new guitar or a BB gun. Or maybe even those boxing gloves he promised me – the ones signed by Muhammad Ali. I guess a book isn't so bad, if it's new. I don't want some old book written in weird words I can't understand. I'm only ten years old. And I haven't even read that book of poems Grandpa got me last year.

'Take it,' Grandpa says, holding the book out to me, his knotty, wrinkled hands shaking with the weight of the book. 'Come on, son.'

I take the small book from his hands and I'm surprised that the mint-green cloth covering the book is soft. Usually the cloth on hardcover books is rough.

The book feels loose, like Jell-O. It just wants to fall apart or fall out of my hands. It can't decide. Just like I can't decide if I should tell Grandpa I'd rather take a trip to his workshop in the basement to see his gun collection. That would be more fun then trying to hold this book together.

'*Black Box*,' I say, reading the title on the cover. 'Is this a kids' story?'

'It's okay for smart kids like you. It's about war and family and . . . well, you'll just have to read it to find out. You'll like it, I hope.'

Grandpa leans forward in his giant leather chair, as if he's waiting for me to open the book and start reading. So I do. And I'm really surprised when I find I can't stop. I don't know how long I've been reading, but my arms start to cramp up from holding the book in front of me. Taking a seat on the sofa across from Grandpa's chair, I continue reading.

Herman always spoke highly of his mother in the company of others, but as soon as he was alone with her, he became a tyrant, throwing one tantrum after another. When Polly attempted to discipline her six-year-old son, he only retaliated with more violence and vile language. He was a very bad boy with a heart as black as soot. That's what his mother always told him. Finally, Polly decided she had no choice but to place Herman in an orphanage.

Herman cried and acted out for weeks, but he soon realized that he didn't want to be thrown away again. And the nuns refused to adhere to Herman's outrage. Within months, he was as mild-mannered as the young girls who had been born in the orphanage. For ten years, he ate his vegetables and wasted not even a crumb of bread. He said good morning *and* good evening *and never forgot a* please *or* thank you. *He helped the nuns with the wash and the milking of their one cow and four goats. He did well in his classes and always offered to read aloud during weekly mass.*

But deep inside the soft curves of his soul, Herman knew that the prickly tyrant he left in Winchester with Polly was waiting.

Now sixteen years old, Herman decided it was time for him to take up a hobby or involve himself in some great cause; something that would keep the tyrant at bay. On the morning of December fifth, Herman pulled on his gray coat and rain boots and set off for a long walk to the town square to enlist in the United States Army.

'How could his mom do that to him?' I asked Grandpa. 'Is that legal?'

Grandpa lets out a raspy laugh then he sits back in his big chair and folds his hands over his belly. The leather patches on the elbows of his maroon sweater squeak a little against the leather arms of the chair.

'It was legal then and it's still legal now, son, so you'd better behave,' he replies with a wink.

I smile as I glance at the page again. 'Is Herman going to war?'

'He sure is, but there's lots more story that comes before that. You just keep reading and tell me what you think when you're done.'

I pull the red ribbon bookmark between the pages to mark my place, then I close the book. 'Why is it called *Black Box?*'

'You'll find that out too, but I'll give you a hint. There's a little blackness inside all of us.'

There's a little blackness inside all of us.

'Don't worry, son, not all stories have happy endings; but that doesn't mean they're not worth the read.'

Chapter Eight

January 3rd

Crush

Staring into Mikki's green eyes, I swear I'm looking into my own. She's hiding something from me that I haven't quite figured out yet, but I'm positive it has to do with her trip to L.A. There has to be a reason someone as skittish as her decided to have coffee with me rather than go home when her flight was canceled. And there's definitely a reason greater than curiosity for the question she just asked me.

If it weren't her asking, this would be the point in our conversation where I begin to suspect her of being an undercover cop or journalist. But it *is* Mikki. And something about this girl tells me she's not here to find out what happened in a dark parking lot three years ago.

'That's a trick question,' I reply. 'If I tell you I've never killed anyone, then you'll think I'm a good guy and you'll stay, because even though it's not a very exciting answer, it means you're safe. But if I tell you I've killed someone, you may find it intriguing or frightening. Either way, intrigued or scared, you'll probably try to get the fuck away from me, and I don't think I'm ready for that.'

She smiles as she looks down at her fingers, which she's tapping on the surface of the bar. 'That's a real suave way to dodge the question. It also sounds like something a murderer would say.'

'Really?'

She looks up and meets my gaze again. 'Who did you kill?'

I pause for a moment as I try to figure out where she's going with this conversation. Then it hits me. 'Do you *want* to die?'

'What?' she asks, shaking her head far too adamantly. 'That's . . . that's a stupid question.'

'Why is it a stupid question?'

'Because,' she snaps at me. 'It's just stupid. I don't want to die.'

She continues to look down at her hands, which are still trembling as she fidgets with her silver thumb-ring. I get an urge to grab her hand again, to stop the trembling and fidgeting, but I don't.

'I'm sorry. I guess that was kind of a stupid question. I was just wondering why a pretty girl like you would hang out with me when you could be at home in your warm bed with your pjs on. Or out with your friends . . . or your *boyfriend*.'

She finally chuckles. 'So, accusing me of wanting to die is your way of avoiding my question or is it just a really messed-up way of asking me if I have a boyfriend?'

'It's just me being a total dick. And . . . do you have a boyfriend?'

'No.' She looks up and fixes me with a steely glare. 'Most guys don't appreciate a girl who's crazy and also doesn't put out.'

I'm not quite sure how to respond to this statement. It's probably best to change the subject or reach for a joke. 'Yeah, I know how you feel. Most girls don't appreciate a guy who can cite Shakespeare and won't put out. Actually, I think that's a line from *Macbeth*.'

Her glare melts into a reluctant smile. 'You're not a total dick.'

'Still not putting out.'

Jimmy, the bartender, arrives a few minutes later and Mikki retreats into herself again in his presence. Jimmy's a cool guy, like me, but he can seem a bit intimidating. At six-foot-three with nineteen-inch biceps, he doesn't have to work hard to keep the rowdy customers in check. But I want Mikki to feel relaxed. And I can see, by the way she's fidgeting with her thumb-ring and her hair, not adding a single word to our conversation, that she's pretty uncomfortable.

'You want to head out of here? We can go get a drink somewhere else.'

She looks up at me, slightly confused. 'Why would

we go somewhere else? We haven't even finished our first drink yet.'

I nod and ask Jimmy to get another round of dirty martinis ready. 'How do you like that martini?'

She picks up the martini glass and guzzles down the rest of the drink, leaving the olive at the bottom. 'Delicious.' She grabs the other glass that Jimmy just set down in front of her and takes another long swig. 'Definitely the best martini I've ever had in Boston.'

'Have you ever had a martini in Boston?' I ask, then I guzzle the rest of my first martini so I can keep up with her.

'Not nice, young lady.' Jimmy chides her and she lifts her martini glass to him.

'Still the best,' she declares, then she finishes martini number two.

Jimmy throws me a brief glance that probably means, *Where'd you find this one?* or, *Am I gonna have to eighty-six her at eleven a.m.?*

'Maybe you should eat a little something before you transform into a walking dirty martini. All you had was half a muffin.'

'The bottom,' she clarifies, looking at Jimmy. 'I'm not hungry.'

'I make a pretty mean green olive and maraschino cherry kabob,' I reply, and Jimmy lifts the condiment tray onto the bar.

I grab a toothpick and stack two olives and two

cherries, then I hold it out to her. Her face looks a little gray as she shoots my concoction a look of disgust.

'I said I'm not hungry. You eat it.'

I pop the toothpick into my mouth and pull it out clean. The bitter brine of the olives hits me first, then the cloying sweetness of the cherries. I take my first chew and it all explodes into a squishy mess in my mouth.

'That's disgusting,' she remarks.

I gulp down the rest of my shit-kabob and Jimmy shakes his head as he sets a glass of ice water on the bar for me to wash it down. 'Yeah, but it got you to stop jonesin' for a martini for two minutes.'

She rolls her eyes. 'I'm more of a beer girl, anyway.'

'You and I are going to get along very well.'

'I thought we were already getting along pretty well.'

I successfully manage to get her to slow her downward slide into Crunksville by asking Jimmy to switch us to tap beer, which he cuts with a little club soda. Then I keep her talking to keep her mouth busy. Soon, three hours have passed and we've only had three more beers. Unfortunately, with the lack of food, she's looking pretty loose as she leans over the bar with the side of her head propped up on her fist.

'And that's the tragic story of why my dad gave Bradley away when I was six.'

She's just spent the past twenty minutes telling me the story of her dog Bradley Snickers, a chocolate Labrador Retriever. The only pet she ever had.

'You took your dog for a walk on thin ice to see if it would hold you both?'

'I'm not saying it wasn't a stupid thing to do, but I was only six years old. I think my dad may have overreacted just a little.' She guzzles the dregs of beer in her glass and looks up at me, her eyes unfocused and a bit teary. 'I loved that fucking dog. It was the only thing I ever loved. I would never have purposely hurt him.' I reach up to brush a piece of hair away from her eyes and she smacks my hand away. 'Don't touch me. I didn't say you could touch me!'

'Sorry. I – I'm sorry.'

'You don't have to be sorry, just don't do it.' She chuckles a little after she says this. 'That's what my mom used to say to me when I got in trouble and I tried to apologize for being bad. She'd say, "Don't apologize; just don't do it." Like it's that easy to always do the right thing.'

'Mikki?'

'What?' she snaps at me as she slides her empty beer glass away so she can rest her head on top of her arms.

'Where are you staying tonight?'

She heaves a deep sigh as she closes her eyes. 'Don't know. Right here seems just fine.'

Jimmy raises his eyebrows as he pretends to be busy popping the seeds out of the lemon wedges he just cut. I can't help but watch her face with a bit of awe. Even with her black hair, her lip ring, and the tattoos on her fingers, she looks so sweet and innocent. I feel strangely protective of her, like I should tell Jimmy to buzz off. She can spend the night wherever she wants. *Can't you see she's broken?*

I can tell by the shiny bit of drool accumulating at the corner of her mouth that she's already beginning to fall asleep. I take a risk and reach for her. Gently grasping her arm, I give it an easy shake. She doesn't flinch this time.

She groans softly and her eyelids flutter open. 'Sorry. I didn't sleep last night.'

'Maybe we should get you a room so you can get some rest.'

She pushes herself up from the bar and blinks a few times. 'If you try anything I'll kill you,' she mutters, reaching for her purse. 'And I don't mean that figuratively. I will actually murder you. I have nothing to lose.'

'Not if I kill you first.'

Chapter Nine

Four years ago
Mikki

Rina lies back on my bed and holds up the piece of paper I just handed her. She reads the poem silently and I watch her; silent on the outside and screaming on the inside: *She hates it.* I take a couple of deep breaths to keep from hyperventilating. I've never shared my poems with anyone.

Finally, she smiles and lets the paper fall from her fingers and float down onto her chest. 'Wow . . . Is that what your first kiss felt like? 'Cause mine was nowhere near as romantic as that.'

'So . . . you liked it?'

She laughs as she sits up. 'Are you kidding me? That was amazing. Do you have more?'

'No,' I reply quickly and she looks confused. 'I mean, nothing that's ready to be seen.'

'That's cool. So . . . the guy in that poem . . . was that . . . *Brad*?'

'No.' I snatch the paper off the bed. 'He wasn't my first kiss.'

'No, he was your first asshole. There'll be plenty more of those. At least, that's what my mom says.'

I fold the piece of paper, where I poured my most intimate thoughts yesterday, and tuck it into the top drawer of my nightstand. 'I'd rather not talk about Brad.'

Reaching into the back of the drawer, I retrieve an amber bottle of pills. I spill one of the green pills into the palm of my hand, then I grab the glass of water from the top of my nightstand and guzzle it down. Rina doesn't stare at me while I do this. This is normal behavior to her. She's seen me popping pills since the day we met on the first day of school six weeks ago. Her mom pops pills too, but for different reasons than I do.

'Hey, I have an idea.' Rina jumps off the bed and spins around to look me in the eye. 'You should submit your poems to the newsletter committee.'

'Hell no! I almost passed out just from showing them to you. I'd die of mortification if anyone else read them.'

'But it's so good! You can't keep that to yourself. That's not fair to the rest of the world.'

I shake my head as I grab my empty glass off the

nightstand and head for the bedroom door. 'No way. End of discussion.' I open the door, opening my mouth to ask her if she wants anything to drink, then I see my mom at the top of the stairs.

'Mikki, have you seen Rina? Her mom just called and said she doesn't know where she is. She's on her way here.'

'Haven't seen her,' I blurt, then I slam the bedroom door shut. 'Your mom's on her way,' I whisper frantically.

Just then, the doorbell rings and Rina grabs fistfuls of her long red hair. 'Oh, shit! What do I do?'

Rina's not supposed to be at my house. She's grounded until next month for cutting class three days last week, but this didn't stop her from coming to my house after school.

'Climb out the window,' I suggest and her eyes widen as she moves toward the window behind her. 'No! I'm just kidding! It's too far down.'

'Not with the patio cover.' She yanks the window open and smiles as she looks back at me over her shoulder. 'Hey, I've got an idea. Put the poems you write here on the windowsill and I'll come by and get them whenever my mom lets me out of jail. You can pretend you're sending them to a fancy magazine or newspaper; something really important. But it will just be me reading them.'

I can hear footsteps stomping up the staircase outside the bedroom. 'Fine, fine! Just go!'

She grins as she carefully lowers herself onto the wooden lattice patio cover in the backyard. She skitters across the cover and deftly lets herself down onto the block fence surrounding the property. From there, she jumps down into the neighbors' yard and gives me a thumbs-up as she races toward the back of their property. Then she disappears through the wooden gate into the alley behind the house.

Chapter Ten

January 3rd
Mikki

By the time Crush settles the bar tab, and we stuff our suitcases and his guitar case into the trunk of a cab, I'm starting to sober up a little. Both the meth and the alcohol are wearing off, leaving behind a warm rush of anxiety that leaves me emotionally conflicted. Part of me wants to tell him I can't get a hotel room with him. He's practically a stranger. Another part of me wants to lay my head in his lap and fall asleep. I guess I'll settle for lying in my own bed in the hotel room.

'Park Plaza,' Crush says to the cab driver, and I laugh out loud as I lean my head against the window.

'Park Plaza? That's a bit fancy, don't you think?'

'It's one of the few hotels in Boston with a two-bedroom suite. Unless you want to sleep in the same room as me. I'd be happy to get us a twin-size bed to share in a hostel, if that's what you prefer.'

'Whatever. How do you know it has a two-bedroom suite? You stay there often?'

He's quiet for a moment, then he clears his throat before he responds. 'My dad is the CEO of a large investment trust and they used to own a large stake in the Park Plaza.'

I pull my head away from the window and sit up straight as I turn to him. He's gazing out the passenger window, probably trying to avoid seeing my reaction to this.

'Define large.'

'Billions.'

'So . . . you're rich is what you're trying to tell me?'

He sighs as he turns to face me. 'Does that bother you?'

'Honestly, it's a little intimidating . . . Okay, more than a little intimidating. But I guess it explains why you look like that, but you talk like Harvard.'

'*Talk like Harvard?* Is that an insult?'

'No way. It's cute,' I blurt out before I can stop myself.

He tilts his head and smiles. 'Cute?'

I shake my head and look out my window. 'I mean, it's cool. It's just, I go to community college. I'm used to talking to assholes who can't form a complete sentence to ask a girl out on a date.'

'Finally, my expensive education will be put to good use.'

I get a weird urge to blurt out *I love you*. I get urges

to blurt out inappropriate stuff all the time, but that's the first time I've ever gotten that particular urge. I should probably take my meds if I'm going to be hanging around someone normal. Of course, how normal can he be with the name *Crush*?

'Are you ever going to tell me why you changed your name to Crush?'

'Are you ever going to tell me why you don't want to go home?'

The cab pulls up in front of the Boston Park Plaza and Crush slips the driver a wad of cash that makes the cab driver spit out incoherent mumblings of gratitude. The driver rushes out of the cab to help with the bags in the trunk and I follow right after him. But Crush is already there and the luggage is standing on the snow-covered pavement in front of the hotel. A bellman races out from under the black awning covering the sidewalk in front of the hotel entrance. Crush tells him to take my bag and I follow them into the hotel, trying not to smile as Crush holds the door open for me even though he's the one carrying his guitar case and dragging his luggage.

My mouth drops when we enter the lobby. An enormous crystal chandelier hangs from the high ceiling in a space the size of four huge lecture halls. Large, square pillars line the right and left side of an open carpeted space beneath the chandelier. Beyond the pillars on the right is the reception desk. Through the spaces between the pillars on the left, I glimpse what could be a fancy lounge area. This place screams historic opulence. I'll bet this was a great place to stay about eighty years ago.

Crush is approaching the check-in counter and I hurry up to join him. I can't help but feel curious about him now. I want to see how the people here treat him.

'Good afternoon, sir,' the woman says as Crush sidles up to the counter.

Crush nods and I swear there's some form of silent agreement going on between these two. 'Good afternoon, Greta. Is the Garden Suite available?'

'Yes, sir.' Her gaze falls onto her computer screen as her fingers move like lightning across her keyboard. 'How many nights will you be staying with us? We have another guest booked in the Garden Suite on Thursday.'

'Three nights?' Crush replies, taking a beat to consider this timeframe. 'That should be enough. We're just waiting for our flights to be rescheduled. The airline should be getting us on another flight in a day or two.'

Greta raises her wispy, blond eyebrows. 'You got here just in time. We were told to expect an influx of guests tonight. They're saying the storm will have all flights grounded for at least two days. Do you want to book another room for Thursday, just in case? Or do you want to wait?'

Crush turns to me and I try not to let him see the panic building inside me. I can't stay in Boston that long. Someone will find me. Even if I'm holed up in a hotel room booked under the name Crush. I'm sure someone working in this hotel will eventually see something on the news or somewhere with my missing person photo.

'Do you want to book another room, so we don't have any problems booking later on once the hotel is rushed with travelers?'

I glance at Greta and she flashes me a guarded smile. I wonder if she knows Crush's real name. I wonder if he's brought other girls here before.

My shoulders slump as I resign myself to my fate. 'Book another room. I can't leave the hotel anyway, so that's probably best.'

'What do you mean, you can't leave the hotel?'

'I mean *we* can't leave the hotel. Just look at that *snow!*' I point at the hotel entrance, my heart racing as I hope he doesn't question this slip of the tongue later.

'Okay,' he says with a smile. He knows I'm bullshitting. 'We'll book another room for Thursday and Friday night, just to be safe.'

'We don't have any two-bedroom suites available, but we do have a junior suite. It has one bedroom and a sofa bed.'

Crush looks to me again and I nod so I don't say anything stupid. 'Book it,' he says to Greta.

Once the rooms are booked and Greta hands Crush the card keys, I turn around and find my suitcase is gone. 'Oh, shit! Where's my suitcase?'

'Over there,' Crush chuckles as he points at a brass luggage trolley on the other side of the lobby.

'I totally knew that. I was just trying to scare you.'

'I highly doubt you could ever scare me.'

I follow him toward the trolley. 'You obviously don't know me.'

The bellman watches as we approach and he falls into step next to us. We cross the lobby and pass the pillars toward a corridor with a few elevators. He punches the call button for us and Crush smiles down at me as we wait.

'What?' I bark at him.

'You're not scary. Not even a little bit.'

'Yeah, well, like I said before. You don't know me. I'm . . .'

I already told him I'm bipolar, but I resist the urge to admit that I'm off my meds. I don't think he or the bellman could handle that kind of news.

When we arrive in the suite, my eyes widen and I get a strange giddy feeling in my belly. 'This place is huge.'

Crush closes the door after the bellman. 'Well, you wanted a separate bedroom, didn't you?'

'Yeah, but this is too much.' I take a seat in a stool at the breakfast bar of our very own kitchen. 'I know you said you're rich, but I feel like I'm taking advantage of you.'

'You're taking advantage of me?' he replies, opening the refrigerator door and pulling out a couple of bottles of water. He sets one on the bar in front of me and takes a swig from his own. 'Somehow, I find it very unlikely that you would ever take advantage of me. Not that I wouldn't want you to.'

'What?'

'Only kidding.'

Suddenly, this huge space feels a little claustrophobic. 'I'm . . . I'm going to take a shower. Is that okay?'

'You don't need my permission. Make yourself at home. I have a feeling we're going to be here for a while.'

'Um . . . where's the bathroom?'

He grabs my suitcase and leads me past the dining area, where a fancy table is set with six sets of dinnerware, and back past the kitchen toward an open door. The bedroom is not huge, but it's private. And the bed, with the fluffy white pillows and comforter, looks a million times more comfortable than my bed at home.

He points at a door in the far left corner of the room and smiles. 'Bathroom's over there. If you're tired, feel free to go right to bed afterward.'

Without warning, my eyes tear up and I quickly wipe the tears away.

'What's wrong?'

I close my eyes so I don't have to see the look on his face. 'Nothing, I'm just . . .' I want to say that I'm taken aback by his kindness, but that would be weird, so instead I say, 'I haven't taken my meds. I have to look for the bottle in my suitcase. I'll be fine. I'll come hang out with you when I'm done. I should at least try to stay awake a little while longer.'

I hastily drag the suitcase into the bathroom and lock the door behind me. Taking a seat on top of the suitcase, I bury my face in my hands as I sob uncontrollably. This is so stupid. I should just take the stupid pills, but the alternative to the odd behavior, the speech problems, and the uncontrollable crying is being a zombie. I want to feel my last days on this fucked-up Earth.

I remove my hands from my face and open my eyes. The bathroom is smaller than I expected in a room like this. It's not even that nice, in fact, it reminds me of something. I begin to undress, removing everything but my bra and panties as I try to remember what this bathroom reminds me of, when suddenly I feel the alcohol in my belly shooting into my throat. I race to the toilet and vomit the last couple of beers I consumed. The liquid burns my throat and leaves a bitter trace of meth on the back of my tongue. I vomit until there's nothing left in my stomach and my eyeballs are ready to pop out of their sockets.

I attempt to stand, but the tiny lights dancing in front of my eyes have me disoriented. Reaching for the wall to steady myself, my hand misses the wall and I tumble forward. I lose my footing and my forehead hits the edge of the tub.

Chapter Eleven

January 3rd
Crush

The retching sounds I hear through the adjoining wall of the kitchen and bathroom cease and I breathe a sigh of relief. Then I grab the phone receiver to call room service for some ginger ale, but a loud thump interrupts my plans. I drop the receiver and rush to Mikki's bedroom.

I knock on the bathroom door, but she doesn't respond right away. 'Mikki!' I shout this with my lips pressed to the tiny crack between the door and the frame and she still doesn't respond. 'Mikki, if you're all right, please say something.'

I wait a few more seconds before I try the doorknob. It's locked. *Fuck it.* I take a step back and land a hard kick just to the left of the door handle, but it doesn't give at all. On the second kick, I hear a small crack in the wood that gives me hope. Seven kicks later, the doorframe splinters completely and the door swings inward. The first thing I see is Mikki's jeans, sweater, and T-shirt tossed haphazardly onto the bathroom sink. Then I see her.

Mikki is lying on her side on the bathroom floor next to the tub, a thin stream of blood trickling from a cut on her forehead. I crouch next to her and put my fingers on her neck to check her pulse. It seems strong, maybe just a tad fast.

'Mikki? Mikki, can you hear me?'

I scoop her up in my arms and that's when I see it. I nearly drop her onto the bathroom floor at the sight of it, but somehow I manage to hold onto her slender body as I carry her into the bedroom. Every step feels like a thousand and I can't seem to get to the bed fast enough. Finally, I get there and, as I lay her down gently, she begins to stir.

'I'm calling an ambulance. You need to get your head checked,' I say, though I feel as if it's someone else saying the words.

'Don't go,' she mutters as her eyes attempt to find me through the haze of the blow to the head. 'Please don't . . . don't call.'

I stare at her in utter fucking disbelief. It's her. I knew it the moment I heard her sigh in the café, but I had hoped with everything inside me that I was wrong. I glance at the dozens of scars on the tops of her thighs – proof that I failed her – then I quickly look away.

Her eyes seem more focused now and she finally seems to realize what's going on. I turn away as she scrambles to hide herself under the covers.

'I can't just ignore the fact that you injured your head,' I reply, unsure how I'm going to bring up the fact that I saw the tattoo on her chest. The same one I saw in that parking lot three years ago. The same image that she used for her Twitter profile four years ago.

'You saw me,' she whispers, and the shame in her voice makes my skin prickle.

'I didn't see anything,' I reply quickly, still facing away from her toward the bedroom door.

Fuck. I didn't think that she would be okay after what happened, but I never expected this. I don't know what to say to her. For the second time in my fucked-up life, I'm speechless. Only this time, it's not by choice.

'You did. Yes, you did. You saw.'

I grit my teeth against the raw emotions threatening to overtake me. 'I'm going to turn—'

'No!'

'Mikki, we need to talk.'

'No, just please don't call anyone.'

'I'm not going to call anyone. I need to talk to you about . . .' I turn around and her eyes are wide with fright as she clutches the blankets up to her chin. 'About April fourteenth.'

Chapter Twelve

April 14th – Three years ago
Mikki

I have this recurring dream that I'm swinging on a wooden swing high above the city. And I'm scared, obviously, but I'm also excited. So I keep pushing myself to swing higher and higher. Finally, I feel that flip in my stomach and a split-second moment of weightlessness. I'm falling, but only for a second because that's when I wake up.

Maybe that's the way life is. We spend our lives going back and forth between courage and fear, afraid of something bad happening. Afraid of falling. Afraid of dying. But what if death comes so fast that it's over before you even know what's happening?

There's a part of me that believes in love and happy endings. A part of me that wants to see the Grand Canyon and swim with dolphins. There's also a part of me that wants to wear sweatpants and lie in bed all day. A part of me that fantasizes about jumping off that swing.

I'm type-two bipolar. I was diagnosed just over a year ago when I got a strong urge to tie my purse strap around my neck – anything to make it stop. I didn't actually tie my purse strap around my neck. Instead, I logged into my secret Twitter account and sent out a mayday signal.

I couldn't log into my real Twitter account. I had deleted that profile months before to stop the harassing tweets. This new account was safe. I didn't expect anyone to respond to a tweet from an unknown person with a cartoon bunny profile picture and the Twitter account name *@burninbushytail.* But he responded, whoever he is, or was. And I'll never forget it.

> **@burninbushytail** This Black Box is yours to keep, to stash your troubles away. Just lock it up and call my name, and I'll be there always.

Instead of ending my life thirteen months ago, I went to my mom and told her everything. I told her about the purse strap. I told her about the bullying. I told her about feeling overwhelmed by my classes. I told her about my anxiety and the confusion, and how I was beginning to feel like there were too many people and too many voices. I told her about the nightly hallucinations and how I just wanted it all to end.

Diagnosed bipolar at age fourteen. Now, more than

one year and three different medications later, I'm almost normal. And I'm about to go to my first 'normal' teenage party. Of course, what the hell is normal when you're fifteen?

Rina picks me up at eight o'clock. My light-brown hair is pulled up in a neat ponytail and I'm wearing skinny jeans and a white hoodie with the name of some taco bar in Cancun where my family went on vacation two years ago. This is the hoodie I wear when I want to feel normal. It's a conversation piece. People always ask if I've been to Beto's Cantina when I wear this, so it's good for a party where I'll know absolutely no one but Rina.

Rina, short for Katrina, is my new best friend. My old best friend, Lucy, ditched me last year so as not to get caught in the bullying crossfire. I changed schools seven weeks before the end of my freshman year. Tomorrow it will be exactly one year and four months since I started going to alternative high school.

Alternative. Why don't they just call it what it really is? A school for kids who've fucked up so royally that they can't even be put in the remedial classes at regular high school. I ditched so many classes last year to avoid Brad and Nellie. It was hard to care about AP Biology when all I heard as I walked the halls were the whispers . . . *slut* . . . *cum-dumpster* . . . *hole.*

Nellie's boyfriend, Brad Winthrop, sat next to me in history class. I was always pretty quiet, but Brad had a way of asking just the right questions to get me talking and laughing. He flirted with me on Twitter for weeks before he came into class one day looking really upset. He said that he and Nellie had broken up and he had been counting on her to help him with a history essay. Being the idiot that I was, I offered my assistance. Little did I know that Brad was just using me to get back at Nellie for not having sex with him. Brad and I never had sex during our study session, but the truth didn't matter once Nellie believed the lies Brad told her.

Eventually, the bullying got so bad, online and offline, that Lucy began avoiding me and I quit going to school altogether. I deleted my Facebook and Twitter accounts and basically refused to get out of bed. That was when the purse strap started looking very appealing.

But that was over a year ago. I'm at a new school now. Rina is nothing like Nellie, or Lucy. I don't have a reputation here other than being a bit quiet. I'm actually getting all As, which isn't very difficult considering the teachers at this alternative high school aren't allowed to give us homework. This may not be what I envisioned for my high school experience, but it's getting better every day. My therapist warned me yesterday that I may be entering a manic period, where everything seems great and I'm motivated to do normal things, like going to parties.

As Rina turns her twelve-year-old Toyota onto Centre Street, my phone vibrates in my back pocket. I slip it out and check the screen. It's a text from my mom.

Mom: Don't forget to text me when you get there and call me if you need me to pick you up. Gold

My mom signs all her texts to me with the word *Gold*, and I'm supposed to sign all my texts to her with whatever code color we've agreed on for the day. Tonight, I have to sign my texts with the word *Black*. This is her way of making sure that I'm not lying in a ditch somewhere while some murderer texts her pretending to be me. Sometimes, I think my mom is almost as crazy as I am.

Rina glances at my phone then looks straight ahead. 'That your mom?'

Other than Rina, my sister Meaghan, and my chemistry lab partner, my mom and dad are the only people who ever text me.

'Yeah, she's just freaking out a little.' I shoot my mom a text telling her I'll call her if I need anything. I end the text with *goodnight*, then my code color, hoping this will prevent her from texting me again later. Rina smiles the way she always smiles when she's trying not to make fun of me. 'What? You know my mom is a freak.'

She shakes her head. 'That's not why I'm smiling.'

'Then why are you smiling, weirdo?'

'I'm giving it up to Heath tonight.' The car swerves a little as she adjusts the radio station and settles on 'Nothing On You' by B.o.B.

Tonight? I want to say, *When you're supposed to be*

holding my hand through the scariest social outing of my life? But I don't.

Rina and Heath met in the computer lab this year. They've been dating less than two months, but she's been talking about losing her virginity to him since day one. They're so wrapped up in each other that Rina and I have been hanging out at Heath's lunch table with all his stoner friends for the past month.

Despite all the shit I went through at Franklin High last year, I never did drugs. The only time I ever drank alcohol, I got so sick my parents had to take me to the emergency room. And I never drank again. The idea of going to a party with a bunch of people who drink and do drugs regularly is not my idea of the perfect Friday night. But the idea of hanging out with them while my best friend is in another room having sex is terrifying.

'I told you I was gonna do it,' Rina says, turning right onto Cary Street. The sound of a car horn blaring behind us makes my heart jump. The guy Rina just cut off swerves around us in his white truck and floors the gas pedal to pass us up. 'Get your head out of your ass, jerkface!' Rina shouts at his taillights.

She's had her driver's license a total of three and a half weeks and she's almost gotten into four car accidents already. Five, if you count this near miss. She reaches for the stereo to turn the music up and I can see her hand trembling slightly.

'Jerkface?' I repeat her insult and she smiles sheepishly.

I want to tell Rina that she'd better not leave me alone all night with Heath's friends, but I don't want to guilt trip her into hanging out with me. I've turned down all Rina's party invitations for over a year, but I've always been honest with her about why. Until they put me on CBZ when I turned fifteen, I had yet to find a medication that eased my symptoms without turning me into an emotionless zombie. Until CBZ, social situations caused too much anxiety. I was always in my head, constantly wondering if people were judging me or whispering about me. It was exhausting.

'Jerkface is a perfectly acceptable insult,' Rina replies, tossing her red hair over her shoulder as she pulls up in front of a gray one-story house on Ashfield Drive. There are three cars squeezed into the driveway and the sounds of music and laughter drift out of an open window. I try to discreetly take a deep breath, but Rina notices. 'Do you want me to take you home?'

'No, you told Heath you'd be here at eight. It's almost eight thirty.'

'Who gives a fuck? He can wait.'

I shake my head and smile. 'Nope. I can't keep avoiding this for ever. This isn't Franklin. I have nothing to be afraid of.'

'You're damn fucking right this isn't Franklin. These assholes don't want to drag your name through shit. They just want to get fucked up. And I think Lars likes you.'

'He does not.' I reach for the door handle, eager to get away from this pre-party pep talk.

'Well, he told Heath that he accidentally touched your hair the other day in third period and it was so fucking soft.'

'What the fuck? That's creepy.' I reach up and twist my light-brown hair around my finger.

'Yeah, but Lars is hot, so that makes it less creepy, right?'

'No, it's still creepy.'

'Whatever. You don't have to hook up with him. All I'm saying is that no one in here is going to make up shitty lies about you. We're just here to hang out.'

I open the car door before I can change my mind and slam the door shut behind me. Right on cue, the screen door swings open and Lars comes outside with a beer in one hand and his cell phone in the other. He grins when he sees me and I feel my chest tighten with anxiety. I force a weak smile just as Rina loops her arm in mine and drags me forward.

'Give me a sec,' Lars says into the phone as we approach. The glow of the porch light gleams in his blond hair, which falls around his face looking purposely messy. 'Hey, Mikki.' His deep voice is wrapped in a soothing warmth that actually puts me at ease.

'Hey,' I say, this time flashing him a genuine smile.

Rina opens the screen door and pulls me in after her. I glance over my shoulder and Lars smiles, the kind of smile they put on billboards. 'I'll see you inside,' he calls out.

My stomach flutters at the thought of this and suddenly I remember how I felt when Brad came to my house to study last year. The fluttering turns into a burning sensation that's worse than the nausea I sometimes get from the CBZ. I close my eyes as Rina pulls me inside and I use one of the anti-anxiety techniques I found online. I count to ten and open my eyes. I imagine that everyone in this living room feels as frightened and self-conscious as I do, and it's my job to put *them* at ease.

I can do this.

I'm not supposed to drink while taking CBZ. So when Cedric Holmes greets me with a plastic cup of keg beer I refuse the drink a few times. Finally, Lars walks in, tucking his phone into the back pocket of his jeans before he takes a seat on the arm of the sofa where I'm sitting.

'If she doesn't want the beer, she doesn't want the beer. Don't be a fucking dick.' Lars takes the beer from Cedric and guzzles some down. 'She probably has to go home soon anyway.'

'No, I don't,' I blurt. 'I mean, I have to be home by midnight.'

Lars grins at me as Cedric laughs. 'It's okay. I'll make sure you get home on time.'

'You can't drive if you're drinking.' *God, I must sound like a total killjoy.*

'I'll be sober by then.' He places his hand on the back of my neck and gives it a gentle squeeze. 'You're safe with me.'

'Don't believe that shit!' Tony shouts from the other side of the living room where he's sitting with his girlfriend Karla.

Tony and Karla are the only seniors here. They probably drove most of these people here in their two cars. Lars' silver BMW was one of the three cars parked in the driveway.

I lean forward to get away from Lars' hand and he cocks an eyebrow at me. 'I'm fine. Rina's driving me home later.'

Lars chuckles. 'Yeah, good luck with that.'

I'm about to ask him what he means by this when I look around and realize Rina has already disappeared, probably snuck away to one of the bedrooms with Heath. Suddenly, this party is starting to seem like a really bad idea.

Chapter Thirteen

April 14th – Three years ago
Crush

The sound of the voices on the other side of the door make me nervous. I stare at the black pouch on the bathroom counter and, with every second that ticks past, the pouch seems to move farther away from me. Cassie's voice can be heard over all the other voices. She's not loud, but she has that deep kind of voice that penetrates through the thickest walls. Suddenly, the idea of doing this with so many people just steps away, laughing and enjoying themselves, seems stupid and selfish – two qualities I've come to despise in myself.

I swipe the pouch off the counter and tuck it into the back of my jeans then pull my shirt down to cover it up. When I open the bathroom door, Cassie is staring at me with that lazy sort of bored expression she gets at these parties. Her dark hair is pulled back in a complicated braid she calls a conch and her blue eyes are accentuated by a layer of violet eyeshadow. She's gorgeous; though, she's not any more gorgeous than the other dozen girls I've fucked since the accident.

'God, can these people be any more dull?' she asks as she squeezes past me. 'Don't keep ditching me all night or I swear I'll take your keys and leave you here.'

'I'm gonna run to the store and grab a bottle of vodka. This thing is BYOB and we didn't bring anything.'

'It's not like you're drinking.' The silence that follows this statement is heavy with all the things we both can't mention. 'Sorry,' she says, realizing her blunder too late.

'I'll be right back.' I plant a quick kiss on her cheek before she disappears into the bathroom.

Cassie and I have only been dating for three weeks. She doesn't know my real name, but she knows why I don't drink. Everyone in Cambridge knows why I don't drink, so it didn't take long for her to figure it out even though she's not from Cambridge.

I enter the living room and no one looks at me. They're all too busy speculating about what classes they'll be taking and who they'll be rooming with when they get to Harvard. I don't need to sit here and pretend I'm excited about dorm assignments. Walking right past them, no one says anything as I walk out the front door and down the brick paved pathway toward my new Jetta.

I deactivate the alarm and slide into the driver's seat, glancing at the front door to see if anyone has followed me out. It's stupid, but part of me wishes someone would notice my hasty exit and figure out what it is I'm planning so they can try to talk me out of it. I don't want to die, but I also know I don't deserve to live.

If I could dig a hole and bury myself in the ground, I'd do that part, too. Unfortunately, somebody will find my body, but I don't want anyone, especially Cassie, to find me dead in a stranger's bathroom. I'll drive around until I find a parking lot or an alley. Some place where no one will find me until it's too late. I have to get far away from here, where no one knows me or my car.

I get off the highway in Brockton. As I drive down Centre Street, the idea that people will mourn my death begins to make me sick. I try not to think of what Jordan would think about my plans. He'd probably encourage me to do it; he had way too much faith in reverse psychology. I tried to tell him that reverse psychology only works when the person you're using it on doesn't know you're using it.

Damn. I fucking miss him.

I continue down Centre Street toward the center of Brockton, then I make a right on Cary. The GPS shows the Ashland shopping plaza is further north. It also looks like there's an industrial lot with some buildings just ahead of the plaza where I can probably park behind. It's Friday night. Most likely, no one will come into that lot until Monday morning.

I turn left into the lot and drive between two buildings before I find a nice row of box hedges where I can hide my car. Once I'm safely parked behind the bushes, I kill the headlights and leave the engine running as I reach for the stereo to turn up the volume. The local pop station is playing dance music for the Friday-night clubbers. I hit the button to change the station and the next one is playing Chopin's Nocturne Op. 9 No. 2 in E-flat major.

I learned to play this four years ago after I found an old record in Grandpa's study. I remembered him playing Chopin while I read *Black Box*. At thirteen years old, I had been playing piano for more than seven years. It still took me five months to learn this piece and play it confidently. But that was four years ago. I haven't touched the piano in over a year. I don't know if I could even play this anymore. All I know is that the melody pulls memories and emotions out of me that I'd prefer to ignore, so I swiftly change the station again until I find some classic rock music.

Opening the glove compartment, I pull out the black pouch I stuffed in there earlier. That's when I see the handgun I placed in there two months ago.

I bought the handgun after the trial ended and I received a vague and anonymous text message threat. The text read: *We both know you're not innocent.*

Yes, I definitely know I'm not innocent, which is why I'm here now. I should have stood up in that courtroom and told everyone the truth. Instead, I listened to the lawyer my father hired and kept my mouth shut. I was the only person who knew what happened the day Jordan died, and I didn't have the balls to speak up on his or my behalf.

Reaching into the compartment, I pull out the gun. I was acquitted of the second-degree murder charge, and the lesser manslaughter charge, but I was still cited for illegal discharge of a firearm within 500 feet of a dwelling. I can't get a gun permit until I'm thirty years old. I was surprised at how easy it was to buy an unregistered gun. All I had to do was mention to Tyler, Cassie's older brother, that I'd been threatened by someone at school and he suggested I get a gun. Tyler's friend Victor knew a guy in Southie who could get me a clean .92 Beretta. Within eight days of that text message threat, I had this gun.

After what happened with Jordan, most people would think I'd never want to see another gun for the rest of my life. But, just as I grew up with music and books, guns have always been a part of my life. My dad first took me out to the range when I was eight years old. By the time I was twelve, I could hit a three-inch target from fifty yards out. My familiarity with guns only made Jordan's death seem even more senseless. It's also the reason I was kept off the stand during the trial. My only defense was to convince the jury that neither Jordan nor I knew how to handle a Ruger .270 – and that I was drunk as fuck.

I shut the glove compartment and lay the gun on my lap, then I reach for the pouch. I'll use both. I'll shoot a lethal dose of heroin into my vein, then I'll pull the trigger.

Unzipping the pouch, my stomach curdles at the sight of the contents. I don't do drugs. Other than the few times I smoked pot my freshman year, drugs have never appealed to me. And I haven't drunk any alcohol since the accident. I have no idea what this stuff will do to me. All I know is that it will kill me.

I slip the lighter out of the pouch and test it before I begin preparing the syringe. It sparks a flame on the first try. As I set the lighter back inside the pouch, a flash of lights gets my attention. A dark mini-van pulls into the lot, rolling to a stop between the hedges and the back of the building on my left. I quickly duck down so they can't see my silhouette in the car through the tiny spaces between the leaves of the bushes. The unmistakable sound of a car door opening is quickly followed by a scream. Instinctively, I pop up in my seat and squint into the glare of the headlights. What I see makes my heart stop.

Chapter Fourteen

April 14th – Three years ago
Mikki

The party sucks. I've spent the last hour trying to appear comfortable as everyone around me laughs and chats about people, places, and memories I'm not familiar with. I sit on the end of the sofa, refusing offers of drinks and tokes. The smell of the smoke has surely seeped into the deepest layers of my clothes. My mom is going to kill me when she smells it.

I rise from the sofa and Lars looks up at me. 'Where are you going?' He looks genuinely disappointed that I might be leaving.

'The restroom.' I flash him a tight smile then set off toward the foyer where I've seen everyone else pass through on their way to the bathroom.

As I step into the foyer, I glance over my shoulder and no one is looking in my direction. Quickly, before anyone can notice, I head toward the front door instead of the bathroom. I open the door as slowly and quietly as I can and slip out into the cool darkness.

Slipping my phone out of my pocket, I hold it at my side as I head down Ashfield toward Cary. As soon as I turn the corner onto Cary, I'll call my mom and ask her to pick me up. I should never have come here. I'm not a party person. I'm better off accepting that truth now to save myself more awkward exits in the future.

'Hey!'

I turn my head toward the sound of the male voice. A guy in a Red Sox baseball cap is hanging out the open passenger window of a dark-blue mini-van. The second thing I notice, which instantly makes me panic, is that the van's headlights are not on.

'Hey, you need a ride?' he asks, and I can hear laughter from inside the van.

I'm frozen as my body aches with fear. I shake my head, but it's so slight he doesn't see it.

'I asked you if you need a ride. I can give you a ride.'

The sound of the van door sliding open snaps me out of my stupor and I take off running for the front door of the nearest house. But I don't make it. A thick arm locks around my torso as a hot hand clamps over my mouth, stifling my screams. I thrash and attempt to bite his hand, but he headbutts me in the back of the head, stunning the fight out of me.

I'm stuffed into the trunk of the mini-van where a chubby guy waits with a pillowcase, which he quickly yanks down over my head. Then he forces me onto my stomach and ties my hands behind my back with a piece of rope. He digs his knee into my back to keep me from moving as the trunk door slams shut. I try to scream, but the chubby guy clocks me on the side of the head with his fist then presses my face into the floor of the trunk.

It feels as if the car is making a U-turn to go back into the residential tract instead of toward Cary Street. I can't breathe. Through the tears and the weight of the guy on my back. I'm going to die.

'Please. I can't breathe,' I plead.

'Shut up!' he roars.

'Ease the fuck up!' another voice shouts from the backseat. 'If you kill her you have to get rid of her.'

These words make my entire body convulse with fear. Still, as the chubby guy eases his knee and his weight off my back, I can't breathe from the guttural sobs wracking my body.

'I said shut up,' he threatens me again, but this time he hits me with an open hand. Even with the fabric of the pillowcase covering my face, the blow stings and I cry out.

'Please stop,' I whimper.

'Maybe this will shut you up.'

He reaches under my belly and fumbles around as his thick fingers search for the button of my jeans. I squirm beneath him, but there's not enough room in the trunk to stretch my legs and get any leverage to kick him.

'Help!' I scream in a voice that doesn't even sound like my own. 'Help me!'

'Shut the fuck up! Do you want to die, bitch?' a voice shouts at me from the backseat.

Though I can't see anything, I still squeeze my eyes and lips shut, trying to shut out the horror my mind and body are about to experience. *Please don't do this, please don't do this*, I beg silently as he lifts my hips into the air and yanks my jeans and panties down.

I wish I could say that at a certain point I'm able to force my mind to go elsewhere; to mentally escape even if I'm unable to physically get away. But there is no escape. I hear every groan, every vulgar insult, and every second of the shrill laughter that follows. I feel every drop of sweat that hits the pillowcase and seeps onto my face. I smell and taste every disgusting second of it. I scream aloud and silently at every burning rip of my insides. And I die a thousand times.

I don't know how long I spend in the trunk of that van. I don't know how many times I'm violated or by how many guys. But when they're done, I can't feel my arms or legs. I'm numb and I'm pretty sure it has to do with the loss of blood. I can feel it pooled beneath me. I'm barely holding onto consciousness, but I can feel that I'm alone in the trunk now as the van bumps along down the road.

They're arguing over whether to drop me off and, after all that, I feel as if I shouldn't care. I should *want* them to just kill me. I should *want* to die. But all I want is my clothes. I don't want to lie here naked for a second longer.

'Dude, turn on your headlights or you'll get pulled over.'

Don't turn on your headlights, I want to say.

The van sets off again and the chubby guy's voice breaks through my consciousness like a knife twisting in my belly. 'Right there! Pull in there!'

Seconds later, the van comes to a stop and, by the shift in the distribution of weight, I'm pretty sure the chubby guy is coming for me in the trunk. I don't have the strength to scream as he opens the trunk and pulls me out backwards by the restraints on my wrists. As soon as my feet hit the pavement, my legs give out beneath me, and I scream as my knees slam down onto the pavement.

'Get up!' he shouts. 'Get the fuck up!'

The tiny bits of gravel on the pavement cut into my knees and the soles of my feet as I struggle to stand up.

He roughly turns me around. 'When I take this off your head, you walk straight and don't look back. You understand me?'

'Yes.'

'If you turn around, I'll kill you and your parents.'

I hear the trunk door slam shut behind me and I jump. 'Hurry up, man!' one of the others calls to him.

His hand on the top of my head sends a shiver through me and he swiftly yanks the pillowcase off my head. I blink a few times as my surroundings come into focus. I'm in a parking lot. The sound of his footsteps moving away from me fills me with a sense of relief, but my instinct kicks in and I turn around to make sure he's walking away. I quickly remember his threat and turn back, but it's too late. He saw me.

Chapter Fifteen

April 14th – Three years ago

Crush

This can't be happening. It has to be a hallucination. I glance down at the pouch in my lap. No, all the drugs are still in the tiny plastic pouch. This is no hallucination. This guy just shoved a bloody, naked girl out of that van. And she's walking very unsteadily in my direction.

My body floods with a surge of adrenaline as I toss the pouch onto the passenger seat and take the gun in my hand. I leave the engine running, and as soon as I reach for the door handle, another scream pierces the air followed by a sickening thump. He's beating her while she's lying naked on the asphalt.

Every second feels like an hour as I climb out of the car and round the hedges. 'Get away from her!' I bellow.

He lands one more kick to her head before he looks

in my direction. The Beretta is pointed straight at his head and he glares at me.

'You can keep her.' He pushes her onto her back with his foot and begins to walk away.

Her face is unrecognizable as a human face. It's covered in blood, as are both of her legs and her torso. How was she even walking a second ago?

I can't stop myself. Every muscle in my body contracts around that trigger.

The shot hits him in the side of the head when he's a few feet away from the van. He falls to the ground and the van door slides shut in a flash. The van skids away, but not before I send three more bullets through the back window.

What the fuck have I done?

I killed a man.

My entire body trembles as I stare at his lifeless body, mesmerized by the way the moonlight glitters on the blood as it forms a pool on the asphalt under his head.

I killed a man.

Vomit bites at the back of my throat and I swallow it down as I tear my gaze away from the man's body. The moment I turn back to the girl, the vomit threatens to come back up. I've never seen a human being more mangled, more devastated by evil. I have to get her to a hospital.

What if they think I did this to her? *Fucking shit!* What was I thinking?

I *wasn't* thinking. And now I need to get her out

of here before those guys come back. I tuck the gun into the back of my jeans and run to her. Her face is a swollen bloody mess and they must have brutally raped her; there's blood all over her legs and all the way up to her exposed breasts. I place my fingers on her neck to feel for a pulse and it's there, though very faint. Scooping her up in my arms, I'm immediately struck by the metallic scent of her blood mixed with what must be the acrid tang of their sweat. I want to vomit, but I grit my teeth and carry her to the car.

Her breath comes in soft, shallow gurgles that make me want to go back and kick the shit out of that guy even though he's dead. *How can anyone do this to another human being?*

There's a little blackness inside all of us.

No, I think to myself as I adjust my hold on her to stop the lolling of her head. This is not *a little blackness*. This is an all-engulfing black hole in the fabric of humanity.

I consider laying her down in the backseat, but I'm afraid she'll start choking on her blood or stop breathing and I won't see it until it's too late. I lay the passenger seat as far back as it will go and lay her down on her side so she'll be facing me as I drive. Her entire backside is smeared with fresh and old blood. *How long have they had her?* Part of me doesn't want to know the answer to this question, but another part of me knows it will probably make me feel even more justified in my actions tonight.

As I drive toward Good Samaritan hospital, I'm tempted to speed through all the lights, but getting myself arrested is only going to delay her care. Eight minutes later, I'm just a few blocks away from the hospital when I realize that . . . this girl saved my life. I don't believe in fate, but I don't know what else could have put her there at that exact moment. The idea makes me both sick and grateful. If they'd gotten there just a few minutes later, both of us would probably be dead.

I reach inside my coat to grab my phone and pull out a small, mint-green book instead. I tuck the book back into my pocket, then I pull out my phone and look up the number for the emergency room. Pulling up about twenty yards beyond the emergency-room entrance, I pull my hood over my head and hop out of the car. I race around the back of the car, thankful that there's no one outside the emergency room to see me. I wrench open the passenger door and easily scoop her up. She can't be more than fourteen or fifteen. Her skin is stretched taut over her bones and now that she's lost so much blood, she's wispy as an angel in my arms.

That's what she is: an angel. A broken, bloody angel. I want nothing more than to stay here with her to make sure she's okay. To thank her . . . for existing. But I can't.

I enter the emergency room through the sliding doors and gently lay her down on a waiting bench near the entrance. The harsh fluorescent lights illuminate her bloody body, and that's when I see the bunny tattoo on her chest. I make a split-second decision to lay my only copy of *Black Box* on the bench next to her head, then I race out the emergency-room doors to my car.

Chapter Sixteen

January 3rd
Mikki

Just hearing the words April fourteenth makes me want to vomit again. 'Who are you?' I scream, covering my eyes with the sheet so I can't see his face.

'I don't want to hurt you.' His voice is getting closer.

'Stay away!' I shriek as memories of my humiliation flash in my mind. 'Don't touch me!'

'You don't understand. I'm not one of them.' His voice is soft and reassuring and it makes me sick.

'Get out!' I want to threaten to call the cops, but I can't.

I'm trapped in this fucking hotel room with one of the few people in this world I can say took my soul from me. My body trembles as my mind flashes to our conversation in the club; how he joked around about killing me. I wonder if he recognized me the moment

I walked into that airport terminal and I just played right into his hands.

This is *not* how I want to die. I want to die on my own terms. I can't let him take that away from me. I have to do it before he does.

I pull the sheet away from my face and I can't stop the tears once I see the hardness in his gaze and the way his chest muscles bulge beneath his shirt. 'Please don't hurt me again,' I plead, sick with myself for once again being so weak. 'Please just let me go.'

His jaw clenches as he stares at me. 'You think I'd do something like that to you.' I don't know if he looks more angry or hurt. 'I'm not one of those pieces of shit who did this to you. I'm the one who found you. I'm the one who took you to the hospital.'

'You're lying.'

'I'm not!' he shouts and I squeeze my eyes shut against the memory of the bottom of a sneaker coming down on my face. 'I'm not one of them,' he says, a bit gentler this time. 'I swear to fucking God, I'm not one of them.'

'You want me to trust you.' I sob into the blanket. 'I'm not falling for that.'

'I can prove it. I left something with you, when I dropped you off at the hospital. A book.'

The trembling stops completely as I think of the book I've been carrying with me for more than three years. There's only one person in this entire world who knows about that book other than me and my sister Meaghan. I pull the blanket away from my face and peer under the sheet at my chest where the tiny tattoo over my heart stares back at me. Is this what gave me away?

'*Black Box*,' I whisper, staring at the bunny tattoo; my old Twitter profile picture.

'It's me,' he responds, and I don't have to look at him to hear the relief in his voice. 'I've been looking for you.'

'Why?' I pull the covers below my chin so I can see his face.

He shakes his head as tears well up in his eyes. 'I don't know. I guess I wanted to know that you were okay.'

'Why?'

His gaze pierces into me, as if I should know the answer to this question. And I *do* know.

He moves toward the bed slowly and, when I don't flinch, he takes a seat on the edge of the bed and buries his face in his hands. 'I'm sorry.'

'Sorry for what?'

'For not staying with you.'

'You didn't have to stay with me. I was in a fucking hospital. Trust me, I was being taken of.'

I wipe the tears from my face as I think of the first shower I took in the hospital bathroom. There's only so much the nurses could wipe away with a sponge bath. The dried blood came loose from every crevice of my body. No matter how hard I scrubbed, more just kept coming, from my hair, my fingernails, my mouth.

'Can you please leave?' I ask, wiping the last tears on the sheet, almost expecting to find blood smeared on the white fabric. He doesn't look at me. He just gets up and silently heads for the bedroom door. 'Just – just wait outside the door, please.'

He looks over his shoulder and nods before he closes the door behind him. I throw the covers off me then scramble into the bathroom to get dressed. Then I head back to the bedroom to dig the book out of my luggage. I lift the flap of my gray messenger bag then I unzip the interior compartment. Digging my hand inside, I come up with the soft, mint-green book. As always, the bloody fingerprint stains along the top edge of the cloth cover make my stomach twist.

I sink to the floor and clutch the book to my chest as the memory closes in on me.

I try to open my eyes, but my left eye is covered with something and my right eye seems to be fused shut. I whimper as my eyelashes are painfully pulled apart by the frantic struggle of my fluttering eyelid.

'Ow,' I mewl desperately.

The pain in my eyelashes is nothing compared to the pain in my mouth and my . . . The memory of the attack starts coming back to me and, through the cotton stuffed inside my cheek and bottom lip, my cries become less like weak whimpers and more like desperate moans.

'Help,' I groan thickly.

A nurse walks in and her eyes are wide with concern. I must look like shit for someone who's seen as much trauma as she's seen.

'Are you in pain, sweetie?' she asks, checking the monitors around me, pressing buttons that mean something to her, but to me they're just bleating reminders of my fragility; my humiliation.

'Yes,' I mutter through the cotton and the knot in my throat. 'It hurts.'

'Where does it hurt?' Her hand clutches the side rail of my hospital bed as she peers down at me with her wide brown eyes.

'Everywhere.'

She nods her head solemnly as she repeats this in a whisper. 'Everywhere.'

She can't hold back any longer. She wipes a tear from her eye as she reaches for the bag of clear fluid hanging from the IV stand. I think it's just a cover, because the bag is almost full.

She turns back to me and sniffs loudly. 'I'm sorry, honey. Your parents will be here soon. Did you want some pain medicine now? It might make you too sleepy to visit with them.'

'They're not here yet?'

The corner of her mouth screws up as she tries to hold back her tears again. 'You didn't come in with any identification. It took a while to find them. But they're on their way.'

'Ow . . . I need medicine, please.' I don't want to feel this pain. This feeling that I've been hollowed out with a dull knife. 'Please.'

She pushes some buttons on one of the machines and a soft pumping sound startles me. It reminds me of the sound of the van as it squeaked up and down beneath me. My fingers tremble as I squeeze the bed sheet in my fist. But my grip slackens quickly as the drugs kick in and soon I drift off into blissful blackness.

When I come to again, my mom is standing next to me, her green eyes bloodshot from crying and her light-brown hair frazzled, as she was woken in the middle of the night and probably didn't bother combing it. She reaches for my hand and I yank my hand back. This sends a sharp pain through my shoulder and I cry out.

'Ow! Don't touch me.'

My mom reaches for a button on my bed, probably to call a nurse, as the soft sound of Meaghan's cries come to me from somewhere near my feet. I lift my head a little, ignoring the pain in the side of my neck so I can see her. The collar of her T-shirt is pulled up over her face so that it covers her up to her eyes. She's trying to hide her tears from me, but she can't hide the way her shoulders jump with each sob.

I lay my head back on the pillow and close my eyes, then I immediately open them again when I see the Red Sox cap. 'What time is it?'

'Seven a.m.' My father's voice comes to me, ragged and reserved, from somewhere near the door of the hospital room.

Seven a.m. I left the party around eleven o'clock. I'm almost afraid to ask, but I have to know.

'How long have I been here?' I ask just as a different nurse enters the room.

'Since two a.m.,' she replies while reaching for something behind me to turn off the nurse call. 'You were in surgery for an hour, then you were sedated for a while. Are you hurting?'

'In surgery?'

My mom covers her mouth as she turns around and steps out of the way for the nurse to check my IV lines. 'Nothing too serious. The doctor will talk to you about it tomorrow after you've had some rest.' The nurse leans in, pretending to adjust my pillow as she whispers, 'I have your book if you want me to bring it to you. I figured I'd let you decide if you want to keep it or let the cops take it.'

I almost ask her what the fuck she's talking about, but my heart starts racing with the prospect of possibly finding some kind of clue as to who did this to me.

'I want it now, please,' I whisper as she's pulling away.

She nods as she turns on her heel and leaves the room. She returns a couple of hours later and insists that my family needs to leave so I can rest. Mom, Dad, and Meaghan wander off to some waiting room or restaurant where they'll surely speculate about what happened to me; maybe even feel sorry for themselves for having to see me like this. The nurse returns a few minutes after they leave with a large plastic zipper bag containing a mint-green hardcover book. Smudges of blood are visible on the cover of the book *and inside the bag. I don't recognize it at all, until she holds it up in front of my face so I can see the cover:* Black Box.

'This Black Box is yours to keep, to stash your troubles away. Just lock it up and call my name, and I'll be there always.'

'This is your book, right?' she asks. I nod slowly and she smiles. 'I'll keep it safe for you until you're discharged. They took way too much from you already, sis. I won't let them take this.'

Chapter Seventeen

January 3rd
Crush

I wait outside the bedroom with my hands and nose pressed against the door, waiting for the slightest noise or vibration. I don't know if I can trust her in there alone. My entire body is on alert, like I'm back in Brockton, driving along Cary Street in the car I torched later that night, praying she doesn't stop breathing.

'Are you okay?' I shout as softly as I can through the door.

I don't know how to shout softly, but I don't want to scare her again. She's so on edge. How could she not be?

She doesn't respond so I wait a few seconds before I call out to her again. A moment later, the bedroom door swings open and I glimpse her back as she walks toward the bed. She drops a book – *the* book – onto the mattress, then she sinks down onto the floor with her back leaned against the foot of the bed.

I move slowly toward the bed and my chest aches when I see the book. It's stained with blood, probably from that night, and I'm almost afraid to pick it up.

'I knew it wasn't them who took me to the hospital. They would have left me for dead. I knew that the minute they stuffed me into that trunk.' I lift the book from the mattress and ease myself down onto the floor next to her. She glances at the book before she continues. 'There's a sense you get around someone new and, instantly, you know if you can trust them. I knew the minute that guy called out to me on the street that I was going to regret leaving that party for the rest of whatever life I had left.'

She draws in a deep, stuttered breath and I wish she would look at me instead of the splintered bathroom door.

'My sister and I have read that book about a thousand times trying to figure out who wrote it.' She turns to me, her face incredulous. 'What kind of book doesn't have any information about the author or publisher? What the hell is *Black Box*?'

I open the book to the title page and trace my finger over the words *Black Box*. The pages were already so worn when I left the book with Mikki, but, even after all these years, I can still recognize that the pages have been turned many, many more times.

'You mean to tell me you've read this book a thousand times and you still don't know what it is?' I close the book and turn it over in my hands to examine every inch of it.

She lets out a soft huff. 'I know what it is. I just want to know how you came upon this book. Who gave it to you? Who wrote it? *Why* did they write it? Because I feel like this book was written for me.'

I smile as I remember the first time I read the last few lines of *Black Box*; how I felt exactly the same way. 'That's because it *was* written for you. And for me. And for my grandfather who gave it to me.'

She finally looks up and the sheen of tears on her cheeks makes me want to kiss her skin. She's silent for a moment before she looks away again.

'You killed that guy.' She's not stating this as a question. There's no confusion about this. 'You did that . . . for *me*?'

I nod, even though she's not looking at me. 'He was going to kill you or just leave you there to die.'

She buries her face in her arms, which are folded on top of her knees, and she cries softly. I want to rub her back or hold her. I can't stand to see her bear the burden of this alone. But I'm so afraid of scaring her away. I've looked for her everywhere. The police and the hospital wouldn't release her information to anyone because she was a minor. I was forced to look for that tattoo. I incurred a long list of one-night stands while searching for it. I can't scare her away now. I have so many questions that only pile up the longer I stare at her.

What happened to her after I left the hospital? Was she treated well? Did she have to identify the body of her attacker? How did that affect her? Would she still be this afraid if they had convicted those other bastards in the van?

I need answers, but, most of all, I need to know that I did the right thing . . . in her eyes.

Finally, she draws in a deep, congested breath and turns to me. 'I'm hungry.'

'How's your head?'

'No more messed up than usual.'

I smile as I hold the book out to her. She stares at it for a moment before she takes it from me. I rise from the floor and head for the door. 'You want to look at the room-service menu.'

She smiles and the glint of light on her lip ring makes my guts feel all warm and gooey. 'You pick something. I trust you.'

Room service arrives twenty minutes later with a cart piled high with plates covered in silver domes. I pretend not to notice when Mikki suddenly needs to get something out of the bedroom when she hears the knock at the door. She comes out of the bedroom a few minutes after the waiter leaves our room, which gives me enough time to set up the plates and accouterment on the dining table.

She eyes the half-dozen silver domes on the table warily as she approaches. It's past eight in the evening, so I'm not surprised to see her wearing an oversized black T-shirt and pajama pants covered in images of anime characters. But I am surprised by how much it turns me on.

I turn my attention back to the food and begin removing the lids from the plates. 'I didn't know what you wanted, so I thought we'd try a few different things.' The first lid I remove reveals a plate of plain spaghetti with marinara sauce. 'I'm not sure if you're a vegetarian, so I told them to hold the meat.'

She shakes her head as she takes a seat at the table. 'I'm not a vegetarian, but I don't eat meat in restaurants. I don't trust it.'

'Well, then you should be happy with the other items I ordered for you.'

I lift the next lid and she laughs when she sees a pile of blueberry muffins with the tops cut off. The woman who took my room-service order must have thought I was crazy when I asked for these, but it was totally worth it to see Mikki's reaction.

'That's a lot of muffin stumps. I can't eat all of those.' She grabs one off the top of the pile and shakes her head as she peels away the crinkled paper.

'You don't have to eat them all right now. We've got at least a few more minutes before the advocates for fair treatment of muffin tops bust down our door.'

Her eyes widen. 'What are you going to do about the bathroom door?'

'It's just a little damage. I'll pay for it when we leave.'

'Just like that, huh?' And she shakes her head. 'I can't believe I was saved by a rich boy.'

'Twice. And why does that surprise you?'

'I don't know.' She shrugs as she takes her first bite of blueberry muffin. 'I guess I just expected it to be some punk kid who spent way too much time on Twitter while hanging out in dark, deserted parking lots.' She takes a swig of the iced water in front of her then looks me in the eyes. 'Why were you there in that parking lot?'

Chapter Eighteen

January 3rd
Mikki

The confident smile Crush was wearing when he unveiled the muffins is gone. A chill lifts the hairs on my arms as I think of the very far-fetched possibility that I've considered for the past three years: that the guy who saved me also raped me, but he had a change of heart when he realized I was about to be murdered. The only thing that stopped me from allowing myself to give in to this theory is that there were two sets of fresh tire skid marks in the parking lot and the trail of my blood led toward a set of tire marks that did not match a mini-van. But that hasn't stopped me from wondering if maybe he used another car to take me to the hospital. And Crush's silence following this question is troubling.

Finally, he looks me in the eyes. 'I'll be honest with you. I've spent the last three and a half years trying to find you while also trying to forget what happened that night. I was in a very dark place.'

'Oh, fuck,' I whisper involuntarily as I begin to feel woozy. 'I need a cigarette.'

'What's wrong?'

I shake my head as I set down the muffin in my hands. 'Were you . . . were you with *them*?'

'What? Fuck, no! I was parked there alone when the van pulled up.' I let out a loud sigh of relief and he continues. 'I was . . . I was thinking about my cousin. Jordan died a year before that. I was with him when it happened.'

I have a strong feeling he's holding something back, but he's been so patient with me today that I think it's time for me to return the favor. 'Hey, look at that. You ordered booze.'

I grab a bottle of beer out of the bucket of ice in the center of the dining table and he quickly reaches for it to take it away. His fingers graze mine and I drop the beer onto the table. Luckily, it doesn't break and he swiftly saves it from rolling off and onto the floor.

'You need a bottle opener for these,' he says, his eyebrows knitted with worry. 'How about I crack these open and we can go out on the terrace for a smoke?'

'Yes,' I reply quickly, bumping my knee on the table as I hastily rise from the chair and make my way back to the bedroom to get my cigarettes and coat.

I yank my coat off the chair in the bedroom and decide I'd better put a sweater on between my T-shirt and coat. Then I pull on two pairs of socks under my boots and head out to the living room. Crush is standing just inside the enormous glass door leading out to the terrace. He's wearing a gray beanie and a serious expression that makes me smile inside.

'Pull up the hood of your coat,' he says, holding out an open bottle of beer as I approach.

'So bossy.' I accept the beer, taking a large swig as he reaches for the door handle.

He twists the handle slowly and carefully pulls the door inward. The snow falls softly over the outdoor tables and chairs. But it's the glow of the city lights, muted by the haze of snowflakes, that's mesmerizing. Crush pulls his coat tighter as he waits for me to step outside.

'I should have changed into some jeans,' I say, my teeth chattering as I trudge through the snow toward the large stone spheres poised atop the iron railing surrounding the terrace.

The terrace is huge. Four wrought-iron tables covered in snow fit comfortably in the space. I find myself imagining rich people in their tuxedos and cocktail dresses hobnobbing on the terrace, sipping thirty-year-old bourbon and discussing the stock market. Crush could be one of those people, though he certainly doesn't look or act like one.

'Where are your gloves?' he asks, shutting the glass door behind him.

'I forgot them.'

'I'll hold your beer.'

He holds his hand out and I shake my head despite the fact that I can already feel the cold penetrating the soft pads of my fingers and into my bones. 'No, thanks.'

The stone spheres on the railing are covered in cone-shaped piles of snow. I brush the snow off the sphere nearest me and attempt to balance my beer on top.

'My granddad used to say that he never left New England because magical things happen in the snow.'

My fingers are really starting to ache, so I guzzle down the rest of my beer and toss the empty bottle onto the snow-covered table behind us. I turn back to the railing and Crush is gazing up at the sky with a wistful look on his face as the snowflakes fall on his cheeks.

'This is the same granddad that gave you the book?'

He looks down at me and my stomach flips. 'This was the last thing he gave me before he died.' For a moment, I assume he's talking about the book, until he reaches into his coat pocket and comes up with a crushed penny. 'It's my lucky penny. I use it every time I have an important performance.'

'You have a lucky penny?'

He gazes into my eyes and nods. 'Do you believe in fate?'

'No.'

'Neither do I. Do you believe in luck?'

'Yes.'

'What's the difference?' His gaze is intense as he awaits my answer.

'I don't know. You're the one with the lucky penny. You tell me. What's the difference between fate and luck?'

He smiles and turns his attention back to the view of the city. 'Fate is for fairy tales. It's a romantic notion. Luck is what happens when you're in the right place at the right time . . . with the right person.'

A shiver travels through me and I tuck my hands inside my coat pockets. I lean over the railing to get a view of the street below and Crush grabs my arm.

'Please don't do that.'

'Do what? I was just looking at the street.'

Not that it didn't cross my mind to leap, but we're only four stories up. Not high enough.

His eyes are fixed on my arm where his immense hand is clasped around my bicep. It takes a moment for me to realize that this is the first time he's touched me and I didn't flinch.

He gently releases his hold on me. 'Sorry. I didn't mean to grab you. Just instinct, I guess.'

'That's okay.' I pull my lighter and pack of Lucky Strikes out of my pocket.

He glances at my cigarettes and smiles. 'You smoke Luckies?'

'My best friend Rina smokes a Blackjack, but I can't do that. I don't smoke just because I'm addicted to the nicotine. I like the flavor.'

'Where's your best friend now?'

I pop the cigarette in my mouth, but the snow and the slight breeze keep stamping out the lighter's flame. Crush cups his hands around my hands and the flame holds as I draw a long pull on the cigarette. His face is less than a foot away from mine as he slowly lowers his hands. I don't notice I'm holding my breath until I begin to choke on the smoke. I turn my head away so I don't cough in his face, but when I turn back he's still there.

'Are you all right?'

'I'll live.'

'Not if you keep smoking those.'

My face twitches with all the things I wish I could say. Instead, I take one more long pull on the cigarette, watching as the cherry burns its way up the cigarette toward my mouth. Then I flick the cigarette off the balcony and exhale as I make my way back into the hotel room.

Peeling off my coat, I toss it onto the round, mahogany coffee table before I plop down onto the sofa in the living room. He comes in a few minutes later and sits next to me. I can feel the cold emanating from his snow-dusted coat and I get an urge to tell him to take his coat off or he'll catch cold.

He pulls off his beanie and tosses it onto the table, on top of my coat, then he leans back on the sofa and stares up at the ceiling. 'I think I know why you don't want to go home.'

My phone vibrates in my back pocket, but I continue to ignore the ringing and the voicemails the way I have been all day. But just a few seconds later, Crush's phone begins to ring. He slips the phone out of his jeans pocket and answers.

'Hello?'

I get a weird, painful sensation in my chest as I watch him on the phone, hoping it's not a girlfriend. I watch his lips as he speaks, unable to hear his words. All I can see is the perfect peaks at the top of his lip; the juicy pink color; and the curve of his mouth – that smile. I tear my gaze away from his mouth. He's smiling because he's caught me staring at his lips.

'It's the airline,' he whispers, pointing at his phone and still flashing me that knowing smile.

I nod as I shoot up from the sofa and grab my coat off the table. I make my way back to the bedroom and slam the door shut behind me. Sitting down on the edge of the bed, I hastily begin removing my boots, but I leave on the sweater I'm wearing over my T-shirt. I curl up on the bed and try not to think about his lips.

I haven't kissed anyone since before the incident at Uncle Cort's house last summer. The last guy I kissed tasted like tequila. It was a few nights before I graduated from alternative high school. My parents were out for the night, playing poker at Aunt Crystal's house the way they always do on Saturday nights. Rina brought over a couple of guys she met at Starbucks and we all got drunk in my bedroom. Both guys were pretty cute, but the one with the darker hair and the lip ring that lined up with mine when we kissed was definitely hotter. I don't even remember his name and it was only seven months ago. But I do remember what he said to me when I refused to do anything more than just kiss.

If we're not going to fuck, what's the point?

He was right. If you're not going to go all the way, what's the point of doing anything? Why get out of bed if you don't have the courage to leave the house? Why make the phone call if you're too afraid to ask someone out? What's the point of existing if you're too chickenshit to live?

Chapter Nineteen

January 3rd
Crush

I consider leaving Mikki alone for the rest of the night, but in the end I decide against it. If I leave her alone, she'll probably stay awake all night obsessing over the fact that I caught her staring at my mouth. I should at least try to ease her embarrassment before I go to bed.

I knock softly and I'm not at all surprised by her immediate response.

'Goodnight!' she shouts from inside the bedroom.

'Don't you want to know what the airline said?' I shout back.

I imagine she's probably letting out a deep sigh as she realizes she can't avoid me. A minute later, the door opens just a crack as she stares at the floor.

'What did they say?'

I take a step back, hoping this will put her at ease.

'The flight was rescheduled to Thursday night at six. Does that work for you?'

She shrugs without looking up. 'I don't have much of a choice, do I?'

'They gave me a number you can call if you want to reschedule, but that's the soonest they could get us on a new flight.'

Her mouth drops open a little. 'What about your song? Will you still be able to record it?'

'I'll call the producer tomorrow and see if we can reschedule.'

'And if he can't?'

She finally looks up and I gaze into her eyes for a moment before I answer. 'Then I'll have to wait for another stroke of luck.'

Her lip trembles and she quickly shuts the door. 'Goodnight.' Her voice is barely audible through the door, and the tears.

'Goodnight.'

I stand just outside her door for a moment, wondering if I should leave. My mind flashes to the screaming red marks and the scars I saw all over the tops of her thighs. I know I can't stop her from *feeling* like she wants to hurt herself, but I don't think I'll be able to sleep tonight worrying about what she may or may not be doing in that room.

I raise my hand and pause for a second before I knock again. She doesn't answer right away like she did last time, so I knock again. She still doesn't answer. I call her name through the door, but still no reply. I try the handle and it's not locked. Turning the handle slowly, I expect her to push the door closed on me, but she never does. And, soon, the door is wide open and the sound of running water greets my ears.

A large crack of light shines into the bedroom through the splintered doorframe. Somehow, she's managed to close the door all the way. *Fuck.* Why do I have such a bad feeling about this? It's not as if she hasn't lived all these years without me around to stop her from hurting herself. But something, some primal instinct, is shouting at me that I need to keep a close eye on her. Something is telling me she wants to die.

And it's not just the cuts on her legs. It's everything I've learned about her since we ran into each other at the airport. The fact that she doesn't want to go home. That she won't answer a single phone call or text, though I've seen her phone buzzing for hours. That she's moving to L.A. to go to community college. Who moves clear across the country to go to community college?

But I think the biggest tell has to be the fact that she brought *Black Box* with her. This shows me that she hasn't let go of what happened that night – how could she? – and that she's still searching for answers.

I should tell her everything. I should tell her why I was there and why I wanted to kill myself. I should tell her exactly what I saw, what I did, and how I covered it all up. But I don't want her to judge me the way I've judged myself. I got away with murder; possibly twice. What does that say about me? How can you not judge someone when you find out something like that about them?

Moving slowly toward the bathroom door, I listen for the slightest sound that would indicate she's okay in there, but I hear nothing. I draw in a deep breath and knock.

She lets out a sharp yelp. 'What the fuck?'

'Sorry! I was just checking to make sure you're okay.'

'I'm taking a fucking bath!'

'I'll get out of here now.'

'Wait!' she calls out as I begin to walk away. 'Wait. I forgot my toiletries. Can you push my suitcase in here?'

'Why don't you use the hotel toiletries?'

'I have sensitive skin!'

I smile as I grab the handle on her suitcase, which sits just outside the bathroom, and wheel it toward the door.

'Close your eyes!' she shouts as I use the suitcase to slowly push the door open.

I close my eyes, but the wheels of the suitcase get caught on something and, instinctively, I open my eyes to see what it is. Catching a glimpse of Mikki's reflection in the mirror instantly gets my heart racing. She's lying in the bathtub and she doesn't know I can see her, but I can still see the anxiety on her face as her eyes are glued to the door.

'What are you waiting for? Just push it in here.' She looks up at that moment and the reflections of our eyes lock.

I let the suitcase handle go and quickly pull the door shut. 'The suitcase was stuck,' I explain to the door, but she doesn't reply.

I incur my walk of shame out of her bedroom and hope I haven't made her too uncomfortable or broken her trust. I can't imagine she gives that away easily. And it must have taken a healthy amount of trust or desperation for her to get a hotel room with me today . . . before she even knew who I was.

She didn't even know who I was.

Shaking my head as I enter my bedroom, I allow my body to fall backward onto the bed. I have to ignore this crazy voice in my head telling me that this whole thing – the storm, the canceled flight, the chance meeting – was fate's way of bringing Mikki and me back together. That kind of stuff only happens in cheesy romantic movies. And, let's face it, if they ever made a movie for Mikki and me, it would probably be categorized under horror flicks. Everything from the moment we met on Twitter to this very moment has been a series of unhappy endings.

I heave a deep sigh before I sit up in bed and begin peeling off all my various layers of clothing. I start with my boots, then I toss my coat, sweater, and T-shirt onto the armchair in the corner before I rise from the bed to remove my pants. Once I'm down to nothing but my boxer briefs, I contemplate taking a shower, but I'm afraid something will happen to Mikki while I'm in there.

Heading for the bathroom, the sound of knocking at the door stops me. 'Yeah?'

'Can I come in?'

Fuck. 'Uh, yeah. Give me a minute.'

Thinking quickly, I scurry into the bathroom and grab the bathrobe off the hook and slip it on, hastily tying it closed. I open the bedroom door and she looks me up and down for a second before she speaks.

'What are you doing in here? Getting a mani-pedi?' she asks with a grin.

She looks beautiful with no makeup and damp hair.

'Very funny. I was just going to take a shower. What's up?'

Her hands are clasped behind her back as she looks off to the side. 'I came to apologize. I didn't mean to yell at you. You just kind of startled me. And . . . thanks for the flight info . . . and for letting me stay here with you until the flight.'

'How about the muffins?' She looks up so she can glare at me, but her eyes glance over my chest. I smile at her as I attempt to pull the robe tightly closed, but this thing must be made for women or scrawny, old dudes. 'Well, since you're in a grateful mood, do you think you can thank me by giving me your phone number?'

She scrunches up her eyebrows. 'Why do you need my number? We're staying in the same room.'

'Yeah, but I was thinking it might be easier to avoid running into each other naked if we can send a text before barging into each other's rooms.'

'You think of everything, don't you?'

I shrug as I open the bedroom door wider and head for the nightstand where I set down my phone earlier. 'What's your number? I'll text you right now so you can save my mine in your phone.' She shoots off the ten digits quickly, probably trying to see if my fingers can keep up. I fire away a text message then smile at her as I look up from the screen. 'You might want to go check your phone. I think you just got a text message from a really hot guy.'

She rolls her eyes as she turns to leave. 'Goodnight, Crush.'

'Goodnight, Mikki.'

She closes the door and I take my phone with me into the bathroom. The hot water is running and I'm about to step into the shower when I hear the buzzing noise of my phone vibrating on the counter. I scoop it up and smile at her reply.

Me: Want to stay in tomorrow and watch movies and order room service all day?
Mikki: Only if we watch Pretty in Pink and you change the ending so Andie ends up with Fuckie.

I laugh out loud at the typo and she instantly sends another text through.

Mikki: Duckie! Duckie! Not Fuckie!

Me: Are you sure you're not talking about Pretty in Kink? I think that's the one with Fuckie.

Mikki: Stupid phone.

Me: Of course we can watch that and if Duckie doesn't get the girl this time, I'll hunt down John Hughes and demand a re-make.

Mikki: John Hughes is dear.

Mikki: Dead! John Hughes is DEAD! Ugh.

Me: Killed by all those Fuckie fans, I'm sure.

Mikki: SMH

Me: Getting in the shower now. Feel free to wake me up later if you need anything.

Mikki: Goodnight.

Me: Sweet dreams.

Chapter Twenty

January 4th
Mikki

The moment I close my messaging app, I see the little red icon telling me I have fourteen voicemail messages. I turn the screen off and the darkness swallows me. I want to slide out of bed, slip into the bathroom, and end it all right now: all the voicemails, the obsessive thoughts, the awkward moments, the memories. But I swore I wouldn't do it in a place where I could be found. And I don't think I can do that to Crush after what he saw in that parking lot.

I have to let my cell phone battery die. Pretty soon it will be twenty-four hours since I went missing. The police will be able to track my phone if it's powered on. Letting the battery die means I won't have to listen to those voicemails, but it also means no more cute text messages from Crush.

Laying the phone on the nightstand, I lie back and

gaze into the darkness. Then I force myself to remember everything. I've stayed pretty high and drunk for the past three years, but sometimes when I'm sober I force myself to remember. I never want to forget that the world can go black in a split second.

The first time I did this was the night before my appointment with the detective who handled my case: Detective Mills. I didn't sleep the night before that appointment. I was up the whole night, forcing myself to remember every detail as I scrawled it down on a million pieces of paper. And somewhere around four in the morning, while crouched on my bedroom floor, sobbing over a pile of messy notes, I realized that I needed to change the facts to make sure the investigation never went to trial. I finally understood why so many rapes go unreported. I didn't want to face my attackers in a courtroom. I didn't want to know what they thought of me. I didn't want to see even a trace of satisfaction in their eyes. I didn't want to deal with questions about what I was wearing or whether I was a virgin or what it felt like to have my soul ripped to shreds.

These are the facts: On the night of April fourteenth, an unknown number of young men brutally raped me over the course of approximately three hours. Then they dumped me in a parking lot, beat me within an inch of my life, and left me for dead. I wasn't going to let the justice system rape me again.

*

I step out of the bedroom the next morning, freshly showered with my makeup and hair in place. When I enter the dining area, I can see him in the kitchen, standing next to the sink with his shirt off, guzzling a glass of water. As soon as he sets the glass in the sink, he spots me and the smile he casts in my direction is just too fucking cute.

'Good morning. You look like you're ready for a day at the library.'

I look down at my clothes, confused by his remark. I'm wearing a pair of skinny jeans Rina and I drew on with clothing markers, a baby-blue Cubs T-shirt – because the sight of it drives my dad crazy – and a black hoodie.

'Do I look like a book nerd or something?'

He rounds the breakfast bar and my breath catches in my throat when I see his gray boxer briefs. I quickly reach for one of the dining chairs and pull it out to take a seat, so I can stare at the table instead.

'I thought of something last night and I—' His voice cuts off and I look up to see what's wrong. 'Never mind. You said you wanted to stay in. I'll go get dressed. Go ahead and order us some breakfast.' He takes off toward his bedroom and I seize the opportunity to watch him as he leaves. 'Order me a steak.'

'With or without blood?'

'The more blood, the better.'

I've never ordered room service before, and I'm certain the guy taking my order knows. He sighs audibly when I don't immediately know what cut of steak I want to order or what I want to drink. A few minutes later, I hang up the hotel phone and Crush walks out of his bedroom looking like the lead character in a blockbuster movie about demon hunters. I press my lips together as I head for the sofa in the living room to keep from smiling.

We both sit down and he begins fiddling with the remote as he searches for something to watch. 'If I can't find *Pretty in Kink*, are you going to be upset? Like, will you start crying or force-feeding me muffin tops until I burst, or something?'

'No, but I might nuke your steak in the microwave and force you to eat that.'

'Fair enough.' He continues flipping through the various apps on the TV, searching for somewhere he can purchase a movie and I pull my feet up on the sofa to hug my knees. 'Maybe we should just read,' he says after a few minutes of fruitless searching.

I turn to him and I can't help but smile, even though I'm so tired from not having slept all night. Reading will probably put me to sleep. Maybe that's not such a bad thing.

'I'll get the book.' I spring up from the sofa, practically skipping as I make my way to my bedroom to retrieve the book from on top of the armchair where I left it yesterday.

When I come out of the room, Crush is letting in the room service guy. The guy sets all our dishes on the dining table and pours us each a cup of fresh-squeezed orange juice and ice water while Crush signs the check. I sit down at the table again, laying the book in my lap as I wait for Crush to take a seat.

'I don't know what's what, so go ahead and start unveiling,' he says, lifting the lid on one of the plates.

He gets lucky and finds his steak on the first try. I lift the lid closest to me and find the warm croissants I ordered. Setting aside the lid, I pour myself a cup of coffee – black – then pull my legs up on the chair to sit cross-legged. I hand the book to Crush so he can place it on the other side of the table, away from all the food and drink, but he opens it up instead.

'Can we start in the middle so we have time to finish it before the flight?' he asks, thumbing through the pages until he finds the first page of chapter twenty-three. I know that chapter. So does he.

'We can start wherever you want. It's your book and you haven't read it in way longer than I have.' I tear off a chunk of the croissant and pop it in my mouth, letting out a soft moan. 'This is fucking delicious. Have you tried these?'

He nods as he pulls the ribbon bookmark down the center of the book and closes it. 'When was the last time you read *Black Box*?'

I wash down my croissant with some equally delicious black coffee before I respond. 'Last week.'

He chuckles softly as he cuts off a piece of steak. The blood runs from the steak and all I can think is that I hope it doesn't run into his scrambled eggs. That would be disgusting. Scrambled eggs should be eaten with ketchup. Not blood.

He swallows his food and gulps down some orange juice before he turns to me. '*Black Box* is my grandfather's story. It's the only book he ever wrote and he never got it published.'

'You gave me the one copy of the only book your grandfather ever wrote?' He nods and continues eating, as if this is no big deal. 'Are you fucking crazy?'

He doesn't flinch at my question. He finishes chewing his eggs then he slowly sets down his fork and turns to me. 'You would have done the same thing.'

'But . . . if that's your grandfather's story, that means . . . The black box exists?' He nods and I feel as if I can't breathe. 'Can we start reading now?' He hands me the book and I push my plate of croissants aside so I can lay the book on the table. I open the book to the page he marked and begin to read aloud.

'Herman's plane landed at Boston airport at seven in the evening. His relief to finally be home after eight months away could only be matched by his utter elation at finally being able to see Leah and June.'

I quickly close the book and cover my face as the tears begin. 'I'm sorry. I can't do it. You have to read it.'

I know why he picked this chapter to start with and I'm almost angry with him. Though I've relived it a million times over the past three years, it still kills me when Herman returns from the war to find his seven-year-old daughter, June, has died. Now, knowing it's his grandfather's story only makes it worse.

'Are you okay?' he asks as he takes the book from me and sets it on the seat of the chair next to him.

'I'm sorry,' I blubber into my hands. 'I just hate that she died. I really wanted him to read her letters.'

I can't stop the tears. In fact, the more I think about it, the more I cry. Suddenly, I feel movement in my hair. I pull my hands away from my face and Crush is touching my hair.

'This isn't your real hair color,' he says, mesmerized as he rubs a lock of black hair between his fingers.

'I've dyed my hair a dozen different colors since that night, but black is my favorite. I'll never go back to my natural color. I don't want to see . . . I don't want to even know what I used to look like.'

'You mean, you don't have any pictures of yourself before that?'

I shake my head as I use the sleeves of my sweater to wipe my face. 'I burned them all.'

He reaches his hand forward slowly and I close my eyes as he brushes a tear from my jaw. 'I think you'd look beautiful with any hair color.' He pulls his hand away and I open my eyes. 'Can you come with me to the library?'

'The library?'

'I know you don't want to leave the hotel, but my

grandfather donated some rare books to the Boston Public Library. They have them in a glass case on the third floor of the McKim Building. I've been too scared to go see them because I've missed him so much. Then Jordan died and . . . Anyway, I think I'm ready to go.'

I want to say yes to him. He obviously needs this. But I can't risk getting caught. I've been planning this trip for too long. I'm not backing out now.

'Can't you go alone?'

He shakes his head. 'I don't think I can. But I'll understand if you don't want to go. I promised you we'd stay in. That's what we'll do.' He places the silver lid over his half-eaten steak and eggs, then he drains the last drops of orange juice from his glass before he rises from the table. 'Let's go read.'

Chapter Twenty-one

Black Box

Herman's plane landed at Boston airport at seven in the evening. His relief to finally be home after eight months away could only be matched by his utter elation at finally being able to see Leah and June. Captain Winters sent his wife's brother to retrieve Herman from the airport, since Leah and Herman didn't own an automobile. The last letter he received from Leah six weeks earlier, she wrote of her outing with June to the marathon finish line. Three runners broke the world record this year. Leah said June was ecstatic to witness such an unbelievable feat.

Terry Knott, Captain Winters' brother-in-law, seemed like a decent enough fellow. He worked as a longshoreman at the Port of Boston, loading and unloading the enormous crates on the cargo ships. He didn't speak much on the drive home, but the ropy muscles in his neck tightened every time he nodded in reply to one of Herman's questions. Herman got the sense Terry was tense about something, but it wasn't his place to pry into William's private life, so he kept quiet.

When they arrived at the apartment on Howard Avenue, the rain was coming down pretty hard. Terry helped him unload his army-issue duffel bag onto the sidewalk then, with a curt nod and a stiff *good luck*, he raced back into the driver's seat and set off in his shiny Ford truck. Herman didn't know if he had offended Terry, but he didn't have much desire to find out. He had to get out of this downpour and upstairs to his two favorite girls.

The three-story, brick-faced home in Roxbury had been converted into six tiny apartments over a decade before. Herman, Leah, and June all shared one bedroom, living room, kitchen, and a bathroom the size of a matchbox. The neighborhood could be rough, but it was home to some of the best jazz clubs in Boston. And, other than his girls, there was nothing he loved more than nursing a glass of bourbon while puffing on a DC and listening to some great jazz.

Herman swung his duffel bag over his shoulder and dashed up the front walk and the six concrete steps, his boots splashing in the tiny puddles accumulated in the cracks of the concrete. The stairs delivered him to the front door of the building and he breathed a sigh of relief. He was home.

He didn't have a key, but the landlord had installed a

buzzer shortly before Herman left for Korea. He lived in apartment four, but he pressed the buzzer for apartment three; the apartment across the hall from theirs. He wanted to surprise Leah.

'Who's there?' the female voice crackled through the speaker.

It was Mrs Yardley; a nice woman who did most of the ironing and mending for the neighborhood. Her husband was a drunk who beat her frequently. One of these days, Herman was going to move Leah and June into a big house in Cambridge and the day they left he'd tell Mrs Yardley that she and her two boys deserved better. But he couldn't do that now. Her marriage wasn't any of his business; even if Mr and Mrs Yardley did keep June up with their arguing on occasion.

'Mrs Yardley, it's Herman. Would you please buzz me in?'

'Herman?' she replied. 'Would you like me to call Leah?'

'No, no,' he answered quickly. 'I want to surprise her, if you don't mind.'

'Oh. Oh, yes, of course. Just a moment.'

A second later, the door buzzed and he nearly broke the rusty doorknob off in his haste to yank it open. The smell of damp wood was heavy in the dark entry hall, but it diminished as he raced up the staircase to the second floor. The sight of the brass number four on the face of the dark wooden door made his stomach drop. He was home.

He knocked on the door and eventually heard signs of slow movement inside the apartment. His heart raced at the sound of the lock turning. Then the doorknob began to rotate and he had to stop himself from throwing the door open.

The door creaked inward and Leah was standing there with her eyes wide and her mouth hanging open; but it wasn't the same Leah. She'd changed.

She'd lost at least ten pounds, and she was already too thin when Herman shipped out. Her eyes were glassy and vacant and she appeared almost afraid. He knew he'd changed a bit over the past eight months; his skin had darkened from hours in the hot Korean sun on the deck of the USS *Los Angeles*.

'Leah, it's me. It's Herman. I'm home.' Her lip trembled as she stared at Herman, still unable to speak. 'Darling, it's me.'

He took one step forward and she took three steps back, bumping into the armchair in the sitting room. Herman dropped his duffel onto the floor and she shook her head adamantly as she began to cry.

'I'm so sorry,' she whimpered. 'I'm so sorry.'

'It's okay. I know I caught you by surprise.' Herman reached for her, but she scuttled around the armchair to keep the distance between them. 'Leah, what's wrong? Where's June?'

Leah continued to shake her head and Herman knew that he had come home too late. Something had happened to June. He tore across the living room and threw open the door to the bedroom. The curtains were drawn so tight, not a crack of light penetrated the space. Herman yanked the chain on the lamp near the door and the bed was empty.

'Where is she?' he roared at Leah from the bedroom. 'Where's June, God damn it?'

Leah crept toward the open bedroom door, tears streaming down her face as she clasped her hands tightly over her chest. 'She's gone. They put her in isolation when she got TB and the medicine they gave her . . .' She covered her face and sobbed into her hands.

Herman grabbed her wrists. 'What about the medicine? What happened?'

But Herman didn't need to know anything more. June's history with psychosis always put her at risk when she needed treatment for any type of illness. Anything could set her off.

'She stole a needle from one of the nurses and stabbed herself in the neck so many times . . . in the middle of the night.' Leah choked on her words. 'By morning, she was gone.'

Herman shook his head in disbelief. Not his little girl. The same girl who filled his world with sunlight could not deliberately turn his world black.

He couldn't voice this aloud. Herman knew Leah would not lie about something like this. She struggled with June's psychosis more than anyone. For many years, she had been certain June's condition was her fault; maybe she didn't sing to her enough as a baby or maybe June had inherited the psychosis from Leah's grandmother who died not knowing her own name. Just one look at Leah's emaciated face and Herman knew she would blame herself for this for years to come.

He wanted to comfort Leah, but there was one more pressing matter to attend to first. He marched across the bedroom and yanked open the closet door to search for the black box. He shoved boxes of shoes and photographs off the shelf in the closet then dug through all the shoes and boxes on the floor and found nothing.

'Where is it?' Herman demanded and Leah pointed to the top drawer of the bedside table.

Herman yanked it open and retrieved the wooden box made out of solid walnut and finished to a mirror shine with black lacquer. He felt around the inside of the drawer for the key to open the box, but came up short.

'And the key?' he asked Leah.

She shook her head. 'I've searched everywhere.'

And just like that, Herman lost his daughter twice in one day.

Chapter Twenty-two

January 4th
Crush

I set the book down in my lap to give Mikki some time to recover. She's in the middle of the sofa with her legs folded under her, using a box of tissues she pilfered from the restroom to soak up her tears. The pile of crumpled tissues on the coffee table in front of us is stained with black mascara and violet eyeshadow. When she's finally settled down enough for me to continue, I'm not surprised to find that most of her makeup is gone. Even the red lipstick she was wearing is now smudged across her mouth, as if she just kissed someone.

'Why are you staring at my mouth?' she asks in a small voice and I immediately look up to focus on her puffy eyes.

'Your lipstick is gone.'

'Oh.'

She stares off into space and my heart rate speeds up as she traces the pads of her fingers over her lips. I just want to shove her hand away and kiss her. Instead, I decide to test the waters by reaching for the damp tissue balled up in her fist. She flinches a little before she hands it over and I know I made the right decision. She's not ready to be touched. Not the way I want to touch her.

'So June was . . . your aunt?' she asks, her eyes pleading with me, hoping I'll tell her that nothing in *Black Box* is true.

I nod and reach for her hand. I trace my finger over the letter *G* tattooed on her right ring finger as I answer. 'She was sick and they didn't know how to deal with her in those days.'

The tears stream down her face again, though her gaze is glued to her finger. 'Do you know where she's buried?'

'She was buried at St Joseph's until my grandfather purchased the estate in Cambridge. She's buried there now.'

'The estate . . . I can't believe this is the story of your grandfather. Herman – I mean, what's your grandfather's real name?'

'Hugh.'

Her fingers close around mine as she continues, but I don't know if she's doing it consciously or subconsciously. 'Hugh blamed himself for her death. He thought if he'd had enough money to get Leah and

June that big house, he never would have had to go to Korea and June would still be alive. He never stopped blaming himself.'

'Jane.'

'What?'

'My aunt. Her real name was Jane. And you're right. Grandpa Hugh never stopped blaming himself for what happened to her. And that's why he bought that rundown hotel just a few months after her death and turned it into an empire.'

She wipes at the half-dried tear tracks on her face then looks me in the eyes. 'What happened to the black box?'

I gaze into her eyes a bit longer, savoring the softness of her skin against mine. 'It's here with me.'

'Here? Like, in this hotel room?'

'Yes. My grandfather left it to me in his will when I was ten, but he didn't leave me the key. He left me a note telling me that when I was eighteen I could go to Boston Public Library where they have the books he donated on display in an exhibit dedicated to Jane. He said I'd find the key there, but I never went.'

'What? *Why?* How could you not go?'

I glance at the book where it rests in my lap and she does the same. 'I didn't go because I gave you the book when I was seventeen. I felt like whatever was inside that box didn't belong to me any more.'

She pulls her hand away suddenly and I feel a flash

of pain throughout my entire body, as if part of my body has been cut off.

'We have to go to the library.'

'We?'

Chapter Twenty-three

January 4th
Mikki

The look on Crush's face, that crazy hope in his eyes, scares me. He still doesn't know why I'm trying to avoid being seen in public. I need to tell him something, even if it's not the truth, so he understands that we can't indiscreetly wander the streets of Boston. Maybe I should tell him I'm a fugitive. Technically, he did kill someone. Even if it was to protect me, that makes him a fugitive.

'But first, I have to tell you something,' I begin, wishing he were still holding my hand.

His skin on mine felt so comforting and natural. It actually put me at ease. I know Crush would never do anything to hurt me. Though I hardly know him, I'm pretty sure he's the only person I can say that about, other than Meaghan.

Meaghan. I hope she hasn't found the note yet. It's

been twenty-four hours since I left for the airport. By now, they'll have called Rina to ask her if she knows where I might be. With my history of attempted suicide, they'll search my room for a note or anything that might suggest where I'd go after the flight was canceled. I don't like to worry my family, especially Meaghan, but the reasons I have for taking my life are still valid.

Crush grabs my hand and tilts his head as he waits for me to spill. 'What do you have to tell me?'

I close my eyes and draw in a deep breath. 'I don't want to lie to you.'

'Then don't.'

I look up at him and, for the first time, I allow myself to take in his features: the vibrant green irises of his eyes, the long eyelashes, his chiseled cheekbones, the perfect slope of his nose, the symmetrical peaks of his top lip. It dawns on me that, except for the slope of my nose, which is still a bit crooked from the attack, all of those features are mirrored in me. My green eyes, long eyelashes, strong cheekbones, and the symmetrical bow of my lips. But looking like someone on the outside doesn't mean you look like them on the inside.

If I tell Crush I'm going to L.A. to kill myself, he'll probably take me to the nearest hospital. That's what the average person thinks is the responsible thing to do. They have no idea what it's like to be committed. They don't know that my desperate desire not to be committed again is one of the things propelling me toward suicide.

'First, let me tell you the small stuff.' I pull his hand into my lap so I can stare at our hands clasped together as I speak. 'I told you that I'm bipolar, but that pill you saw me taking yesterday wasn't my medication. I've been off my meds for a couple of weeks now.'

'Why?'

'Because I want to be free,' I reply defensively. 'I don't want to just exist. Existing is not enough. I want to feel everything. I want to live my life *my* way, not the way everyone else thinks I should, suffocating in a cloud of psych meds. I want to breathe and not wonder if it's my last breath of freedom. Is that too much to ask?'

He's silent as he reaches for my face. The backs of his fingers are warm against my skin as he pushes a piece of hair out of my eyes. 'You're so afraid.' He grabs my chin and gently turns my face toward him. 'But I don't want you to be afraid of me. I'm not going to force you to take your meds or go home or anything like that. I'd never force you to do *anything* you don't want to do. You believe me, don't you?' I nod and he flashes me a warm smile. 'Then, can you tell me the real reason you're going to L.A.?'

'To kill myself,' I say, holding my breath as I look into his eyes, awaiting his reaction.

His gaze falls. 'I was afraid of that.'

'I don't want to lie to you.' He lets go of my face and

stands suddenly, leaving me with the painful ache of rejection. 'Where are you going?'

'To get the black box. We have to go to the library. I want to know what's inside that box. I just . . . I have a feeling it will change everything.' His gaze burns into me. 'I hope it will change everything.'

Though Crush called concierge and asked them to have a cab ready for us, I still pull my hood tightly over my head to cover as much of my face as possible. I decide not to reapply my makeup. After getting rid of all of my old pictures, I made sure to never again take a picture looking all fresh-faced and innocent. With my hood pulled tight and no makeup, I have a good chance of not being recognized.

We slide into the cab in front of the hotel and I pull my feet up onto the seat to hug my knees. It's freezing out here and this cab is not much warmer.

'You cold?' Crush asks as the cab makes a sharp left on Park Plaza, pulling me toward him. He laughs as the inertia holds me against him. 'I guess that's a yes.'

I roll my eyes as I scoot back to my side of the seat. 'You wish,' I reply, my teeth chattering.

He smiles. 'It would be my honor to keep you warm.'

'Shut up.'

'Why?'

The driver takes the curve onto St James Street and I hold onto the door handle to keep from sliding. 'Because you're making me feel weird.'

'Weird? Like you may start discussing your toe jam at any moment or weird like you're uncomfortable with this conversation?'

I narrow my eyes at him. 'Both, and . . . weird like my insides are all tangled up.'

'I know that kind of weird. I *like* that kind of weird.'

'Of course you do.'

He smiles and my insides become even more knotted. The driver makes a right at Dartmouth then another quick left on Newbury, and I don't bother fighting gravity. I allow myself to be pulled toward him and his expression is serious as he wraps his arm around my shoulder to keep me from sliding back. I hold back my tears as I lay my head on his shoulder and he lays a soft kiss on my forehead.

Ten seconds later, the cab pulls up in front of the McKim Building entrance on Dartmouth and I don't want to get out. Reluctantly, I push myself up so Crush can pay the driver. Once we're on the sidewalk, I'm feeling weird again, like I can't look at him.

He places his gloved hand on the small of my back, then leans over and whispers in my ear. 'I want to kiss you, but I want to do it when you're least expecting it. Is that okay?'

I nod, pressing my lips together to suppress my grin. He plants another kiss on my temple and I try not to melt into the sidewalk. How sick is it that I love knowing he killed someone for me? I don't know the answer to that question. All I know is that I'm feeling pretty high on Crush right now. I just hope I don't crash any time soon. At least, not before that kiss.

The pavement in front of the library has been cleared and most of the snow is piled up around the curbs, street lamps, the steps leading to the library doors, and the concrete platforms holding up the statues on either side of the entrance. A pathway has been cleared down the center of the six steps and Crush grabs my hand as we ascend.

'Watch your step. It could be icy.'

'*You* could be icy.'

'That doesn't make any sense.'

I shrug. 'Just sticking up for the stairs. Somebody has to.'

There are three sets of glass entrance doors and he holds my hand tightly as he leads me toward the one in the center. Maintaining his grip, he uses his other hand to open the door for me. I enter first and he scurries ahead of me again to pull me farther inside, but I'm rooted in place.

'Holy shit,' I whisper as I stand in wonder of the entrance hall.

The floor, the walls, the ceiling, everything is covered in marble. On our left are a large bronze statue and a marble staircase leading up to another level. Directly in front of us is a marble staircase leading down through a marble archway into a vestibule, which, by the looks of it, is also covered in marble. On each side of the top of the staircase is a marble statue of a lion, each bearing a bronze dedication plaque.

'This place is epic.'

Crush chuckles and I realize I said that aloud.

'It's the most beautiful thing I've ever seen,' I continue.

'It's a book lover's paradise,' he says with a proud look on his face.

'Can we live here?'

'Only if you do all the cooking.'

'Fine by me, as long as you don't mind eating muffin stumps for the rest of your life.'

He smiles and nods toward the staircase on our left. We climb the steps up to the mezzanine level and I pull him toward the marble railing so I can peer down on the entrance lobby from this level. The space is bursting at the seams with silence. If I get recognized and whisked away from this library today, it will have been worth it.

'When was the last time you came here?' I ask, ogling the mural on the wall opposite the railing.

'A long time ago,' he says, pointing at the mural. 'This mural has been here since eighteen ninety-five. It's a replica of a painting by a French painter whose name I can't remember right now. But even the door in the center of the mural is a replica of the door in the painting.'

I follow him toward the archway on our left, trying

not to roll my eyes. 'Are you trying to avoid my question? How long has it been since you last came here?'

He sighs as we pass through the archway. 'I haven't been here since before I gave you the book?'

'Why?' I ask as he presses the call button for an elevator.

'I used to come here almost every weekend with my grandfather before he died when I was ten. After he died, I didn't have anyone to bring me. So, once I turned sixteen and got my driver's license, this was one of the first places I visited.' We step inside the elevator and he pauses to press the button for the third floor. 'I saw the exhibit with the books my grandfather donated and there was no key in the display. That didn't surprise me since his will said I could retrieve the key when I was eighteen. But . . . Jordan died a few months after that, and I never came back.'

We arrive on the third floor and the silence is even heavier now. I want to say something to lighten the mood, but all I can think is, *That fucking sucks*, and I'm sure he already knows that. When we enter the rare books lobby, I'm surprised to find that it looks like it hasn't been updated since the fifties. The room is long and narrow, with oak study tables and card catalogs running the length of the space. There's only one patron sitting at the far end of the row of tables. Midway down, a woman sits at a desk reading a hardbound book and I can't help but smile. This is a place where books are treasured – books that hold the sweetly magical smell of history; books that crackle when you open them and sigh when you close them; books that weigh heavy in your hands, not just your heart.

'Stay close to me and don't touch anything,' he says, pulling me toward a doorway that appears to lead into a very dark room. 'There are surveillance cameras everywhere and you will be severely reprimanded if you touch something you're not allowed to touch.'

We pass through the doorway and my breath catches in my chest. The room is dimly lit, probably to protect the books from UV damage. There are two levels of bookshelves surrounding the room, all enclosed in glass and dimly lit from within. A couple of glass cases in the center of the room display ancient books and manuscripts.

'Many of the books in here are bound in animal skin.' He lets go of my hand as he wanders toward the smaller display case on the other side of the room.

This gets me breathing again, and that's when I smell it. It smells like the first time I opened up *Black Box*. My stomach clenches and suddenly the messenger bag I have strapped across my chest feels as if it's holding lead bricks instead of a book and a wooden box.

'It's not here.' Crush's voice is barely louder than a whisper, but it's so quiet in here, the sound of it instantly pulls me back to reality.

'What's not here?' I ask, going after him to see what's inside the glass case he's peering into.

'The entire exhibit. It's been replaced . . . with original music scores by Mozart.'

'Let's go ask that lady out there about it.' I grab his arm and gently pull him away from the glass case.

Crush approaches the woman at the desk and she looks up from her book with a smile. 'May I help you?'

'Yes, ma'am. Can you tell us what happened to the . . . Slayer exhibit?'

Slayer? Is that his grandfather's last name? Is that *his* last name?

The woman narrows her eyes at Crush, as if she's sizing him up, and I wonder if she recognizes him. 'The Slayer articles are part of the Jordan collection. They were rotated out two and a half years ago.'

I watch Crush to see his reaction to this news. He appears confused, and I think I know why. His grandfather told him to view the exhibit after his eighteenth birthday, but it's not here. Not to mention the fact that the stuff his grandfather donated is now part of the *Jordan* collection.

'Can you show us where the articles are now?' Crush replies.

Again, she looks Crush up and down for a moment, then she turns her attention to me. 'They're no longer on display. Slayer requested the exhibit be put away on July 28, 2011.'

His eyebrows scrunch up in despair at this news. 'The day after my eighteenth birthday,' he whispers to himself, and the woman behind the desk narrows her eyes at him again.

'Are you his grandson?'

'Yes,' I reply for Crush.

The woman smiles. 'Just show me some identification and I'll have a guard take you there.'

Crush shakes his head. 'I don't have identification. Well, nothing that will have my real name on it. I changed my name three years ago . . . the day after my eighteenth birthday.'

Chapter Twenty-four

January 4th
Crush

My mind draws back to the first day I returned to school after Jordan died. The whispers filled the corridors and followed me everywhere; how fitting my name was considering I was responsible for his death. I got in a lot of fights and my parents were forced to get me a private tutor for the remainder of my junior year and my entire senior year. It worked out in the end because the one-on-one attention helped me bring my grades up after Jordan's death and it gave me more time to focus on music. Even with mediocre grades, I still would have gotten into Harvard by flashing my dad's alumni status and donations. But I wanted to make it in on my own merit, which is just one of the reasons why I changed my name before my freshman year.

Mikki looks crushed by the prospect of not being able to see the articles in my grandfather's exhibit. But the woman behind the desk makes no move to call a guard to take us to it.

'Give me the box,' I say to Mikki, and she quickly lifts the flap on her bag to retrieve the black box.

'How about this?' she whispers, holding the bag open so I can peer inside and see the spine of the book.

No one knows this book exists other than my family and Mikki's family. And my family thinks it's tucked away in a safe in my off-campus apartment. If this woman finds out I have a book written by Hugh Slayer, their most generous donor in the last fifty years, she'll probably tie me to a table and torture me until I cough it up.

I shake my head and pull the flap closed on her bag, then I place the black box on the desk. 'This was given to me by my grandfather; actually, he left it to me in his will with instructions to come to the library on my eighteenth birthday to retrieve the key that opens this box.'

'*The Secret Garden* key.'

'What?'

'The key was added to the exhibit the week before the entire exhibit was taken down, per Mr Slayer's instructions. It's one of the staff's favorite exhibits, and a bit of a mystery around here as to why he wanted the exhibit taken down just one week after his estate's donation of the 1911 copy of *The Secret Garden* and the key.'

'What key are you talking about?'

'The key to the secret garden on Slayer's estate. That's what the exhibit says the key is for. We're dying to know what's inside the garden.'

I chuckle at this. 'There's no secret garden on the family estate. That key is not for a literal secret garden. It's for this box.'

I pause for a moment as I try to remember everything I can about the book, *The Secret Garden*. All I can remember is that, after I read the book, I realized that it didn't really matter whether the main characters found the key to the secret garden. In fact, it didn't even matter *what* they found inside the garden. All that mattered was that the garden brought them together and changed them.

'Oh my God, *The Secret Garden*? Have you read that?' Mikki asks me excitedly, then she turns to the woman without waiting for my reply. 'Can you please just try the key on the box?'

The woman stares at Mikki and, for a moment, I'm nervous that her face may have already been featured on the local news this morning. But Mikki doesn't seem to share the same worry. She turns back to the woman and meets her gaze, her eyes pleading with the woman to help us.

'All the articles in that exhibit are housed in an off-site storage facility. Slayer's instructions for the exhibit were specific. The only person allowed to view the articles without a formal request is his grandson, William Slayer. Is that you?'

'It is, but I have no way of proving it,' I reply, trying not to look at Mikki. I can feel her gaze pointed at the side of my face. She now knows my real name and identity. And now, just one Google search and she'll know everything about me up to the night we ran into each other in that parking lot.

'You have the box,' Mikki says, her voice soft and reassuring, 'William.'

Hearing her say my name makes my hair bristle. I always hoped that if I ever met her, she'd never know the person I was before she saved my life. It seems my desire to change my name isn't so different from her need to dye her hair. I want to reach inside her and erase the name from her memory.

'That's not my name any more,' I say, turning to her.

Her green eyes are locked on mine, but the words that come out of her mouth are addressed to the woman behind the desk. 'Believe me, lady, this guy is who he says he is.' She turns back to the woman. 'Please take us to the key.'

The woman eyes the box on her desk and presses her lips together as she considers our request. Finally, she lets out a defeated sigh. 'Oh, okay. But if you aren't who you say you are and something happens to that exhibit, I'm telling the police you threatened my family.'

Mikki chuckles. 'You've been reading too many crime novels.'

The woman looks a bit embarrassed by Mikki's

overly honest remark, but she picks up the phone on her desk and dials a number. After a brief conversation, she hangs up the phone and shakes her head.

'I can't believe you all are going to open that box and I won't be there to see what's inside.' She looks up at me and I know she finally believes me. 'Please consider donating the box to the exhibit. That is, if your grandfather would have wanted you to. I don't know what's inside there, but all this mystery has got my wheels turning. And, yes,' she says, turning to Mikki, 'I read a lot of crime novels. I love a good mystery.'

Mikki smiles. 'So do I. Thank you . . . ?'

'Mary,' the woman replies.

Mikki and I exchange a look. I don't know what she's thinking, but I just remembered the name of the main character in *The Secret Garden*: Mary Lennox. I shake my head. Total coincidence. It's a common name.

Mary instructs us to head down to the orientation room on the first floor where we'll meet a security guard named Jason who will take us to the off-site archival facility in Roxbury, nine miles away.

'Roxbury,' Mikki whispers as we settle into the backseat of the white SUV bearing the logo of a private security company.

'I know.'

Roxbury is where most of *Black Box* takes place. It's just a coincidence that it also happens to be where we'll find the City of Boston Archival Center. It's probably not a coincidence that Grandpa Hugh asked for the exhibit to be housed there after my eighteenth birthday. Roxbury was Jane's home.

Fifteen minutes later, we arrive at a large, box-like building on Rivermoor Street, and Jason escorts us to the entrance of the facility. Inside, he speaks with a woman sitting behind a waist-high counter in a small lobby with walls so white they're almost blinding. It dawns on me that, based on Mary's comments about her and her co-workers' curiosity, at least a few of the BPL employees have driven out here to the archival center to view this exhibit.

'The Slayer exhibit?' says the girl behind the counter, then she cranes her neck to get a better look at us.

She's young and average-looking, so I smile at her, hoping it will help get us back there quicker. She smiles back and beckons me with her hand. I grab Mikki's hand as I approach the counter.

'Are you William Slayer?' the girl asks, and it sounds as if she's trying to hide her Southie accent.

'That would be me. Did Mary call you?'

'Yeah, she called. You're supposed to book an appointment before you come here, you know.'

'I know. But our flight leaves tomorrow, so this is sort of an emergency.'

She sighs then she asks us a few questions about the box and examines it for a couple of minutes. Once she's satisfied the box isn't a bomb, she hands Jason a set of keys and he leads us back to the BPL archives. Jason guides us into a huge warehouse packed with rows of twenty-foot-tall metal shelving units, each one stacked with boxes and boxes of archived documents. He takes us past the rows of shelves and into a small room about as big as a walk-in closet. The walls are lined with bookshelves, enclosed in glass like the ones in the rare books room at BPL.

He walks directly toward the back wall of the room and unlocks the glass door on the left. He reaches into his pocket, pulls out a pair of latex gloves, and pulls them on before he squats down and reaches for something on the bottom shelf. My heart is pounding as he stands up and turns around.

'Hand me the box,' he says gruffly. I hand him the box and he carefully slides the key into the lock. 'Seems to fit.' He attempts to turn the key, but it doesn't budge. 'But it don't turn.'

'That can't be. I know that's the right key. It has to be,' I insist.

Jason doesn't acknowledge my protests, he continues gently in his attempts to turn the key, but it's not working.

'Let me try,' Mikki says.

Jason shakes his head. 'Nuh-uh. I can't let you two touch this or I'll be toast.'

'But remember in *The Secret Garden*? It's Mary who finds the key and opens the garden gate. Please just let me try.'

'What the fuck is she talking about?' Jason asks me as if she's not in the room.

'She's right. It probably has to do with the pressure on the lock. Just let her give it a try,' I say, trying not to punch him in the mouth.

He rolls his eyes and holds the key out to her. Mikki takes it from his hand and I get a pang of jealousy when I see her hand touch his. He holds the box for her as she inserts the key into the lock again, but it appears to go in a bit farther this time. She turns the key and, instantly, the lock clicks and the lid pops open just a quarter of a centimeter as the latch gives.

Chapter Twenty-five

January 4th
Mikki

Jason catches the key in midair as it falls from my fingers. I can't believe I'm about to see what's inside the box I've been reading about for three years. I almost don't want to know for fear it will be something ridiculous like a dry-cleaning receipt. I place my hand on the lid and Crush immediately places his hand over mine.

'Wait. We should open it at the hotel,' he says, and he doesn't have to glance at Jason for me to know why he's suggesting this.

'Okay.'

Crush takes the box from Jason's hands and we all head back to the security vehicle. Once we're back at the library, Crush tells Jason to tell Mary that we'll try to make it back to share the contents of the box with her when we get home from Los Angeles. As we exit the library and descend the stairs, I'm overwhelmed by a dark dread.

'I don't want to know what's inside the box,' I say as we approach the sidewalk to hail a cab.

'What do you mean? You don't want to find out tonight? We can wait.'

'No, you don't understand. I don't want to know at all.'

I'm afraid if I find out what's inside that box, I won't want to go to L.A. any more. I want to tell him this, but I'm still so afraid of being committed. He said he won't do it, but he'll change his mind at the last minute. I know it.

'Why don't you want to know?'

He waves down a cab across the street and the driver slowly maneuvers a U-turn to get to us. We quickly hop inside to escape the cold, but I don't bother putting on my seatbelt.

'Because I don't want you to think that knowing what's inside that box will change anything. I don't want you to get your hopes up. I'm still me and my life is still my life. And it still sucks and everything still sucks. Just because you're beautiful and you're here when I need you doesn't change anything. I'm still me! You can't fix what's inside here,' I say, poking my temple. 'Nobody can. That's why they've all given up on me.'

'Who's given up on you?'

'Everyone.' I pull my feet up on the seat and bury my

face in my knees so the driver can't see me crying in the back of his cab. 'My parents, my therapist, my fucking best friend. The only one who gives a damn about me is my sister, but I can't stay here just for her.'

Crush's silence makes my whole body ache with shame. I want to be the type of person who makes plans for the future and finds beauty in a speck of floating dust, but that's not me. That's me only when I'm tripping on ecstasy or acid. Or when I switch to a new type of medication that *really seems to work!* Until it doesn't work any more, then I'm back to being me. And I'm just so *tired* of being me.

'I'm exhausted,' I say, laying my cheek on my knee so I can look at Crush.

He reaches across and brushes his thumb across my cheek. 'We're almost there.'

By the time we reach the hotel room, the tears have stopped, but I'm still so tired. All I want to do is collapse onto my bed and stay there for the next two days until our flight.

Crush sets the black box on the kitchen counter and I stare at it for a moment, wondering if my curiosity will win over my demons today. I look at him and he's looking in my direction, but not anywhere near my eyes. He's already thinking he needs to distance himself from me.

'I'm going to bed.'

'Wait.' He grabs my hand as I turn to leave. When I look at him, he pulls me toward him so he can cradle my face in his hands. 'Don't go,' he pleads, laying a soft kiss on the corner of my mouth. 'It's only three o'clock. We don't have to look inside the box. Just . . . stay with me. Please.'

'Why?'

He tilts my face up so he can look me in the eyes. 'Because I want you with me. I . . . I think you're supposed to stay with me.'

'*Supposed* to stay with you? What does that mean?'

'It means that I . . . *Fuck.* I think I've loved you for longer than I care to admit and I'm just starting to understand why. And I want you to stay.'

He lays another soft kiss on my nose and I clutch his forearms to keep from collapsing.

'You love me? But . . . you hardly know me.'

He fixes me with a stern glare. 'How many people know the things I know about you?'

I shake my head. 'Nobody.'

'Don't tell me I don't know you when I've spent the last three years trying to forget you.'

I grab the front of his jacket and pull it to me, burrowing my face in his chest so he can't see me sob. He kisses the top of my head as he rubs my back. It takes a while before I finally catch my breath and slow the flow of tears enough to pull my head away from his chest. I immediately wipe my face, though I'm pretty sure all my tears are soaked into the front of his coat.

I take a deep breath before I look up at him. 'Okay. Let's open the box.'

*

We decide to go back to my bedroom and sit across from each other while we open the box, which rests on top of the unmade bed between us. My fingers tremble as I reach for the lid of the box.

'Are you sure you don't want to be the one to open it?'

'I'm positive,' he replies quickly. 'Go on.'

I lift the lid slowly and my heart aches when I see there's only one folded piece of paper in the box. It's not bursting with letters from June to Herman; or, rather, from Jane to Hugh. It's just a single sheet of white paper, folded in half and lying in the center of a black box lined in chestnut-brown velvet.

'You want to read it?' he asks and, though I really don't want to read it, I know I have to.

I lift the sheet of paper out of the box and a photograph falls out, landing back inside the box. Crush picks it up and holds it up so we can both see. It's a handsome older gentleman who looks a lot like Crush, wearing a dress shirt and a fedora and a little girl with short blonde hair dancing next to a stage where a man is playing the saxophone. The stage looks very familiar.

'Is this your grandpa?'

'Yes, so that must be Jane.'

'Was this taken at Wally's?'

He nods as he gently lays the photograph inside the box. 'Read the note.'

I unfold the paper and my stomach aches when I see the messy scrawl of a child.

Daddy,
I can't remember the song you sang to me. I'm sorry, Daddy. They won't stop hurting me and they won't let me see Mommy. I don't want to be sick. I miss you and Mommy. Please give Mommy my box so she can read this too.
Love,
Jane

I drop the note and it lands on the bed next to the box as I try to imagine why Hugh would want his grandson to see this. Why would anyone? My thoughts are interrupted by a dreadful realization. I reach into my pocket for my phone, but it's not there. Glancing to my left, I see it lying on the nightstand where I left it, dead. I have to call Rina and tell her to get the note from the windowsill. I can't let Meaghan see that.

Chapter Twenty-six

January 4th
Crush

'What are you doing?' I ask Mikki as she stretches across the bed to reach for her cell phone on the night-stand.

'I don't know,' she replies, clutching the phone against her chest. 'I think I made a big mistake.'

'What kind of mistake?'

'The kind that hurts people.' She pulls the phone away from her chest and stares at the screen for a moment before she sets it down on the bed. Then she lets out a very unexpected chuckle. 'My phone is dead.'

This is such an inappropriate response to the letter she just read, it makes me uncomfortable. 'Are you okay?'

'My phone is *dead*.' She repeats this as if I should know why this is so significant. 'I just got a strong urge to tell my friend Rina to get rid of the suicide note I left on my windowsill.'

I quickly slip my phone out of my back pocket and hand it to her. 'You can use my phone.' She stares at the phone in my hand, but she doesn't reach for it. And I'm beginning to understand why the people in her life are often frustrated by her behavior. 'Make the call.'

'I can't.'

I know why she can't make the call. She doesn't want to ruin her plans in L.A.

'Fine. If you can't call it off, then go to one more place with me tomorrow.'

She sighs as she pushes my hand back. 'Look. I know what you're trying to do. You get me to go on this adventure to the most gorgeous library I've ever seen. Then you show me what's inside the black box I've been obsessing over for three years. And now you're probably going to try to take me somewhere to have a good time so I can see that I do have something to live for. While I appreciate the thought behind the gesture, I'd appreciate it more if you could let me do what I came here to do.'

'You forgot to mention that I also told you I love you. You forgot to belittle that, as well.' She appears stunned by this remark, so I continue. 'You think I don't understand how you feel? I *do* know how you feel. You're afraid.' I reach for her face and she turns her head. 'You're afraid of being vulnerable, physically and emotionally. You're afraid of loving completely. Most of all, you're afraid you'll live your whole life without ever being truly happy because you don't even know what it is that will make you happy. You're afraid of not being passionate enough or brave enough to live. But you are. You are brave because not only did you go to the library with me today, you were the one who insisted we go.'

'That was curiosity, not bravery.'

'When you were drunk at Wally's yesterday, you told me that, other than going to and from school, you haven't left your house in four months. So I'd say what you did today was pretty brave.' She shrugs, unimpressed with this explanation. 'And looking inside this box . . . reading that note aloud . . . that took huge fucking balls.'

This gets a tiny smile out of her. 'How do you know so much? You sound like my shrink, minus the balls comment.'

I swipe my hand down my face and take a deep breath as I prepare myself to confess. 'I know what it's like to feel so exhausted with your life that you feel as if you might be better off snipping all ties. Before I changed my name, there was a time when I thought suicide was the answer.' Her smile disappears as she waits for me to continue. 'That night in the parking lot . . . I was there to kill myself. That's why I had my gun ready and I was able to save you . . . because when you stumbled into my life that night, you saved me too.'

I hang my head, unable to meet her gaze. I know

she probably won't judge me for wanting to kill myself. But I'm afraid she'll think I'm not strong enough to care for her.

Her hands enter my field of vision as she pushes aside the black box and reaches for my face. Looking up, I find her wearing a soft smile as she looks into my eyes. She doesn't speak as her fingertips roam over my face, caressing every curve and hard line.

'I never saw your face that night.' She swallows hard and my heart begins to race as she traces her thumb over the rim of my bottom lip. 'But I never forgot your scent. Sometimes, I'd be sitting in class or walking through the corridors between classes, someone would walk by and the smell would hit me like a kick in the face. But I'd still close my eyes and breathe it in for as long as the scent lingered. You may have tried to forget me, but, as painful as it was for me, I didn't want to forget you.'

She wraps her arms around my shoulders and buries her face in my neck. I can hear her taking a long sniff as I wrap my arms tightly around her waist to hold her against me. She's trembling a little and it kills me to know that she may have had trouble separating my scent from *theirs* in the early days after the attack.

'I feel like I've known you all my life,' I whisper in her ear. 'I don't want that feeling to go away. I want to know you all my life.' She squeezes me tighter, but she doesn't say anything. 'Come with me to Wally's tonight. I want you to hear the song I wrote for you.'

'For me? You mean . . . the song you're going to record in L.A., you wrote that for me?'

'Yeah, take one guess at the title of the song.'

She pulls her head back and looks me in the eyes. 'Muffin stumps?'

He laughs briefly then fixes me with an intense glare. 'Come with me. I've been working on this song for three years and no one has ever heard me sing it. I want you to hear it first.'

'Me and a roomful of strangers. Just play it for me here, pleeeeeease.'

'It will sound so much better at Wally's. Besides, I'm beginning to think I should probably perform it for a crowd at least once before I play it for Kane.'

'You think so?' she replies sarcastically. I lightly dig my fingers into her ribs to tickle her and she yelps. 'Don't tickle me!'

'Why?' I chuckle.

Her body goes rigid and I can sense something has shifted. I quickly remove my hands from her sides and she scoots away from me. Her hands tremble as she crosses her arms over her chest.

'I'm not going to tickle you,' I assure her, but she's not looking at me any more. She's somewhere else. 'Mikki?'

'I have to take a shower.'

'Okay, do you want me to order you something to eat?'

'No, just leave. I have to take a shower then I'm going to sleep.'

I sigh as I rise from the bed. 'I didn't mean to upset you. I'm sorry.'

'Go, please.'

I close her bedroom door softly and I listen for a bit before I make my way back to the kitchen to grab a beer out of the refrigerator. Taking a seat on one of the stools at the breakfast bar, I sip the beer slowly as I try not to think about what could have made Mikki react that way. She hasn't told me everything those pieces of shit did to her that night, and I'm not sure I even want to know. Any more details might send me on a revenge rampage.

I head back to her bedroom door to listen. The sound of the shower running puts me at ease, but it's quickly followed by another sound. I can't decide if it's sobbing or whimpering; either way, I have to check on her or I'll never forgive myself if I find out she's hurt herself.

When I open the bedroom door, the bathroom door is wide open and, along with her cries, thick clouds of steam are billowing out into the bedroom.

Chapter Twenty-seven

January 4th
Mikki

I ball up my fists and try to grit my teeth against the pain, but I can't suppress my cries. They come out like high-pitched gasps as the stinging hot water hits my chest, sanitizing me. Washing away the thoughts I just had.

The shower curtain is yanked open and I scream as the water is suddenly ice cold. I turn to escape the shower and I land in Crush's arms.

'Don't touch me!'

'Fucking shit! Look at your chest. You have to get under the cold water, now!' He forces me to turn around so my back is against his chest and the icy water blasts the front of my legs. 'I won't look at you, just please get under the cold water.' He lets go of me and pulls the shower curtain closed. 'Get under the water or I'm calling an ambulance.'

I gasp as I step forward into the cold water. 'Ow,' I whimper, as the pressure and coolness of the water against my chest stings and soothes me at once. 'I'm sorry,' I say, sinking down onto the floor of the bathtub.

'Are you in pain?' he calls from the other side of the shower curtain, his voice so close and comforting.

'Yes.'

After ten minutes under the cold water, Crush sticks his hand through a crack in the shower curtain to turn the water off and give me a towel. I yank the curtain open, holding my breath as he looks me in the eye. He quickly unfolds the towel and holds it up for me. I step out of the bath and he wraps the towel around my shoulders. I wrap my arms around his waist as I lay my cheek against his solid shoulder. He's so warm.

'Do you want to tell me what that was about?' he asks, lifting my hair out from underneath the towel.

'I don't think you want to know.'

It's the only part of the attack that I didn't write down the night before the detectives came to my house. It's the only part of the attack I wish I could completely forget.

'Anything you want to talk about, I want to know. Even if you don't want to talk about it, I still want to know. I just want to know why you're hurting. Even if I can't make the hurting stop.' He reaches for another towel and drapes it over my damp hair as he tilts my head back to look me in the eyes. 'How's your chest?'

'Okay.'

He pulls the towel tight around my shoulders to cover me up, then he kisses my cheek. 'I'll be right outside the door.'

As much as I'd like to keep this part of the attack a secret for the rest of my life, I know there's no way I'll be able to do that if I want Crush to understand what just happened. Shame is the worst emotion we can carry inside of us; and I've been a nuclear reactor for shame for more than three years. Because it wasn't enough for them to violate me. The one with the Red Sox cap wasn't happy until I was completely humiliated.

I come out of the bathroom wearing the bathrobe I've been ignoring up until today. True to his word, Crush is standing just outside the door. He steps aside so I can get past him. The black box is gone and the comforter is pulled nice and smooth, as if nothing happened.

I sit on the edge of the bed, staring at my clasped hands in my lap. 'They only took the pillowcase off my head once,' I begin, as he sits next to me. 'The one in the Red Sox cap wanted to see my face. But . . . that wasn't enough. He wanted me to . . . to smile, like I was enjoying it.'

'You don't have to talk about it if it's too much.'

'No, I need you to hear this.'

'Okay.'

Digging my fingernails into the palm of my hand,

I force myself to remember it. 'He . . . kept asking me to smile, but I couldn't. I couldn't stop crying. So he started tickling me and I couldn't help it, I laughed a little and that got him excited. He started kissing me on the mouth. I thought of trying to bite his tongue, but they had my hands tied. I couldn't fight them off. Then he started moving down, kissing my neck and . . . and my chest, and . . . He wouldn't stop. He refused to stop until I . . . I let go. So I did. I'm so disgusting.'

I double over as my stomach cramps up, then I bury my face in my trembling hands as I weep for everything I lost that night. Everything they took. Everything I *gave* in exchange for my life. A life I don't even want any more.

'I've never had . . . consensual sex,' I say, my voice muffled by my hands. 'I never did what they said I did when all those rumors spread in ninth grade. I never even got close to having sex after they . . . they raped me.' I can hardly breathe now. I've never said those three words aloud. 'I don't know if I ever will because they ruined that. They ruined me.'

'They didn't ruin you.' His voice is thick with emotion and it makes my stomach ache. 'You're beautiful, inside and out. And those . . . those fucking animals are the ones who are ruined. I wish I had killed them all.'

'Don't say that.'

'It's the way I feel.'

I take a few deep breaths before I sit up and tuck my

damp hair behind my ears. 'I'll understand if you don't want to sing that song for me any more.'

'What? You think what you just told me changes the way I feel about you?'

I shrug. 'That's the way it's always been. No guy wants to be with a girl who doesn't fuck.'

He hangs his head and takes a beat before he looks up at me and responds. 'Mikki, I fell in love with a girl I knew three years ago for all of twenty minutes. A girl who wasn't even conscious. Either I'm one sick bastard or I don't really care about whether or not you're the kind of girl who doesn't fuck.' He reaches for my face so I'm looking at him. 'Look at me. I knew when I saw that tattoo on your chest – the bunny – that you got that tattoo because I had saved your life the day we met on Twitter. And I hate that you had to go through what you went through for us to meet again in that parking lot, but I knew from the moment I carried your limp body into my car that that was it. I knew that fate would never stop bringing us together. No other girl could ever – *will* ever – compare to the only girl who's meant for me. Do you understand that?'

I nod, unable to speak, and he nods in return.

'Good,' he replies, brushing the tears from my cheeks. 'Now, will you go to Wally's with me so I can make an idiot out of myself in front of you?'

I nod again. 'As long as you don't make fun of me when I cry. No one has ever written a song for me.'

'Well, you'd better get used to it cause I just started writing another one called "Muffin Stumps" that's sure to be a hit.'

I smile at him, though the tears have started again. 'Fuck muffin tops.'

Chapter Twenty-eight

January 4th

Crush

'You should get dressed,' I say, planting one more kiss on her temple just to feel the softness of her skin. 'I'm going to order some food and threaten the concierge with bodily harm if he can't get *Pretty in Pink* on our TV.'

'God, you're so mean,' she says with a smile as I rise from the bed.

Once she's dressed in her pajama bottoms and a T-shirt, she comes out of the bedroom holding a hair-brush. She's got a sly grin on her face.

'The movie is paused and ready to watch whenever you're ready,' I say as she holds the brush out to me. 'What's this?'

'Can you brush the back of my hair? My sister usually does it when it gets like this.'

I chuckle as I take the brush from her hand and

she sits on a stool at the breakfast bar. 'Is it going to hurt?'

'Probably, but it's even worse when I try to do it myself. I get frustrated and make a mess out of it.' She closes her eyes and draws in a deep breath, preparing herself. 'I know it's because my hair is so damaged from the dye, but I don't care.' I bring the brush to the crown of her head and she immediately protests. 'No! Start from the bottom and work your way up . . . please.'

'Whatever you say, your majesty.'

I brush the bottom wisps of her damp, black hair, which are hardly tangled at all. But by the time I reach the middle, my heart is racing and I'm practically sweating just imagining how much pain I'm inflicting on her.

'Are you sure you're okay?' I ask for the twentieth time.

'Yes! I'm fine.'

When I'm done, my arm is aching and my stomach is in knots, but she just smiles and thanks me as she heads off to put the brush away. The food arrives shortly after that and Mikki and I sit on the sofa eating the pizza I ordered while watching *Pretty in Pink*.

'Blane has crazy eyes,' she mumbles through a mouthful of pizza. 'I don't believe a word he says. Andie should have ended up with Duckie. He really loved her. And he didn't have that psychopathic glare.'

'Yeah, but this wasn't Hughes's best film,' I say, pausing the movie. '*The Breakfast Club* was his best, and Molly Ringwald ends up with the right guy in that film, right?'

She turns to me with an incredulous look on her face. 'They all go their separate ways at the end of *The Breakfast Club*. She doesn't end up with anybody.'

'Exactly. Bender was an asshole and the other guys were pussies. She ended up with the right guy.'

She shakes her head as she sets her slice of pizza down on her plate on the coffee table. 'Most guys think Bender is the cool guy in the movie.'

'Yeah, well, I have a sister. And I wouldn't want her dating a douche like him.'

'How old is your sister?'

'She's four years older than me. *Oh, shit.* That reminds me. Harlow's birthday is next month. She'll be twenty-six.'

She smiles as she leans back on the sofa and puts her feet up on the edge of the coffee table. 'You're protective of your older sister?'

I shrug. 'Well, she's smart as hell, but she used to have terrible taste in guys.'

'Yeah, Meaghan has the worst taste in guys. She once dated a guy who had escaped from juvenile detention.' I laugh and she holds up her hand. 'Wait. That's not the worst part. His eyebrow was partially shaved.'

'Now you're just making shit up.'

'I swear, every word of that is true,' she replies. 'So how about now? Does your sister still have bad taste in guys?'

'No. She got married to a total geek last year and they're expecting their first baby soon. I can't wait to be an uncle.'

She removes her feet from the table and sits up suddenly. 'I need a cigarette.'

'Is that your first cigarette today?' I reply, setting down my pizza.

'Fifth.'

'Are you smoking in secret?'

'I've been trying to.'

'Why? I have no problem with you smoking.'

A puff of laughter accompanies her eye-rolling. 'Yeah, I highly doubt the girls you've dated at *Harvard* smoke cigarettes.'

'What girls? I mean, I won't lie. I've slept with a lot of girls, but I've only dated three girls in the last four years and none of them went to Harvard.'

She's silent as she contemplates this. 'I want to know about the girls you've dated.'

'Why? I already told you that no one will ever compare to you.'

She hangs her head as she's overcome with a bashful smile. 'When you say stuff like that, I feel like I'm having a fucking out-of-body experience; like I'm so high I can't tell if this is real life.'

I place my finger under her chin and gently tilt her face up. 'This is real life.'

We look into each other's eyes and everything else

seems to blur. Her gaze falls to my lips and I take that as a signal that now is the time; the moment I've been dreaming about for far too long.

My hands reach up to cradle her face and she grasps my wrists as I lay a soft kiss on her forehead. I trace my lips down her temple until I reach her ear. 'Can I kiss you?' She nods and I pull my head back to look at her. She's trying not to smile. 'You can smile,' I say, planting another kiss on the corner of her mouth. 'I love your smile.'

'My smile is crooked because of the scar.'

I tilt her head up a bit more so I can kiss the scar that runs from the bottom of her lip to the point of her chin. She relaxes her grip on my wrists as I kiss the other corner of her mouth. Finally, I turn my head so our noses are almost touching; my lips hovering over hers as I wait for the moment where I can feel her need to be kissed. Then I see it; her chest heaving, nostrils slightly flared, eyebrows knitted together in anticipation.

I kiss her softly; a tender, closed-mouth test of her boundaries. Her lips taste like pizza and I can't help but smile.

'Why are you smiling?' she whispers.

I press my lips to hers again, ignoring the distraction, and she tightens her fingers around my wrists again. Brushing my lips lightly over hers, her lips part just enough for me to know she wants more. I take her top lip into my mouth and she whimpers as I gently suck on it.

'I love you,' I whisper against her lips so she can both hear and feel the words.

She's breathing heavily, but I wait a moment before I finally slip my tongue into her mouth. Tilting my head, our mouths locked, we just fit; the way I always imagined we would. She parts her lips a little wider, beckoning me further into the depths of her as she removes my hands from her face and places them on her waist. She grabs my face and her kiss becomes hungrier as she sits up on her knees.

She's taller than me in this position and I pull my head back so she can look down at me. Her green eyes are bright with passion, but there are tears glistening in the corners.

'Let's watch the movie so you can get some rest,' I whisper and she sinks down a little until she's sitting on her feet. I gently place my hand over her heart. 'Does your chest still hurt?'

'Only on the inside.'

'Come here,' I say, leaning back and beckoning her to lay her head on my chest.

I turn the movie back on and we watch in silence for a few minutes before she chuckles. 'I can hear your heartbeat. It's strong, like a drum.'

I sweep her hair behind her ear so it's not in her face and kiss the top of her head. By the time the movie is over, I can tell she's fallen asleep by the way her breathing has slowed. It's only 7:30 p.m., but something tells me she didn't sleep much last night. I consider trying to slip out from underneath her, but I really don't want to risk waking her. So I don't move. And somewhere in the middle of the late show, I fall asleep.

Chapter Twenty-nine

January 5th
Mikki

I wake with the right side of my head aching and I quickly realize the reason. I must have fallen asleep on Crush's ridiculously hard chest. I feel almost as if I'm hungover or like I overslept. *What time is it?*

I peel my cheek away from his warm chest and he draws in a sharp, startled breath. 'What time is it?' he asks groggily.

'I don't know.' *My phone is dead*, I almost remind him, but I'd rather not bring up that subject again.

'It's light outside,' he says as we both sit up. He leans forward to slip his phone out of his back pocket and check the time. 'Eight a.m. You slept more than twelve hours.'

'I guess I was tired.' I press my fingertips against the side of my head and roll them around to massage the aching.

'You have a headache?'

'I'm fine. I just need a shower.'

'Another one?' I don't know how to respond to this, so I don't respond at all, but he quickly notices my unease. 'If I ever say something stupid like that again, feel free to punch me. Right in the face, or the ear, or anywhere.'

'It's okay. I'll be right back.' As soon as I stand, he stands with me. 'I'm not going to hurt myself. I'm just going to take a shower.' He nods, though I can see the worry in the curve of his brow. 'You should go take a shower, too. You smell like pizza.'

'That's because you were drooling on me all night with your pizza breath. Did you sleep okay?'

'I don't remember the last time I slept that okay.' He smiles as he looks at me with that look; the look that makes me question everything I know to be true about life. 'I'll be right back.'

In the shower, I have to keep my back to the water and the temperature set to barely warm since my chest is still pretty red and raw. I try not to remember the thoughts that brought on this injury, but it's hard with the water prickling every nerve in my skin.

I've had guys ask me what I'm into, not willing to accept my answer that I'm not into anything. One guy, who shared a computer class with me, asked me if I was into rape fantasies. I told him that I don't have rape fantasies; I have rape nightmares. Then I locked myself in the school bathroom and called my mom to pick me up.

I let the conditioner soak into my hair for a while so I don't have to ask Crush to brush my hair again, then I rinse off and grab a towel. I stand on the rug in the center of the bathroom floor as I wrap the towel around my waist, staring into the mirror. The water from my hair drips down my body and, for a split second, I think I might glimpse what Crush sees when he looks at me.

I chuckle at this thought. He's seen me half-naked once and fully naked another time. And yet I don't feel horrifically ashamed of this; only slightly ashamed. Sort of the way I felt when we took a family trip to the water park when I was twelve. I've always been thin and awkward. I was five-foot-seven by the time I was twelve. Now I'm five-eleven without heels. Not that I wear heels any more, unless I'm wearing boots. I hate dressing up. Some would say my black hair and tattoos are a way of attracting attention, but they're not. They're a way of warding off the wrong kind of attention.

When I come out of the bedroom, fully clothed and made up, Crush is waiting near the door to the hotel room with his coat on and a smile dressing his gorgeous face.

'You going somewhere?' I ask, taking a seat at the breakfast bar. 'I thought Wally's doesn't open till six.'

'They don't, but we have to eat breakfast and I'm tired of room service.'

I sigh as I realize he wants me to go somewhere to have breakfast. 'I really don't want to go out in the daytime again.'

He steps away from the door and into the kitchen so he can look at me across the bar. 'Can I ask what you think will happen after they find your note?'

'Well, to be honest, they've probably already filed a missing persons report. I'm sure they've talked to Rina to see what she knows. Rina has heard me talking to my advisor at Santa Monica College. I made sure she watched as I booked the flight and hotel room. She believed I was going there for a job interview. I guess it all depends on whether she's smart enough to check the windowsill. I've left notes for her that she didn't check for weeks. Sometimes, she finds them hours later.'

I try not to think about the emotional repercussions of the note. Every suicide note I've ever written has always been an apology to my parents and Meaghan. I considered not leaving a note this time, but I didn't want them to launch a decades-long investigation into my disappearance. Especially when they'd know, in their hearts, what had really happened.

Crush looks like he's getting frustrated with me. 'So what do you think will happen if you try to catch a flight after a missing persons report has been filed?'

'The rescheduling of the flight was not a factor in my plans.'

He rests his elbows on the kitchen counter and leans forward. 'Can you please just admit that your plans are shot to hell? And call your friend to get rid of that note?'

'You don't understand. I should just leave,' I say, sliding off the stool.

'Don't go,' he insists, following me to my bedroom. 'I'm just trying to figure out how this is going to work for you. You obviously can't get on an airplane if they've filed a report.'

'Maybe they already found the note and the search is off.'

He stops at the threshold after I say this, but I don't bother looking back to see his reaction. Then the gravity of the situation hits me and I fall to my knees next to my suitcase in the corner. All my meticulous planning has been wiped away like snow from a windshield.

'Have you ever been in a mental hospital?' I ask, my gaze focused on the emblem on my suitcase. 'As a patient?'

'No.'

'Like I said. You don't understand.'

'You're right. I don't understand. We'll stay here. I'll go order some breakfast.'

I lean forward, resting my forehead on the top of my suitcase, as I think of that bottle of pills in my purse. It used to be tucked safely next to my copy of *Black Box*, but it's not my book any more. It belongs to Crush.

That's when I begin writing a new suicide note in my head.

*

Crush can sense something is wrong. I haven't cried once today while we hung out waiting for six p.m. to arrive. Of course, I've carefully avoided all potentially emotional subjects. When he asked me about Rina, I told him that she's the only person crazy enough to still be friends with me, but she keeps herself at a distance. She likes to go out and have fun and I don't. She sticks with me, but only when she doesn't have other plans. When he asks me about my mother and father, I tell him they love me so much that, after my second suicide attempt, they got a court order saying they have power of attorney over my health care.

'I don't think that's something to joke about,' he responds from his side of the sofa.

'Neither do I. Believe me, I take it very seriously.'

He hangs his head because he knows something has shifted. I'm not the same person who fell asleep on his chest last night or the girl he rescued three years ago. I'm the person he met two days ago.

'What would you do if your sister told you she wanted to die?'

'This is not the first time someone has asked me that question,' I reply immediately.

'What would you do?'

I shrug and turn away from him so I don't have to see that look on his face.

'Please answer the question.'

'I don't know. I'd . . . I'd . . .'

'You can't answer that truthfully, can you? You've

been so honest with me the past two days and *now* you want to start lying to me? After everything I've shared with you?'

I turn to look him in the eye and address his accusation. 'Yes, after everything you've shared with me, I still want to die.'

'That's not what I said. And, *fuck*, I still want to die sometimes. I understand that. I *don't* understand the lack of honesty. I've already told you that I'm not going to make you do anything. I'm not going to make you go to breakfast with me or call your parents or check yourself into a mental hospital. Your body and your mind are yours. Do *you* understand that? Do you believe me when I say that?'

'But they're not mine. They haven't been mine since the day I started taking meds when I was fourteen. And people just continue to remind me of this. My body and my mind, *anyone's* body and mind, belongs to whoever feels like owning it, whether it's a bunch of fucking perverted assholes or a board of assholes in white coats. I will never have full control over my body or my mind as long as my parents have the power to commit me and the state has the power to drug me. Do *you* understand now?'

The muscle in his jaw twitches as he nods. 'Yeah, I understand.'

I look down as I feel a surge of emotion rising inside me. 'So that's why I can't stay, no matter how I feel about you or Meaghan, because neither one of you can give me back my life.'

He reaches forward and grabs my hand off my knee. 'How *do* you feel about me?'

'I don't want to talk about it.'

'I won't make you talk about it, but . . . can you please consider telling me before . . . you know?'

Looking up at him, I'm taken by the hopeful expression in his eyes. 'I hate you,' I begin. 'I hate the way your lip curls up when you're confused. It's sickeningly adorable. I hate the way your arms are so fucking strong. It kind of scares me.' He smiles and I take a deep breath, trying to keep from crying, but it's so hard. 'I hate that your smile makes me want to cry and I don't know why. I hate that you know how to look so together on the outside when you're screaming inside. I hate that you always know the right thing to say. I hate the way that I already know what you're thinking just by the way you're looking at me.' He wipes the tears from my jaw and I close my eyes. 'I hate that you saved me. But, most of all, I hate that you love me because now I love you and I don't know how to make it stop.'

He pulls me into his arms and I try not to think of the new suicide note. Instead, I think of the song he's going to sing for me tonight. It won't change the fact that if I go home, I'll be committed. But maybe Crush will work a marriage proposal into tonight's performance. Then Crush and I can get married and we can have that stupid power of attorney nullified.

Nope, I don't have rape fantasies. I have courtroom fantasies.

Chapter Thirty

January 5th
Crush

I hold onto her tightly, stroking her hair to calm her. I know it must have taken great courage for her to say what she just said to me. And I hope I'm not being foolish in thinking that I can fix this.

I know I can't fix Mikki, but I think I can get her to change her mind about killing herself. I just have to figure out a way to prevent her parents from committing her. The thought of going behind Mikki's back to contact her family makes me sick. I need her to contact someone who can convince her parents that she's safe, as long as she's with me.

'I love that you love me,' I whisper in her ear.

'I hate you, too. Don't forget that part,' she replies with a loud sniff.

'I love that you hate me, too. Both of those emotions require a lot of energy. Don't make me go all Harvard on you and tell you the scientific difference between loving and hating someone.'

She laughs and her breath tickles my neck. 'Please do tell.'

'Basically, love and hate activate similar circuits in the brain, but hate also activates the circuits used for rational thought. Which means, when you hate my adorable lips, you're thinking quite clearly, unlike when you think of how I love you and you turn into a pile of irrational mush. In other words, you love me with all your circuits.'

She tilts her head back to look at me. 'I love you with all my circuits . . . I like that.'

I plant a soft kiss on her chin and she smiles. 'So do I.'

I don't bother with a cab this time. I've hired a car to take us to get some dinner at Toro, a tapas restaurant in South Boston, then it will take us straight to the club and back to the hotel. I don't want Mikki to be recognized any more than she does. I want us to spend this last night together without any interruptions. If all goes according to plan, I'm hoping that after I perform for her she'll be willing to call someone to talk to her parents. I don't want to think of what will happen if I'm wrong.

We arrive at Toro at 6:30 p.m. and the place is pretty packed considering it was snowing just a few hours ago. You'd think most people would want to stay inside and snuggle up under the covers with a book or a loved one. But this place is buzzing. It probably has to do with the neighborhood. With the revitalization of South Boston, this neighborhood is slowly becoming hipster central. Recently, it's become a breeding ground for trendy eateries and hangouts. I brought Mikki to Toro because I doubt that most of the people here watch local news. They're probably too busy listening to NPR and browsing Pinterest.

'For two?' the hostess asks with a phony smile.

'Yes,' I reply and she leads us to a long community dining table in the center of the restaurant adjacent to the bar.

We scoot in about six feet from the end of the table until we're sitting across from each other and next to two strangers; an older couple. Mikki looks a bit uncomfortable and, though I don't want her to get wasted, I'm thinking a couple of drinks might take the edge off.

'You want something to drink?' I ask and she raises her eyebrows. 'I know you said you're a beer girl. They've got some great IPAs and imports here. But they also have some great cocktails.'

'I'll have whatever you're having,' she replies, picking up her menu to examine the offerings. 'See if we're on the same circuit.' She's quiet for a moment then she gasps. 'Oh my God, there's bone marrow on this menu.'

The woman sitting on her right throws her an

annoyed sideways glance, so I glare at her, unimpressed with her snootiness. 'It's pretty far from Brockton and the airport. And I know you're not a big meat eater and this place serves mostly meat dishes.'

Mikki looks up from her menu, confused by this information, then it finally dawns on her that I brought her here because no one would look for her here. 'Oh . . . How sweet.'

The woman must think we're even crazier now, but I really don't give a shit. I reach across the table, grab Mikki's hand and bring it to my lips, laying a tender kiss on the *W* tattooed on her middle finger.

'I'll always look out for you,' I say and she rolls her eyes.

'So chivalrous.'

'They have some good meat-free dishes. Do you want me to order something for you?'

'Please do. We all know I'm not capable of making sound decisions on my own.'

'That's not what I meant.'

'I know, I know. Just order me something,' she says, waving off my explanation. 'I'm trying not to take my life too seriously for the next four hours. That is how long this date is going to last, right?'

'More like three hours and forty-nine minutes, but who's keeping track?'

'Good, cause I have a feeling it's going to be a real tear-jerker. Nice to get a break from those every now and again.'

'Speaking of tear-jerkers, do you want to finish reading the book tomorrow before the flight?'

'The flight?' I open my mouth to remind her, but she cuts me off. 'Oh, my God! I forgot to tell you. When you let me use your phone to call the airline, they told me our flight might get pushed again. They said a lot of the flights from Newark were being rerouted through Logan and to make sure to check the status of the flight online before we head to the airport. She said it should be updated within twenty-four hours before takeoff.'

I let go of her hand and quickly pull my phone out of my back pocket. Sure enough, the flight has been pushed back two more days to 9:15 a.m. on January eighth. *Shit!*

'What's wrong?' Mikki asks, seeing the disappointment I'm unable to hide.

'Nothing. I just have to see if I can reschedule the appointment with Kane.'

'You can't reschedule. They'll think you're one of those spoiled rich boys who thinks everyone should do whatever they want.'

'I have no choice.'

She shakes her head in mock disgust. 'If you're so rich, why don't you just charter a plane to get there?'

I sigh as I tuck my phone into my pocket. 'Because I don't want to.'

'Why? Are you one of those rich boys who likes to purposely make his life difficult just to spite his parents?'

Fuck. She hasn't even had a drink and she's already taking this conversation into uncomfortable territory.

'Look. I didn't charter a plane because I wanted to have some coffee with you after the flight was canceled. Then . . . well, as I'm sure you're aware, things got complicated.'

'Wait a minute.' Her face lights up and her eyes widen. If we were cartoons, there'd be a light bulb flashing over her head. 'You can charter a plane and you don't need a plane ticket for that . . . Can you take me to L.A.?'

'No.'

'Why?'

The waitress arrives to take our order and deliver our drinks, but Mikki doesn't acknowledge the waitress or the beer in front of her. Her eyes are locked on mine awaiting my answer. I spout off the food order then take a long swig of beer, trying to give myself time to think of any response other than, *Because I don't want to help you kill yourself.*

'I can't charter a plane to L.A. because my dad has people who monitor my spending. Chartering a plane will raise a red flag. He'll ask me what the trip was for, and I don't want him to know anything about this trip to L.A.' She lowers her head, looking so disappointed. 'I'll be honest. I'm sorry that you're disappointed, but I'm not sorry that I can't help you with this. And, if I'm being brutally honest, I think you'd be even more disappointed if I agreed to help you.'

She leans forward and sighs as she rests her cheek on the heel of her hand, looking totally bummed for a moment, then it's gone.

She sits up straight and smiles. 'Can I sit with you on that side?'

'Don't get up. I'll come to your side.'

'No, no. Stay. I want to go to *your* side.'

She slides off the stool and rounds the long table to make her way to me. There's a spring in her step that I don't think I've seen at all since the day we ran into each other in Terminal B.

She eagerly climbs onto the stool next to mine and leans over to whisper in my ear. 'Don't look now, but that old guy next to you thinks I'm crazy. He kept shooting me nasty looks and I was getting tired of looking at his sausage face.'

I turn my face to her so I can kiss her. Otherwise, I might clock the guy on my other side. Mikki's lips are soft and they still taste a little like the fruit plate she had for a light lunch at the hotel. When I pull away from her, she's clutching the front of my hoodie and staring into my eyes.

'You . . . you're going to give me a short circuit.'

I smile at the compliment and kiss her nose. 'Drink your beer.'

Chapter Thirty-one

January 5th
Mikki

The food and beer Crush ordered for me at Toro was better than any of the food we've had at the hotel, but I won't admit to this. Not even after I've had another two beers and one Mamacita: a cocktail that tastes like a margarita mixed with beer. I have a pretty high tolerance for alcohol, but I think these IPAs Crush ordered for us must have more alcohol than tap beer; or maybe it's the fact that I've hardly had anything to drink since we went to Wally's two days ago. Or it could be that these tiny plates of food are not doing enough to slow the absorption of alcohol into my bloodstream. Whatever it is, I'm feeling pretty tipsy after two hours and four drinks at Toro.

Crush pays the check then I clumsily slide off the stool to leave. He lays his hand on my shoulder as I squeeze between the tables and bodies to make my way toward the entrance. Then I see it; a blue Red Sox cap.

Never forget that, in an instant, your entire world can go black.

This mattress is too firm. This isn't my bed.

I open my eyes and the first thing I see is black clouds. Then I see Crush and he's smiling.

'Are you okay?' he says with a nod.

He wants me to say I'm okay.

I nod back.

He turns away and all the sounds come in: the crackling static of a radio; the muffled whoosh of cars driving by through the snow; the whispers. All of it is intelligible white noise, but it tells me the story of what just happened.

I must be lying on a gurney in front of Toro.

'Did I pass out?' I whisper, my throat feeling a bit raw.

No one hears me, but I can hear Crush now. 'She doesn't need to go to the hospital. She had one too many beers. Look, she's fine now.'

I try to sit up, but my torso is strapped to the gurney. 'Get this off of me!'

Crush immediately reaches for the straps holding me down. I attempt to focus on my breathing to block out the thoughts of my time in High Point. The medic in the uniform blue parka attempts to push Crush's hands away and Crush shoves him back so he can finish releasing me. I sit up quickly and lock my arms around his shoulders as he lifts me off the gurney.

'It's okay. They're not taking you anywhere,' he whispers in my ear. 'I won't let them take you.'

'We need to take her vitals one more time. It's policy,' the guy in the parka says from somewhere behind me.

'Make it quick,' Crush replies, relaxing his grip on me.

Reluctantly, I loosen my hold on him and he grabs my face to kiss my forehead. I sit on the gurney as the medic presses his stethoscope to my chest and I flinch.

'Just check her wrist,' Crush says. 'She has a sunburn on her chest.'

Tears spill from the corners of my eyes as I'm overcome with an overwhelming sadness for everything he's doing to keep me from going to the hospital. Love shouldn't be this much work. He shouldn't have to lie for me. He shouldn't have to worry if I'm going to slit my wrists every time I go to the bathroom.

'I don't deserve you,' I whisper and he looks me in the eye without saying anything.

'Pulse is still a little weak, but it's stronger than it was ten minutes ago. Next time, don't drink so much,' the medic says, moving out of the way so I can stand.

'I won't.'

Crush holds out his hand to help me up from the gurney and he pulls me aside so we're a few yards away from the small crowd now making their way back inside Toro. I stare at the silver zipper of his hoodie to keep from looking into his eyes. I don't want to know that he agrees with me that I don't deserve him.

His fingertips are gentle on my skin as he lifts my chin. 'Are you ready to hear your song?'

'Yes.'

The drive to Wally's in the backseat of the town car is short. Is this what life is like for rich people? You need something, you just call someone and they make it happen. Need a plane? Charter one. Need a ride to a club and don't want your crazy girlfriend to be recognized . . . Look at that, already referring to myself as Crush's girlfriend. I have definitely blown a fuse.

'Do you want to talk about what happened back there?' he says, giving my hand a soft squeeze.

'Just the usual stuff that keeps me locked in my house. It was . . . the guy in the Red Sox cap.'

'He was in there?' he roars, sitting bolt upright.

'No,' I reply quickly, grabbing his arm to settle him back into the seat. 'It wasn't him; it was just a guy wearing a Red Sox cap.'

He looks at me with such heartbreak in his eyes. 'You react that way whenever you see a Red Sox cap?'

'Sometimes . . . if I'm caught off-guard.'

'God. I'm so fucking sorry for what they did to you. I'm sorry I wasn't there to stop it before it happened.'

I laugh at this response. 'You don't need to apologize. You didn't even know I existed until you saw me in that parking lot.'

The car pulls up outside Wally's, but the driver

makes no mention of it. He allows us to continue talking and, again, I'm struck by how it's the little things like being allowed to talk instead of being shoved out of a cab that rich people probably take for granted.

'I did know you existed, remember?' He lightly presses his fingertip over my sweater where my bunny tattoo lies beneath. 'I was on Twitter that night because it was two weeks since Jordan died and I was meeting with a ballistics expert the following day who was supposed to record video of me loading a shotgun. The video was going to be used as evidence to show that I didn't know what I was doing the night Jordan died . . . I got on Twitter that night hoping to confess that I did know what I was doing. Or, at least, I thought I did.

'I clicked the local tweets button, hoping to find someone who had heard about the case. I was ready to tell a complete stranger, in less than 140 characters, that I did know how to load a Ruger .270. But then I saw your tweet and . . . it changed everything. I knew Jordan wouldn't have wanted me to come clean. You showed me that.'

'I showed you what?'

'That sometimes the truth hurts more than the lies. That's why you're here, because you couldn't be honest with your family about the real reason for your trip to L.A. And that's why I'm here, because I never told anyone what really happened the night Jordan died.'

This time I squeeze his hand and turn his head so he can look at me. 'What would have happened if you had confessed? You would have been found guilty of manslaughter and you might have still been in jail a year later.'

He's silent for a moment and I want to ask him what happened that night, but I don't want to push him. He's been so patient with me, never pressuring me to open up about the things that happened to me.

'But you said it yourself, you hate that I saved you,' he replies. 'And now you want to die. Maybe I should have just confessed instead of sending you that tweet.'

'I think the thought of never having met you is worse than what happened to me that night.' I take his hand and close my eyes as I lay it over my heart. 'This black box is yours to keep.'

He kisses me tenderly and I slowly lose myself in him. All I can feel is his hand on the back of my neck and the light caresses of his tongue on mine, making my stomach flutter. The way our mouths fit together makes me think of a lock and key. I guess the key I was searching for yesterday was right next to me all along.

Chapter Thirty-two

January 5th
Crush

'Come on, or Leroy will kick my ass for keeping him hanging tonight,' I say, pushing the car door open.

The sidewalk in front of Wally's is pretty desolate on a Wednesday night at 9:08 p.m. There's a group of regulars who show up just about every night. As soon as we're inside, Mikki and I squeeze in at the end of the bar so I can wait my turn, and so I can fill her in on the regulars' basic information. I don't want her to feel uncomfortable, like she's sitting in a roomful of strange men. I give her a quick and dirty profile on John, the accountant who's in the middle of a messy divorce; Ken, the high-school teacher who sometimes brings his students papers in to grade at the bar while he listens to the music; Rowan, who's in the music program at Harvard, two years under me; and Elijah, the seventy-year-old saxophone player who once played with B.B. King.

'Elijah tells the best stories of anyone I know,' I say as Jimmy slides two glasses of water across the bar. 'He hardly ever repeats a story either. He has a great memory for that kind of stuff. Sometimes, I wish he would slip up and repeat one of my favorite stories he ever told about his sister who sang backup for Led Zeppelin on one of their US tours, on "The Battle of Evermore." Her impression of the band was hilarious.'

She's looking at me with a weird expression. 'How long have you been playing music? The way you talk about it, it seems like it's in your blood. Your face just lights up.'

I shake my head, trying not to let her see how her comments have made me feel a bit exposed. 'I started playing piano when I was six, then I started playing the guitar when I was nine. But my grandpa is the one who gave me an appreciation for jazz and blues. None of my friends were ever really into it, which is why I moved out of the dorms last year. Got tired of annoying the shit out of everyone with my music and practicing. I guess it is in my blood, cause I don't think I could live without it.'

'So . . . tell me more about your thesis.'

I chuckle. 'No, you don't have to pretend to be interested in my thesis. Let's talk about something else.'

'I'm not pretending. I really want to know what you

know about music. I want to know the science behind the song you wrote for me.'

'No. There's no science behind the composition other than general music theory and the standard stuff anyone can learn in a songwriting course. That's not what my thesis is about. It's not about writing a song specifically to draw emotion. It's about figuring out what it is about music that draws emotion across various cultures.' I study her face as I let this sink in. 'The more you try to write something solely for one purpose, the more you lose sight of all the other reasons it needs to be written. So it's better not to write a song to evoke emotion. It's always best to write a song for a person. A person is not a purpose, so when you write a song for someone, you give everything up to the song. Those are the kinds of songs that evoke emotion. At least, that's what my thesis is trying to prove.'

Her eyes well up with tears, which she quickly wipes away. 'Well, now I really want to hear that song.'

'Do you want to sit on stage with me?' She shakes her head as I reach for a bar napkin for her to wipe her tears. 'Are you sure? I don't feel comfortable leaving you down on the floor with a bunch of guys. I'd rather have you next to me.'

'Is that jealousy or over-protectiveness?'

'Both.'

'Okay, but only because the thought of being more than a few feet away from you in here is making me sick to my stomach.' She takes a sip from her water and grabs the front of my hoodie, and I have to temper my reaction so she doesn't know how much this turns me on. 'Now I want you to tell me how you got away with it.'

The question catches me off-guard. At first, I think she's talking about Jordan's death, then I realize she's talking about the fat piece of shit who raped her then left her for dead in that parking lot. Then a dark thought materializes in my mind and I'm afraid to even think it. She was covered in so much blood, it was pooling underneath her when I lifted her off the asphalt. I didn't see any knife or gunshot wounds, but then again I wasn't really looking for them. God, I hope my instincts are wrong.

'The gun I used wasn't registered, so I didn't hesitate when I shot that guy. And I made sure to pull up at least twenty yards ahead of the emergency room entrance, instead of right next to it, in case there were cameras. And so I could make a quick getaway after I left you there.'

She stares at my chest as she asks this next question. 'And the evidence? How did you get rid of the gun and the car and your clothes? I mean . . . you must have been covered in blood.'

'I burned my car and my clothes, then I cleaned up the gun and sold it.'

'That's it?'

'That's it. I figured they probably wouldn't be banging down doors, doing a hard investigation into who killed the guy who did that to you. And, with the guy dead, he couldn't rat out which of his friends were with him that night. And even if they were picked up for questioning, I highly doubted they would want to admit to seeing me there; that would be like admitting their guilt. Can I ask you a question now?'

'Go ahead.'

'Did they ever show you mug shots or pictures of potential suspects? If they had that guy's body, they must have known who his friends were.'

She grabs her glass of water again and wraps both hands around it as she holds the rim against her lips. 'They did, but I told the detectives I didn't recognize them.'

'Why?'

Her hands are trembling so I take the glass and put it back on the bar.

'Because the first two pictures they showed me were of guys I'd never seen before. I knew they had mixed in photos of unrelated criminals. And I found myself hoping that the next picture would not be one of them either. That's when I realized I couldn't do it. I couldn't pick them out in a picture or sit in a courtroom with them. I never wanted to see them again.'

Jimmy smacks the bar in front of us and we both jump. 'Hey, hotshot. You're up.'

'Thanks,' I shoot back at him, then I turn to Mikki. 'Are you okay to go up there?'

She nods and I wrap my arms around her one last

time, to draw a little more inspiration, and the way she hugs me back fills me up with it. I think I could stand here like this for the rest of my life.

She gives me one last squeeze then leans in to whisper in my ear. 'Blow out their circuits.'

Chapter Thirty-three

January 5th
Mikki

A guy in a black T-shirt and gray newsboy cap delivers Crush's guitar to him on the side of the stage from wherever they were holding it for him. It's a black acoustic-electric that looks sort of like the guitar Meaghan's ex-boyfriend Randy used to carry around with him everywhere. He clips a black leather strap onto the body of the guitar then slings it over his shoulder with such ease, as if he's done it a million times; and he probably has.

'What are you grinning at?' he asks, reaching into his back pocket.

'You look so cool, like you were born to do this.'

He chuckles as he rubs the crushed penny his grandfather gave him between his thumb and forefinger. 'I guess we'll find out if you're right very soon.'

'Some folks just got it,' Leroy says into the microphone as he glances at Crush, eliciting a few hollers from the crowd. One of them sounds like a female squealing and a jealous fire sparks inside me. 'Please welcome to the stage the boy who spends so much time here I'm gonna have to start charging this fool rent. The one, the only, Cruuuuushh!'

'Come on.' Crush nods toward the stage.

I take one step up onto the tiny stage where two white wooden stools await us. I take a seat on the stool on the left and watch as Crush plugs in his guitar and positions both microphones in their stands: one for his guitar and one for his mouth. My heart is ready to pound out of my chest and he seems so calm.

I want to look out at the people sitting and standing just a few feet from the stage, but I'm afraid I'll have a panic attack or throw up. Instead, I keep my gaze focused on Crush as he sits in the stool next to me and tilts the microphone until it's right next to his lips. He winks at me before he turns his attention toward the crowd, and it's this simple gesture that puts me at ease.

'Most of you already know me, so I won't bore you with any further introductions. Tonight's not about me, anyway. Tonight is about this girl.' I bury my face in my hands in embarrassment, sensing dozens of eyes on me, hearing their laughter as I attempt to hide in plain sight. Crush places his hand on my knee and gives it a gentle squeeze. I slowly lower my hands and he reaches for my face. 'This is a song I've been working on for a while,' he continues, and I can't help but grin. 'This is called "Black Box", for the girl who holds the key to mine.'

My stomach is bubbling with so much nervous energy, I'm afraid I might vomit. I take a few deep breaths as I try to focus on Crush. He brushes the flattened penny across the strings and the sound sends a chill over my skin. He takes a moment to tune a couple of the strings, then he clears his throat and begins. From the very first notes he plucks out on the guitar, I can tell that the melancholy acoustic melody is going to make me cry. It has a loose, bluesy feel that reminds me of hot summer nights, lying in bed with a fresh pad of paper and a pen. I find myself hoping that some day he'll sing me to sleep with this tune.

Then he sings the first line and his voice . . . it's like salted caramel, smooth and richly sweet with a grainy finish.

Hope can cleanse the darkest soul
Wash away the blue
And hope is all I can recall
The night I met you
Washed up on this shore of mine
A shell broken, cracked
Never could have known this time
You'd turn my world black

This black box
Is yours to keep
This black box
Will help you sleep

This black box
Don't know your name
This black box
Loves you just the same

Time don't pass for the lonely
Seasons all look gray
Time stands still when you hold me
Knowing you won't stray
Love don't come to the wicked
Get what's coming back
Oh, love ain't no white picket
No, our love is black

I don't believe in coincidence or fate
But I know one thing for sure
Your face was meant to be
Burned into the deepest reaches
Of my blackest memories.

He sings the chorus a couple more times then he slings the guitar behind his back as the crowd cheers. He takes my face in his hands as his green eyes are fixed on mine. The sounds of applause and cheering fade away. Our eyes close and I hold my breath until I feel his lips on mine. I take a deep breath, breathing him in, then I part my lips and he swallows my exhalation.

I have never been kissed in front of anyone, much less a crowd of strangers, but I know this is a kiss I'll never forget. Because I've never felt more safe or loved in my entire life than I do in this moment. And with each passing second, I find myself longing for more than just his kiss.

He pulls away and chuckles as I lean into him, seeking more. Some others must have noticed as I hear a few brief strains of laughter from the crowd.

'Are you ready to go?' Crush asks and I nod hastily.

Yes, I'm ready to go. I want to do that again.

We make out in the back of the car all the way back to the hotel. Just kissing, with one of his hands on my knee and the other clasping the back of my neck, I've never felt more alive. Every tilt of his head and stroke of his tongue, every brush of his lips against mine, sends sparks of longing through me. This is what it feels like to want someone. It's beautiful and frightening and I don't know if I should stop it.

I push him away as I begin to feel his weight pressing me into the corner of the backseat. 'Wait.'

'I'm sorry. Am I pushing you?' He sits up straight and scrunches his eyebrows. 'You're shaking.'

'I'm scared. Not of you,' I clarify. 'I'm scared that my memories from the past will get jumbled up with my memories of you, and I don't want that to happen.'

'You don't have to explain. All you have to do is say *no*, or *wait*, or *stop*, or *piss off*, or *leave me the fuck alone, dipshit*. I'll never force you to do something you don't feel comfortable doing and I'll never make you feel guilty about that. Okay?'

I nod as the car pulls up in front of the Park Plaza. 'Okay. But . . . is it okay if we do that some more?'

'Do what?'

'Kiss.'

'We can do that as long as you want.'

In the elevator on the ride up to the fourth floor, he steals another kiss and I freeze, my body tingling as his lips travel across my jaw and up to my ear. 'Tonight is our last night in this room. Do you still want to switch rooms with me tomorrow?'

I smile with relief as the doors slide open and I pull him out of the elevator. 'Yes.'

I run down the corridor, giddy with excitement, like this is the last day of school. He walks behind me with a smile so warm it could halt a blizzard. I watch him as he catches up to me outside the door of our room, then I throw my arms around him.

'You make me feel normal.'

His smile disappears and I feel like I've said something wrong, but he turns away and looks at the door suspiciously. 'Do you hear voices in there?'

I don't have time to answer before the door swings inward, pulled open by a policeman. Standing not more than ten feet behind him are another policeman, my parents, Meaghan, and Rina.

Chapter Thirty-four

January 5th
Mikki

Rina looks pissed. 'What the fuck, Mikki?'

'Honey!' My mom rushes me. 'Get your hands off of her!' she shrieks, pummeling Crush's arms until he lets me go.

'Mom, stop it.' I position myself between her and Crush. 'Stop it!'

'Excuse me, sir. Can you please step inside?'

The officer who addressed Crush is well built and looks like he might want to do Crush some bodily harm. Crush glances at me, pure confusion in his eyes, then he squeezes past my mom and me and steps over the threshold. My mom throws her arms around my waist and her fingertips dig into my back as she hugs me tightly.

I pat her on the back then push her back. 'I'm fine.'

'Why didn't you call us?' She sounds more pissed

than worried as I pry her arms from around my waist and follow Crush inside, ignoring her question.

'Ma'am, were you being held against your will?' The officer asks me this quite seriously as I step into the hotel room and I can't help but laugh.

'Are you kidding me? No, I am not being held against my will. We're staying here cause our flight was rescheduled.'

'Why haven't you tried to get in contact with your family?'

The other officer with the mustache standing between Rina and my father asks this question in an accusatory tone.

'My phone died,' I reply defensively.

'You could have called before it died or used the hotel phone.' Meaghan's pale cheeks are glistening with tears and my stomach vaults inside me knowing I'm the cause. 'You lied to me,' she continues. 'You said you were going to L.A. for an interview.'

The devastation and betrayal in her eyes kills me. 'I'm sorry. I wasn't . . . I didn't know . . . how it would affect you. I just wanted to leave. I just . . .'

I take a few deep breaths to try to stop the tears, but I can't. And I can't speak the truth aloud, that I just wanted to die, or these officers may take me in. But I don't have to say it aloud for Meaghan to know what I mean when I say I want to leave.

Her jaw is set as I approach her. 'You pissed all over the meaning of that book.'

'I'm sorry,' I whisper, taking her into my arms.

Her arms remain slack at her sides and I bite my lip as I realize she's right.

'What book?' Rina looks confused and slightly betrayed over this reference.

I've never shared *Black Box* with Rina for one simple reason: She doesn't read books and I didn't want to see how uninterested she would be in something that meant so much to me. I do share almost everything with her, but a part of me also feels she doesn't deserve to know about anything that happened after she ditched me at that party three years ago.

The past four months of community college have been absolute hell for me. I've had three panic attacks in class. I blacked out in the middle of the quad when I heard a voice behind me that sounded like one of my attackers. And everyone just keeps trying to convince me that it will get easier with time. It probably will get easier, but it's not getting easier any time soon. So, what? I'm just supposed to suffer with this fear that permeates every cell in my body? I know that eventually another predator will recognize that fear. Whether they will act on it is something I can't know, but it's a dark fear I live with daily.

The day I was raped I was taught an important but harsh lesson: An individual's body does not belong to them if they can't walk the streets at night without fear of being violated. The first time I was committed I learned another lesson: A person's mind does not belong to them if simply wanting to die is cause to lock them up and pump them full of anti-psychotic meds. Self-ownership is an illusion. This is a lesson I learned at a very young age. How can anyone expect a teenager to cope with that kind of realization?

'Show them the book.' Crush's voice is smooth and comforting, but his words startle me.

I can't show them the book. It's *our* book. It holds the story of our fate and all the secrets of how we came to know each other.

I let go of Meaghan and her eyes are wide as she finally pieces together the identity of this guy I've been shacking up with. 'It's him?' I nod, the tiniest of nods, and she immediately runs to him. He chuckles as she throws her arms around his waist. 'Thank you,' she whispers.

'What's going on here?' My dad's voice – a voice I seldom hear – feels like needle pricks in my ears. 'How does she know him?'

I turn to the police officers. 'Look, I'm fine. I'm *better* than fine. Can we please drop all the questioning?'

The officers turn to my parents then back to each other. 'You're an adult. We ain't got no problem with what you do in hotel rooms. But you left a suicide note. We have to take stuff like that seriously. Are you planning on taking your life?'

'No,' I reply quickly.

'Don't believe her.'

I turn to my mom and fix her with the most determined stare I can muster. 'I am *not* going to kill myself. I wrote that note in a low moment. It was a stupid thing to do.'

I don't add that, yes, I do still want to die. But I think I can make it through another day. If I can just get a handle on the fear consuming me. And if I can be with Crush.

'She's tried to commit suicide twice before,' my mom adds.

Twice that you know of, I think to myself.

'She's not going to hurt herself.' Crush gently pulls Meaghan off him so he can stand next to me. 'I won't let anything happen to her.'

'And who the hell are you?' my dad asks and, for the first time in years, I hear a bit of passion in his voice.

My father has hardly spoken to me since the night I was raped. He doesn't even look at me unless we bump into each other in the hallway. I know he thinks I'm damaged now. He's right. My body and my mind are damaged, but I'd like to think that my heart is still worth something.

'I'm William.' Crush extends his hand to my father, but the handshake is not accepted. 'I've been taking care of Mikki while we wait for our flight.'

'*Taking care of?* What does that mean?'

'Exactly what it sounds like,' I reply, unsuccessfully trying to temper the anger in my voice. 'He gave me a place to stay in the city and he's been keeping me safe. I'm safe here, Da.'

'She's safe.' Meaghan's voice is small and a bit nasally with congestion, but I can hear the relief in her voice. 'This is the safest place for her, Daddy.'

A tugging on my sleeve gets my attention and Rina's eyes are pleading with me to tell her what the fuck is going on. 'I'll tell you later,' I whisper.

He's hot, she mouths.

That jealous fire lights inside me again. Yes, he is hot. And he's *mine*.

I slide my arm around Crush's lower back and he drapes his arm across my shoulders as he plants a soft kiss on my forehead. My mom covers her mouth as she watches us, but she doesn't say anything. She's never pushed me to have a boyfriend, but she has dropped hints here and there. *Look how happy Meaghan is with her new boyfriend . . . Rina has a spring in her step. Is it that new boy she's seeing?* Like all my problems will suddenly go away if I have a boyfriend. She's probably looking at Crush and me now and thinking that she was right all along.

But welcoming Crush into my life did not solve my problems. I still want to die. I just want to die a little less today than I did three days ago. But I won't deny that it's Crush who elicited this change in me. It's amazing how different – how much better – an average day can feel when you know you are safe and loved.

The policeman with the mustache turns to my dad. 'You and Mrs Gladstone have the directive. You make the call here.'

'Mikki Gladstone.' Crush whispers this in my ear, sending a chill racing through me. It's the first time he's heard my last name.

'You can't let them take her!' Meaghan shouts at my father and I bury my face in Crush's neck to hide my tears. 'If you take her you'll have to take me. I'll kill myself.'

I gasp as I pull my face away and look at her. 'Don't say that.' I let go of Crush and grab her arms to make her face me. 'Don't ever fucking say that!'

I pull her into my arms and squeeze her so tight, I can feel her bones shifting.

'They can't take you away,' she blubbers.

'Don't you ever say that again.'

She sobs into my shoulder, whispering an occasional apology. I can't hear what everyone else is discussing, but I know something is going on when someone taps my shoulder. Instinctively, I latch onto Meaghan even tighter.

'They're gone,' Crush assures us.

Meaghan and I slowly loosen our grip on one another and she's wearing a sly smile. I shake my head. Unlike me, she has always been very good at getting her way with my parents.

'How did you find me?' I ask my mom.

She pries her gaze away from Crush to answer me. 'One of Aunt Crystal's friends saw you in the lobby and recognized you from the tattoos on your fingers. She tried to follow you guys outside to see where you went, but you were gone by the time she got out there. But this hotel must really take privacy seriously. It took a while for the hotel desk to release any information about you guys. They wouldn't do it without a warrant.'

Meaghan laughs. 'I was so mad. I wanted to drag that bitch over the counter and pound her right there. After we looked at the security feed, she said, "She doesn't look like she's in any danger."'

I can't help but laugh as I think of Greta at the reception desk who seemed to have some kind of silent agreement with Crush. I'm certain she knows his real identity as the son of a huge hotel magnate. I'll have to ask Crush to thank her for stalling the police, even if it did make my family worry even more. If she had given up Crush's information sooner, they may have tracked us down and ruined his performance at Wally's.

'Get your stuff. We're going home.' My dad issues this command with a cold gruffness, without looking at me.

'I'm staying here. My flight is in a couple of days.'

'You're still leaving?'

Meaghan and Rina ask this question in unison. Only then does it dawn on me that I really have no reason to go to L.A. any more.

Crush looks down at me questioningly. 'Are you going to the studio with me?'

I nod as I draw in a stuttered breath.

'What studio?' my mom asks.

'Cru— William is recording a song.' Using his given

name feels weird. I dig my hand into my messenger bag to retrieve the book. 'And he gave me this book the night he saved my life.'

He smiles hugely at this announcement; not at all peeved or afraid that I just basically confessed to everyone in this room that he killed a man in that parking lot.

He takes the book from my hand and gives it to Meaghan. 'I think this belongs to you now.'

She takes the book and hugs it against her chest. 'Thanks.'

My dad shakes his head. 'I don't know what the heck is going on here.' He turns to Crush and addresses him directly. 'But if what they say is true. If you saved my little girl . . .' He pauses to clear his throat as his eyes begin to water. 'I guess I should be thanking you.'

He holds his hand out to Crush. When Crush takes his hand, my dad yanks him into a rough man-hug. My mom seizes the opportunity to give me one more hug. Rina and Meaghan get in line behind her. I'm beginning to think I'm all hugged out, until my father reaches for me.

I go to him tentatively and he's so gentle as he takes me into his arms, as if he's afraid he'll break me.

'Please call us later.'

I nod vigorously, thinking that I'd probably do anything he asked me to right now.

By the time they leave, my throat and face are raw, and I'm considering a nap, until I close the hotel room behind them and turn around to find Crush leaning against the kitchen counter. He looks so serious it kind of scares me.

'What's wrong?'

'Were you lying when you said you'd go to the studio with me?'

'Oh, no,' I whisper, racing to him so I can hold him. 'I'm sorry if that's what you thought. I wasn't lying. I want to go with you . . . if you'll let me.'

Burying my face in his neck, it's as if a switch is turned back on and that longing I felt when we were out in the corridor a few minutes ago is back. I brush my lips over the rough stubble under his jaw and he gently pulls my face away to look at me.

'Of course I want you with me. I want you to go everywhere with me.' I lean forward to kiss the corner of his mouth and he chuckles. 'Are you listening to me, Mikki Gladstone?'

'Oh, God. You'd better not start calling me by my full name.'

He pulls my head back again so he can look me in the eyes. 'Thank you.'

'For what?'

'For sharing *Black Box* with your sister.' He takes a beat as I try to think of a response. 'And for giving me the best night of my life.'

I definitely don't know how to respond to this, so I kiss him. An easy, tender kiss that slowly becomes hungrier and I find myself leaning hard against him, pushing him into the counter as I try to get more out of this kiss. But he hardly moves. He's solid as a stone wall; a stone wall with very kissable lips.

'Lay with me,' I whisper into his mouth. 'Please.'

Chapter Thirty-five

January 5th
Crush

She leads me by the hand to her bedroom, keeping her face forward so I can't read her expression. I have to keep reminding myself to temper this longing that keeps growing inside me. Though I know I won't go any further than where she's comfortable going, I still don't want her to get the impression that I'm frustrated or disappointed with her because of this. She switches the light on as we enter the bedroom then turns around to face me once we're standing next to the bed.

'I know it's probably not a big deal to you, but this is huge for me.'

'You don't have to explain.'

She holds up her hand to stop me. 'I know I don't have to explain. I want to. I just . . . I've never had a boyfriend. I've never slept in a bed . . . with a guy. The fact that I fell asleep with you on the couch is amazing and a testament to how safe I feel when I'm with you. I've never even laid down with a guy, other than you. I've always made out with guys while sitting up and the moment they try to force me down I kick them out.'

'I'm serious. You don't have to explain.'

'Shut up. I'm trying to say something.' I press my lips together to hold my tongue and she continues. 'I just want to lie next to you. It's such a normal *nothing* sort of thing, but it's huge for me and I just want to do that. But . . . I need you to just lay still and talk to me. Even with the lights on, I think I still need to just hear your voice. Can you do that or is that too weird?'

'It's just weird enough to make me fall a little more in love with you.' I grab her hand to stop her as she heads for the other side of the bed. 'Thank you for trusting me.'

She nods as she lets go of my hand. I wait for her to reach the other side and lie down before I do. Once we're both settled onto the bed, I decide it's time to start talking.

'Can I tell you about Jordan?'

'I would love for you to tell me about Jordan.'

I smile at the ceiling as the first memory comes to me. 'We grew up together like brothers. My mom and his mom had us three months apart – he was three months younger. When I was six, I had this pair of overalls that were my favorite. My mom hated them. They must have been a present from someone because she was always dressing me in polo shirts. I remember this one time, I put on my overalls and Jordan and I went out to the pond on the north side of the property and I waded into the pond, hoping to catch some fish in my overalls and take them home to keep as pets.

'I ended up going out a bit too far and breathing in some of the scummy pond water. Jordan pulled me out and laughed at me as I cried and basically hacked up a lung. I ended up getting pneumonia from the bacteria in the water and Jordan asked his mom, my Aunt Deb, to buy me a get-well fish. I had my pet goldfish Guppy for three years before he went belly-up.'

I know she wants me to be still, but she's being so quiet that I have to turn my head to look at her. She's staring at the ceiling with tears streaming down her temples.

'What's wrong?'

'Just keep talking.'

I draw in a deep breath and focus on the ceiling again. 'One of my favorite memories of Jordan is the time we ditched class our freshman year and went to hang out at Harvard. We joked that we were going to find us some Harvard girls to be our sugar-mommas. Once we got there and realized how scrawny we were compared to all the guys there, we decided to just sneak into the music hall and sit in the back and smoke a joint.' I smile as I think of that day and how such a simple decision changed my life. 'As soon as we walked in there and found a place to sit in the back, both of us forgot about smoking. We were mesmerized by the music. So mesmerized, we didn't see the music teacher, Professor Whitman, sneak up on us from behind. Whitman threatened to call our parents until I told him I was only there because I was trying to scope out the program.'

I don't know what I said, but Mikki chooses this moment to reach across and grab my hand. I give her hand a reassuring squeeze and continue.

'He told me the only way he'd believe me is if I played something on the piano. He got on stage, stopped the concerto, and announced to the entire music hall why I was there and what I was going to do. There were dozens of people in the seats and on all sides of me, holding their instruments and waiting for me to fuck up so they could go on with their session.' I pause as I remember how nervous I was, shaking from head to toe as I slid onto that piano bench. 'I took a seat at the piano and began playing "In A Sentimental Mood" by Art Tatum. When I finished, the entire hall was completely silent, until Jordan pumped his fist in the air and shouted, "That's my boy!"'

'What happened with the professor?'

'He asked me to audition for a scholarship, but I told him I didn't need one. I told him who my dad was and he understood. But he kept in touch with me over the years and I've been in about eight of his classes. Whitman's one of the few people I can talk to about music who not only knows what the fuck I'm talking about, but who totally understands how it makes me feel.'

She laces her fingers through mine, then seems to second-guess this and lets go of my hand. I try not to feel disappointed, but it's hard when I've become so accustomed to the feeling of her delicate hand in mine. Just as I open my mouth to continue talking, the bed bounces a little and she scoots in next to me to rest her head on my shoulder. I wrap my arm around her shoulders and resist the urge to kiss the top of her head, even though her hair smells so good. It's one of my favorite things about her. I don't know what kind of stuff she uses for her sensitive skin, but I'm going to have to make sure she's stocked up.

'Keep talking.' She mutters her command into my shirt.

I tell her a few more stories about Jordan. By the time I'm done telling her the one about the time Jordan and I stole one of my dad's cars to go to Dairy Queen, I'm pretty certain she's asleep. I kiss the top of her head, breathing in her clean scent, and her fingers curl around the fabric of my shirt.

'Do you want me to go back to my room?' I whisper.

She's silent for a moment, then she uncurls her fist from my shirt. I can feel her heart pounding against my chest. I want to get up and leave so she doesn't feel like she has to put herself through this.

She sits up suddenly and her nose and eyes are

rimmed pink, but her face is dry. She must have stopped crying a while ago.

'No, I don't want you to go.' Her hands are clasped in her lap and she stares down at them for a moment before she continues. 'Can you sit up and face that way?'

She points at the wall on my left. I sit up immediately and swing my legs over the side of the bed so I'm facing away from her toward the wall.

'Can you . . . can you take off your shirt?'

She whispers this and I can hear the shame she feels for asking me to do something so simple, as if I haven't already seen her without a shirt three times in her life. I pull my shirt off slowly and toss it onto the carpet.

'Just please stay still.'

The mattress shifts as I imagine she's crawling toward me. I can feel the heat of her body behind me, though she hasn't touched me. Then I feel her fingers on my right bicep, light as a soft breeze. She traces her fingers over the curves of my arms and I glance to the right to see what it looks like. She's tracing the lines of muscles, as if she's trying to become acquainted with them, so she doesn't have to fear them.

Removing her fingers, she sits back for a moment before she lays both her hands on my back. I try to regulate my breathing so she doesn't see how much she's turning me on. I expect her to begin tracing the muscles in my back, but instead I feel something else against the back of my neck. Once I feel her breath, I realize it's her forehead.

'Are you okay?'

She nods and her forehead rubs against my nape, sending a chill through me. From the way her breath hits my back, I can see she's trying to calm herself, too, though probably for much different reasons. Finally, she lifts her head off my neck and her hands begin to explore my back. She traces the fingertips of her right hand lightly down my spine and I begin to relax again. After a few minutes, she wraps her arms around my waist and lays her cheek against my back. We sit like this for a few minutes while I think of how lucky I am to be the one person she trusts this way and how I can't ever do anything to fuck that up.

She lets go of me and I smile when she lays a tender kiss on the back of my shoulder. There's more movement on the bed and I imagine this is as far as it will go tonight. Then I feel a whoosh of air as her shirt flies past me, landing on the carpet next to mine, followed closely by her bra.

'Turn around, please.'

Chapter Thirty-six

January 5th
Mikki

His skin is so smooth and warm against my cheek. The soft thump of his heartbeat is comforting. Just sitting here, holding him like this, reminds me of summers swimming in Uncle Cort's pool when I was a kid. Grabbing onto the blow-up dolphin as I wrapped my arms around it, I'd close my eyes as I laid my cheek against the warm vinyl and float; no fear of sinking, just letting the water carry me.

It's not just people who change. The world changes when we change. You can't deny it or prevent it. The minute you glimpse a future that isn't entirely filled with loneliness and despair, the world becomes a different place. Maybe the world isn't black. Maybe it's more like a murky gray with flashes of color here and there. Blink and you'll miss them.

I breathe in the scent of his skin one last time before I release him. Scooting back on the bed, I sit on my feet and marvel for a moment at the definition of the muscles in his back and arms. It may sound stupid, but it fills me with pride. Like he was built this strong to protect me.

My heart pounds painfully against my ribcage as I reach for the hem of my shirt. I close my eyes as I slowly pull it over my head and toss it onto the floor next to Crush's shirt. With his back to me, I can't see his reaction, so I seize this small moment of courage and quickly tear off my bra.

It's not like he's never seen me naked, but it was never my choice for him to see me like that. My hands are shaking again and I can feel the tears stinging the corners of my eyes. I ball my fists at my sides and take a few deep breaths to get a hold of myself.

'Turn around, please.'

I whisper this request so softly, I'm not sure he heard me, until he slowly begins to turn around. I force myself to hold my hands at my sides instead of using them to cover myself up, the way I desperately want to.

'What do you want me to do?' His voice is soft and some of the tension in my stomach eases. 'Just say the word.'

I open my eyes and he's looking at my face, his gaze so reassuring. I lift my hands and reach for him and he gently takes me in his arms. The moment my chest touches his, I feel as if I've been electrocuted. A surge of physical pain lights up every nerve in my body, but it only lasts a split second. It's the fear. I hold on tighter, burrowing my face into the crook of his neck and he slowly tightens his hold on me.

'Is this okay?' he murmurs.

'Yes.'

'I love you.'

'I know.'

'With all my circuits.'

I laugh and a sudden urge to tackle him overcomes me. Instead, I pull away from him slightly so I can take his face in my hands and press my lips to his. The curve of his smile against my lips fills my insides with a rush of warmth. I kiss him slowly, my body shivering as his hands slide down to each side of my waist. That intense longing begins to grow inside me again and the sound of my whimper startles me. I pull my head back and he looks confused.

'Are you okay?'

I nod, letting my gaze fall as my hands do. I try to look away from his sculpted chest, but I can't. It's so beautiful.

'Can we go to sleep now?'

'Of course.' He rises from the bed and reaches for our shirts on the floor.

'Leave the shirt,' I blurt out hastily. 'Just . . . just turn the light off.'

He smiles as he lets the shirts drop onto the carpet,

then reaches for the switch on the lamp on the bedside table.

'You still have your shoes on,' I remark and he shrugs. 'You can take those off.'

'Thank you.'

As soon as the lights go out, I pull down the comforter and sheets to slip underneath. I fold the covers back for him to lie down, then I hold my breath. I can't see where he is, but I can feel the bed moving.

'Turn the light back on.'

My voice is something between a strangled whisper and a soft shriek. The light comes on instantly and he's standing next to the bed, his eyebrows furrowed with worry.

'Maybe I should just go back to my bedroom.'

'Please don't.' I turn onto my side to face him, willing myself not to pull up the covers to hide my chest. 'But do you mind leaving the light on, just until I fall asleep?'

'Of course I don't mind.'

I pat the mattress for him to lie down and he smiles cautiously before he lies next to me. We stare into each other's eyes for a moment before I take a deep breath and snuggle up next to him. The soft flesh of my breast is pressed against his solid muscle, and it just fits. He kisses my forehead again and I press my lips to the place where his neck meets his jaw.

'Can I say something?'

'Yes,' I reply.

'I love the feeling of your body against mine.'

'So do I.'

'Can I say something else?'

I chuckle. 'You don't need permission to speak.'

'Well, then, let me just say that you are the most beautiful person I've ever laid eyes on. And I'm not saying this to gain favors. I just want you to know that what I saw tonight, and what I felt in your touch . . . was unforgettable.'

I try to wipe the tears before they fall from my face onto his skin, but they come too fast. 'I'm not as beautiful inside.'

'Don't say that.' He kisses my forehead then tilts my chin up so he can look at me through the darkness. 'Please don't say that.'

I push his hand away so I can bury my face in his neck again. 'I need to tell you something.'

'You can tell me anything.'

The tears come faster now and I can't even open my mouth. The words are caught in my throat, razor-like realities.

'I can't have kids.' I try not to remember the pain, but it's right there. It's everywhere, the way it was that night, and I can hardly breathe from the weight of it. 'I was so scared and so confused. I didn't know what they were doing. All I knew is that it hurt so much, and when it was all over, I was covered in blood with nothing worth anything left inside of me.' I sniff loudly, lips trembling as I try to catch my breath. 'They took so many things from me. So many things. And the worst part is that they knew what they were doing. One of them laughed and said something about . . . about sterilizing me.'

Crush hasn't said anything or moved in the last minute and it's worrying me. He probably wants nothing to do with me now. I lay my palm against the middle of his chest to push off and he places his hand on top of mine.

'Where are you going?'

'You probably don't want to sleep with me any more.'

'Are you fucking kidding me?'

His voice sounds different. I reach up to touch his face and feel the moisture flowing from the corner of his right eye.

'You are not damaged.' His words are blazing with fierce urgency. 'What they took from you isn't anything that should matter to anyone who truly loves you. So don't ever fucking think that you're broken or incomplete or anything less than beautiful, *inside* and out. Do you understand me?'

'Yes.'

I climb on top of him so I can drape my body over his, then I shove my hands under his back to squeeze him. He wraps his arms around my neck as I lay my head on his shoulder. After a few minutes, my body relaxes and I begin to feel drowsy, as if this position is the equivalent of a sleeping pill.

He gently nuzzles his scratchy jaw on the top of my

head and I groan groggily. 'Inside and out. Don't you ever forget it.'

'I love you,' I mumble.

'Goodnight, beautiful.'

Chapter Thirty-seven

January 6th
Crush

The first indication that my world has been turned upside down is when I wake up sleeping on my belly. I never sleep on my belly. Then I follow the length of my arm to where it's draped loosely over Mikki's back as she sleeps belly-side down with her face pointed at me. I was hoping to see her mouth hanging open and drool pooling on the pillow, but her mouth is closed and I can barely feel the rise and fall of her breathing under my arm. I want to pull her close so she can wrap those gorgeous arms and legs around me. But she looks so peaceful. I don't want to disturb her.

I lie still, watching her sleep, for at least an hour as I think of things for us to do today and tomorrow before we head to L.A. For someone who's hardly left the house in months, I could probably take Mikki anywhere and she'd be at least somewhat fascinated. But I think I'd rather take her somewhere she'll feel comfortable.

When her eyelids finally flutter open, I reach up to brush her hair out of her face. She blinks against the very dim light in the room. I don't think she's opened the drapes in her bedroom once during our stay in this hotel.

'What time is it?' Her voice is a bit thick with sleep. She begins to turn onto her side when she realizes she's still topless. She turns back onto her stomach and I pull my hand back.

'It's just after eight. We have to check out of here and into the new room at noon. Plenty of time for you to shower and pack your things.'

'I hate packing.'

She sounds like a petulant child and I have a sudden urge to tickle her to erase the sour look on her face. Tickling is such an innocent, playful act of affection shared between two people. We don't understand how much those small moments of closeness mean to us until they're taken away.

Her gaze is locked on my bare chest. I reach up, laying my hand on the side of her face as I brush my thumb over her cheekbone. She grabs my hand and slowly turns onto her back so she can hug my arm against her chest. Her heartbeat is racing, thumping wildly under my hand.

We stare into each other's eyes for a moment before

she brings my hand to her mouth and kisses my palm. 'Kiss me.'

I prop myself up on my elbow then cradle her face with the hand she just kissed, trying to find a position that I don't have to lie on top of her. She must see my trepidation as I slowly lean into her. She coils her arms around my neck and pulls me close so my chest is touching hers again.

'Kiss me or I'll make you pack my suitcase,' she says with a soft smile. I plant a quick kiss on the corner of her mouth and she shakes her head. 'Kiss me like this is a movie and we're madly in love and we're seeing each other for the first time in three years, eight months, and twenty-one days.'

I let out a short burst of laughter, then I quickly compose myself and go for it. With every passing moment, every taste of her mouth, every whisper of her fingertips over my skin, the friction between us gets hotter. I can feel myself growing inside my jeans and I'm afraid she'll feel it against her hip.

'Why are you scooting back?' She sounds hurt and the look in her eyes confirms the rejection in her voice.

'I don't want to make you uncomfortable.'

She gazes into my eyes as she considers this. 'Can you lie on top of me? I just want to try it out.'

'Are you sure? You don't have to do this.'

'I know.'

I nod as I gently place one of my legs between hers, watching her face for any negative reaction. She seems to be watching my legs as I move. My hands are on either side of her head now, my face hovering over hers, and I've got one knee pressed against the mattress between her legs so I don't have any weight on her yet.

She reaches for my chest with both hands and she runs her hands over my pecs. I close my eyes when her hands skate over my abs, drawing in deep breaths so I don't scare her with my excitement. She grabs the back of my neck and pulls me down on top of her so she can wrap her arms around my shoulders. Then I kiss her like I haven't seen her or anyone in decades.

A few minutes pass before she begins to shift beneath me, as if she's trying to get away. I instantly pull my head back and she nods.

'I'm going to take a shower. Can you wait in here?'

'Absolutely.' I kiss her forehead then roll off of her, extremely relieved that she knew when to stop and that she still wants me around. 'I'll put your phone charging while you're in the shower.'

'Thanks.'

After her shower, she asks me to brush her hair again, but there doesn't seem to be many tangles. Once I'm done, I head back to my room to take a shower and pack. When I come out of the bathroom wearing nothing but a towel around my waist, I find Mikki sitting on the edge of my bed in her pajamas.

'Hey! I didn't expect to see you in here.' I don't know if I should head back into the bathroom or reach for one of those tiny bathrobes again.

She smiles. 'I'm fine. I've seen plenty of naked guys on TV. And you look way better than them.'

'Really?'

'Yeah, but don't let it go to your head.' She covers her mouth and laughs as she realizes the double entendre.

'I promise I won't. So what's up? Are you here to watch me get dressed? And why are you in your pajamas?'

'I don't want to go down to the lobby with you to get the key to the new room. Can I just stay here and you'll come get me when you have it?'

'Sure. But why don't you want to go down there?'

'I'm just so embarrassed that my mom probably told that girl at the front desk that I was planning to commit suicide. She tells everyone my business all the time. She thinks it makes her seem like she's proud of me despite my defects, but I don't give a fuck if she's proud of having a mentally ill daughter. I don't want anyone to know. I just hate seeing the pity and the judgment staring back at me.'

'You don't have to go down there. I'll get the key by myself. So, does that mean you don't want to leave the hotel? I was kind of hoping we could see a few more things before the flight.'

She heaves a deep sigh and looks up at me with an apology in her eyes. 'I'm sorry. I'm just not that kind of person.'

I take a seat next to her on the bed. 'What kind of person?'

'The kind of person who seeks adventure. I prefer

staying at home, reading a book, watching a movie. I'm boring.'

'That's not boring. I'd much rather stay home and read a book or learn a new piece on the guitar than go out drinking or tearing shit up with my buddies.'

'You never talk about your *buddies*.'

'They're just buddies. We're not BFFs like you and Rina. I lost my best friend four years ago.'

She reaches up and runs her fingers through my damp hair. 'I'll be your best friend.'

By the time we're packed and we've hauled our stuff to the new junior suite, I'm ready for a nice, big lunch, but I'm tired of room service. With Mikki's desire to not leave the room, I have to be creative. I wait until she leaves to use the bathroom, then I call down to concierge and explain what I need. Anthony is eager to accommodate my request.

'I ordered lunch.' I pat the sofa cushion for her to sit with me while we wait for our food. 'You look hot in those anime pajamas.'

She sits next to me and curls her legs under her as she reaches for the remote in my hand. She snatches it away and begins flipping through the channels until she settles on a cooking channel where a buff guy who looks more like a Marine than a chef is explaining how to butcher a whole salmon into filets.

'You think that guy is hot or are you thinking of becoming a chef?'

She looks at me like I'm crazy. 'He is kind of hot. And, no, I'm not going to be a chef. I just like watching cooking shows. It's an art, but it's so precise; so controllable.' She sets down the remote between us and stares at it for a moment. 'It's not like poetry.'

'Do you write poetry?'

She nods then turns her attention back to the TV. 'I wrote a poem about you.'

'Me? When?'

'This morning. After you left the room to get the key.'

'I was gone, like, twenty minutes. You wrote a poem in twenty minutes?'

She shrugs and leans back, propping her feet up on the coffee table. 'It's not finished and it's not any good. Maybe I'll show it to you in a few years.'

My stomach flips inside me; not because she wrote a poem and not because she's going to make me wait that long. But, because she's implying that she'll be around in a few years.

'I'll wait as long as it takes.' I kiss her cheek and she giggles.

'Get your pajamas on,' she says, pushing me away. 'We're not leaving this room today.'

'I don't sleep in pajamas.' She eyes me suspiciously and I chuckle. 'I'm just being honest. I sleep in my boxers and I doubt you want me walking around here like that.'

She shakes her head. 'I feel bad that you're sitting here in jeans and I'm in my comfy *Death Note* pjs.'

'*Death Note*?'

'It's my favorite manga series.'

'I've never understood the difference between anime and manga.'

'Manga is like a comic book and anime is an animated series. *Death Note* was turned into an anime series, which was excellent, but I prefer the original manga series.'

She launches into an excited explanation of the plot and characters, which is actually pretty fascinating. The knock at the door startles both of us and I hurriedly answer it to get the stuff I ordered. I tip the guy generously and shoo him away so I can roll the table into the sitting area myself. Mikki watches with a skeptical smile on her face as I approach.

'Aren't you just the humble rich guy? Doing the servant's job?'

'I have a surprise for you.' She removes her feet from the coffee table so I can set down the covered plates.

'An engagement ring in a glass of champagne?'

'Not quite. Do you really think I'd go for a cliché like that?'

'Just tell me what it is.'

I stick my fingers in the ventilation holes on the top of the domed lids and she watches anxiously. 'I had them make us something special.'

'It better not be muffins.'

I lift the lids on both plates and she doubles over with laughter. Her pizza is baked in the shape of a bunny with slices of red and yellow bell peppers sticking out of the bunny's tail as if it's on fire: burninbushytail. My pizza is baked in the shape of an eyeball, with green bell peppers fanned out to form a circular iris, and it looks as if the pizza has been stepped on.

'Crushed eyes,' she says, giggling as she points at my pizza.

'crushedeyes' was my Twitter username at the time I found Mikki on Twitter. It was an inside joke Jordan and I had. Whenever we went to restaurants, we'd ask the server if we could get crushed eyes in our drinks. Most of the time, they wouldn't notice and they'd just nod in agreement. But some of them would look at us like we were crazy or ask us to repeat the request, then we'd ask for crushed ice to make them think they were hearing things. It was so stupid, but it made us laugh every time.

But as I watch Mikki trying to compose herself I realize it's no longer an inside joke just between Jordan and me. In the process of finding the girl I fell in love with three years ago, I found my best friend.

Chapter Thirty-eight

January 6th
Mikki

I eat half of my pizza – the half with the olives as bunny eyes –and Crush devours his pizza after pretending to find a hair in the sauce. We watch the cooking channel for a couple of hours while snuggling on the sofa. I even respond to a few texts from Rina and Meaghan, though Rina's comments about Crush's hotness just piss me off and I stop responding to her.

As I lie with my head on his chest, I begin to have interesting thoughts about what Crush looks like underneath all this clothing and the things I'd like to do to him. I want to taste the smooth skin on his chest. I've heard songs and read books about sex, but I've never been able to imagine having sex with someone I actually know. I've had fantasies about celebrities and one particularly hot guy in my Women's Studies class. Okay, maybe he appeared hotter than he actually was because he was taking Women's Studies. But Crush . . . there's no denying it. The guy oozes sexiness and he is definitely the hottest guy I've ever made out with.

'You can change out of those clothes. It won't make me uncomfortable,' I say this as casually as I can, keeping my eyes focused on the TV.

He chuckles. 'It's okay. I don't think you can handle this.'

'What?'

'This,' he says, running his fingers down the length of his body. 'You can't handle this.'

'Oh, please.' I push off his chest so I can sit up and glare at him.

'Fine. But don't say I didn't warn you.'

I shake my head as he gets up and heads for the bathroom. 'Wait.' He turns around and looks at me. 'You can use the bedroom.'

Up until now, even though we slept in the same bed last night, it's been assumed that he would be sleeping on the sofa bed tonight. He mentioned it earlier when he propped up his suitcase and guitar case next to the sofa bed. I didn't say anything because I knew it was just his way of showing me that he wouldn't pressure me to sleep in the same bed again. He would wait for me to ask.

He nods as he heads for the bedroom to undress. I feel like I'm being really bossy with him, but I know he won't do anything unless I ask him to. I'm ready to start asking for more.

He walks out of the bedroom with his head bowed a little, but I can still glimpse the bashful smile on his face. 'You happy now?'

Oh, God. My mouth instantly begins to salivate at the sight of his abs. I swallow hard and his expression gets a bit serious.

'Are you okay?' he asks, standing next to the sofa, so close I can smell the scent of his skin mixed with the freshly laundered scent of his gray boxer briefs.

I nod, pulling my legs up on the sofa to sit cross-legged. 'Sit.'

He laughs, but he doesn't sit down. 'Are you getting a kick out of telling me what to do?'

I can't take my eyes off the deep creases that run diagonally from his hips toward his . . . bulge.

'Are you sure you're okay?' he repeats the question and I nod again.

'Yes.' I tear my eyes away from his body and look him in the eyes. 'I'm okay. And, no, I don't like telling you what to do. I'd rather you just do what you want to do for a little while. Is that okay?'

He looks a little confused by this request. 'What do you mean?'

I take a deep breath, then I stand up so we're nose to nose. 'I want you to take the initiative. I know you'll stop when I need you to stop. I just want to feel like you want this as much as I do.'

His hand lands softly on my hip as his lips barely touch mine. 'Oh, I want this. You don't have to doubt that or let it make you do something you don't want to do.'

I cradle his face in my hands and as I look him in the eyes. 'I want this, too.'

He kisses my forehead and takes my hand so he can lay a soft kiss on the inside of my wrist. 'Do you think you'd feel more comfortable if we showered first?'

I smile as I realize he knows me better than I know myself. 'Yes.'

'You want to go first?'

'No.'

'Okay, I'll go first.' He lets go of my waist and turns to leave, but I grab his hand to stop him.

'I don't want you to go first either. I want to go . . . together.'

He doesn't ask me if I'm sure, and I'm so grateful for that. I need him to trust that I know my own boundaries. Though I'm scared shitless at the idea of showering with him, I'm also really excited to do something so normal and sensual with him, knowing that he's not expecting to have sex in the shower. We're just going to get clean.

He tightens his grip on my hand and I allow him to lead me to the bathroom. On the way there, I stop at my suitcase to get my toiletries. Once we're standing in the bathroom, I begin to feel really awkward, like maybe this was a bad idea.

'Can you get undressed first, then I'll decide if I still want to do this?' He nods and attempts to close the bathroom door, but I stop him. 'Leave it open, please.'

He leaves the door wide open, then he holds out his arms. 'Come here.'

I hug him and he holds me gently as he rubs my back. We stand like this for a while until I feel more relaxed. Finally, I let go and nod for him to continue. He places my toiletries inside the shower then turns it on, holding his hand under the water until it's the right temperature. When he turns around, he flashes me the most adorable half-smile as he reaches for the waistband of his boxers.

He slides them down slowly and I don't realize I'm holding my breath until he stands upright and looks me in the eye. I let out the breath I'm holding, then I reach for the bottom of my shirt and quickly pull it over my head. His eyes flit down to my chest then return to my face. I close my eyes, pushing out all the dark thoughts clawing at the periphery of my mind, then I push down my pajama bottoms and my panties.

I open my eyes and he's still looking into my eyes. 'You're beautiful.'

He pushes the shower curtain back and I take one step forward, then another, until I'm right next to him. I step inside the shower and the water is the perfect temperature. I get under the water to make room for him to climb in. Once he's inside, I'm hit with flashes of happy memories of running through the sprinklers in the yard. We're just playing in the water. That's all.

Chapter Thirty-nine

January 6th
Crush

I try to keep my gaze from falling below her face, but it's like trying to keep a lead weight from sinking in water. She said she wanted me to do what I wanted, so I allow myself one glance down the length of her body, then I meet her gaze again. But she's not looking at my face. Her eyes are transfixed, completely focused on my crotch. I wonder if this is like a victim of a robbery being shown the gun they were robbed with. I want to cover myself up or get out of here, then she holds out her hand.

'Come here,' she says, repeating my words back at me.

I take her hand and she gently pulls me toward her. We stand under the water, holding each other, for a while. Her body trembles a little despite the warmth of the water. Finally, she pulls away, keeping her eyes focused on mine.

'Can you give me my shampoo?'

I reach behind me and retrieve the shampoo I set down on the small ledge of the bathtub. I hand it to her and she smiles as she squeezes some into her hands.

'Can I do that?'

She nods as she smears the shampoo onto the top of her head and turns around. I've shampooed plenty of girls' hair. It's just something that happens when you have shower sex and I've had plenty of that. But not knowing whether this is a prelude to sex makes this even more sensual and comforting. I massage the shampoo into her hair, gently rubbing my fingertips in circles over her scalp to help her relax. Her shoulders fall slightly as her muscles slacken.

The eternal struggle begins inside me. I want to kiss her shoulder. She told me to do what I want. She trusts me not to go any further than what she feels comfortable with. I just hope she hasn't foolishly trusted me.

'Turn around so you can rinse.' She turns around and smiles and I take that as a sign that I'm doing okay. Then she reaches for my ear and pinches my earlobe.

'What are you doing?' I ask with a chuckle, hoping she doesn't see how close she came to giving me an erection just now.

She shrugs and continues to smile as she closes her eyes and puts her head under the water. I seize the opportunity to look at her body. Her breasts are perfectly round and perky, nipples slightly pink. Her waist curves down to small hips. She's a little too thin, but she's already not quite as thin as she was three days ago. My gaze slides down a bit farther to the scars on her thighs, and suddenly I see her hand reaching out to me again.

'Kiss me.'

A painful longing fills my chest to the point that I feel I might burst. I place my left hand on her face and my right hand on her waist, ready to put some distance between our hips in case I get too excited. Then I pull her lips to mine and kiss her slowly. Her hands land on my chest, then slide down and around to my lower back. I try to focus on anything other than being inside of her, but it's so fucking hard.

'Ow,' she whimpers.

I pull my head back, completely embarrassed that I just bit her lip without realizing what I was doing. 'Sorry. I got a little carried away.'

'It's okay.' She shakes her head and leans into me. 'Don't stop.'

I kiss her again, this time a bit harder and she moans into my mouth. *Oh, fuck.* I push her hips back a little and she groans.

'Why are you pushing me?'

'I can't do this.' I clear my throat, unsure how to explain this to her. 'You're getting me too excited.' She tries unsuccessfully to suppress her grin, so she covers her mouth with her hand. 'You think that's funny?'

'No. I just think it's kind of cool that I make you feel that way, and that it scares you.'

'You think it's cool that I'm scared of making you uncomfortable?'

'Okay, maybe it's not cool, but it's very sweet. You can turn around if that makes you feel better. I should probably wash your hair now anyways. You stink.'

I kiss her and she's caught off-guard, which elicits an immediate whimper. It's such a fucking beautiful sound. Her hands reach up and she clutches my hair to hold my head still as she kisses me back.

'I love you.' The words sound slightly garbled by the water flowing into my mouth as I kiss my way down her jaw and to her neck. 'I love you so much. I don't want to hurt you.'

She leans her head to the side, opening herself up to me, like a flower waiting for a honeybee. I kiss her neck, sucking gently so I don't leave a mark, but enough to fully appreciate the taste of her skin.

'Crush?'

'Yes, baby.'

'I think . . . I think I want you to touch me.'

Pulling my head back, I gaze into her eyes to make sure she's ready, because her words sounded unsure. Her chest is heaving as she meets my gaze straight on and nods.

I place my left hand behind her neck and pull her toward me so I can kiss her. My other hand lands gently on the small of her back, waiting for another needy whimper or moan to tell me she's ready. And, sure enough, seconds later she gives it to me.

I slowly slide my hand over her abdomen, giving her the opportunity to stop me, but she doesn't. I keep moving down until my hand is between her legs and she gasps.

'Are you okay?'

'Oh, I—' She seems unable to speak so I quickly remove my hand. She grabs it to stop me from pulling away. 'No, I'm fine. I just did *not* expect it to feel like that.'

'Does it hurt?'

'No!'

I kiss her forehead and this brings her smile back. 'Maybe we should just get washed up and go watch some reality TV.'

She sighs as she stares at my lips. 'Okay. But I won't forget that you rejected me.'

'I'm not rejecting you. I want to make you feel how much I love you, but I want to do it out there where I can dote on you. Not in here where I can't even see what I'm doing. Is that okay?'

She nods and I feel a huge weight lifted from my shoulders. Something about this didn't feel right. We'll both know it when it is. And when it's right, it will be that much more amazing for both of us.

After two excruciating hours of cuddling on the sofa, watching reality TV while thinking of nothing but all the ways I'd like to have sex with Mikki, I switch off the TV and ask her something I've wanted to ask ever since she told me she wrote a poem about me.

'I have a favor to ask you.'

'You want to sleep in my bed tonight?'

'Ha-ha. Actually, I was wondering if you'd help me with my song.'

She lifts her head off my chest and looks up at me. 'What song? "Black Box"?'

'Yeah. Ever since you said you write poetry, I was thinking maybe you could look at the lyrics and see if there's anything that could be improved.'

'There's nothing that can be improved. It's beautiful. Besides, just because I write poetry doesn't mean I'm any good at it. I kind of suck.'

'Somehow, I doubt that.'

'You have too much faith in my artistic abilities. I do write better when I'm not on my meds, but not as good as I do when I'm stoned. Just being honest.'

'Okay, you don't have to help, but can you just look at the lyrics with me and see if *maybe* you see some room for improvement. I need to work on the song just a little more before Saturday, especially now that I'm going to be performing it live in front of Kane instead of recording and editing it. I want it to be perfect and I'm still not completely happy with the second verse.'

I grab my phone off the table, ignoring the notifications of missed calls and texts, and go straight to my music-writing app. I open it up and it shows all the tabs and lyrics for the song, and it's all editable.

'That's a cool app. They make an app for everything,'

Mikki remarks as she watches me scroll through to the second verse.

'You're going to think this is even cooler or totally lame, but this is *my* app. I hired an app developer to help create an app where I could write music. None of the apps I found had all the features I wanted.'

'That is very cool. So you're the only person who has this app, like *Black Box*?'

'No, it's for sale and it's been downloaded millions of times.'

'That is why you're rich and I'm not. I need an app.'

'But when you meet my parents, you can't mention the app. They don't know anything about it. I've kept the app and the revenue it generates a secret.'

She smiles. 'When I meet your parents?'

'Stop grinning. You know it's bound to happen.'

'Why don't you want them to know about the app or all the millions you're making? Don't you think they'd be proud?'

'Probably, but I'm keeping it a secret until I graduate in May. I can't wait to see the look on their faces when I tell them I don't need their trust fund.'

She sits up and looks at me, appearing confused. 'Why don't you want your trust fund?'

I sit up straight so I can look at her straight on. 'When you grow up privileged, the way I have, you live your whole life balanced over a safety net with no holes. No fear of falling. Even when you screw up and cause your best friend's death. I'm tired of living like that.' I run my hand down my face, trying to block out the image of Jordan's face the moment he realized a large fragment of the shotgun shell had lodged in his neck and he was hemorrhaging. 'I want to live my life with a little less control. I kept this a secret so that I wouldn't disgrace my father when everyone at school finds out I rejected the trust fund. Anyway, I'm hoping to do some traveling after I graduate.'

'Traveling to where?' She looks a little worried at this news.

'Wherever you want to go.' She smiles and I pat my lap for her to sit with me.

She straddles my legs and drapes her arms over my shoulders. 'I want to go to Australia. They speak English, but there's all kinds of poisonous animals, which makes it sort of exotic.'

'We'll go to Australia.'

'Where do you want to go?' She musses up my hair and I turn my head to bite her arm playfully.

'I want to go home. Will you go to my apartment with me tomorrow?'

Her eyes widen with excitement. 'Yes!'

I laugh at her enthusiasm. 'It's not as exotic as Australia, but I promise there are no poisonous animals.'

'I can't wait.'

Chapter Forty

January 7th
Mikki

Finally, I'm the first to wake up and I'm not at all embarrassed to find the drool spot on my pillow once I see the tent Crush is creating with the comforter. I'll just slide out of bed to go to the restroom. Maybe he'll wake up on his side while I'm in there, relieved that I didn't see his morning wood. But as soon as I move, he groans and I quickly turn away from him so he doesn't see my smile.

He reaches for me and I can't hold it in. 'Stop!'

I look over my shoulder at him, trying not to laugh at the adorable confused look on his face. Then he reaches under the covers, feels around a little bit, and shakes his head.

'I'll be right back.'

I check my phone messages while I wait for him. A few minutes later, he returns from the bathroom, smelling like toothpaste. He gets right back under the covers with me and I smile as he beckons me to spoon with him.

'How embarrassing was that?' I ask as he wraps his arm around my waist and I back up into him so his chest is flush against my back.

'On a scale of one to ten, um . . . quadrillion.'

He brushes his lips over my neck and I close my eyes, trying to stay relaxed, but it's more difficult when I can't see his face. I spin around in his arms until I'm facing him.

'I finally checked my voicemail messages. I had about thirty messages from my mom and Meaghan and two messages from my therapist.' My stomach clenches inside me as I think of her words and the hint of emotion I heard in her voice. 'She said she wanted to talk to me and would be willing to come in after hours or on the weekend . . . The power of suggestion. Like, if she suggests we should talk on the weekend, I'll subconsciously try to stay alive to fulfill this prophecy.'

'But you *will* be alive this weekend. And the weekend after that?'

The way he says this as if it's a question makes my chest tighten. 'I can't promise I won't be hit by a car or die in a fiery plane crash, but I can promise that I won't take that bottle of pills in my purse and swim out into the open ocean.'

The muscle in his jaw twitches. 'That's how you were going to do it.'

I nod as I think of that bottle of pills. 'Can you go in my purse and flush that bottle of pills? And, while you're at it, break all those cigarettes?'

'Are you sure about the cigarettes?'

'Yes. I think . . . and this is so hard to admit because it makes me feel disgusting and stupid, but I think the drugs were making me worse.'

He brushes my hair out of my face and kisses my forehead. 'You are neither disgusting nor stupid.'

'Yeah, but that doesn't change the fact that I *feel* that way. The only good thing about drugs is that they make you forget how awful you feel about being a junkie. Just get rid of them. All of them.'

'Anything else you want me to do before we head out of here?'

I bite my lip as I work up the courage to ask him, then I decide I'll wait until we're at his apartment. It will be better when we're in his domain.

I kiss his nose and shake my head. 'Nope.'

I insist on us showering together to save time, but the truth is I just want to feel at ease with him the way I felt yesterday. I want to step into his apartment knowing that barrier has already been broken. I want to feel comfortable with every part of his body. He is not the one who scarred me.

The entire journey through the hotel and down to the car, I'm worried that the hotel staff will recognize me as the suicidal girl in the Garden Suite. The moment we slide into the backseat of the town car, Crush kisses my cheek and my body relaxes a little. He's grinning like a fool and it dawns on me that he doesn't care what any of these people think about us.

'Why are you smiling?'

He shoots off the address to the driver before he answers my question. 'Just really fucking excited to show you my place. Put your seatbelt on.'

I smile as I reach for the seatbelt and pull it across my chest. He helps me get the buckle in and seizes the opportunity to steal another kiss. It's a soft peck on the lips, his mouth lingering just long enough for me to know he wants more, but he'll wait.

The car turns the corner onto the highway and I sigh as I lean back and think of how many times Crush has saved my life. I hope he never has to save my life again. I have to call my therapist and see if I can get in for an appointment as soon as I get back. I need a referral so I can change my meds – again.

Having a mental illness is like riding a really fast merry-go-round that never stops. There's no escape. You're stuck. But once in a while, you can give the operator some good drugs and he'll slow it down a little; just enough for you to see the trees and the normal people as they stroll by. But that ride operator needs to be supplied often. And sometimes, like any typical junkie, he's just plain unreliable. He stops showing up and you're spinning again. You can't see clearly.

Sometimes, I guess, you can supply that merry-go-round operator with something else that feels like a drug: Love. It's probably only temporary, and I'm sure my inner junkie will soon need something more than love to get by. But right now, I'm going to sit back and enjoy getting my circuits blown out by William 'Crush' Slayer.

Fawcett Street is a small one-way street running almost parallel to the train tracks that seems as if it curves into nowhere land or some type of industrial area. But as soon as the driver takes the curve, the huge building on the left is obviously not industrial. The brick- and slate-faced apartment building is approximately the length of a city block and about six stories tall. A girl bundled up in earmuffs and snow boots and carrying a paper bag of groceries wrenches opens one of the three sleek silver entrance doors and disappears inside.

Crush gets out of the car, but the driver beats him to my door. The driver opens the door for me to get out and I flash him a tight smile as I take Crush's hand so he can help me out.

'Watch your step,' he says, indicating the curb that's almost entirely buried in fresh snow.

We hustle to get inside and out of the storm. The moment we step through the silver doors, I'm mesmerized by the entrance area. All the furnishings and architecture are sleek and precise; from the cherry reception counter on our left to the sitting area directly ahead of us where three people are sitting in boxy armchairs in front of a fireplace, their fingers clicking speedily over the keyboards of their laptops and phones.

Crush leads me past the reception desk to an elevator. I feel really uncomfortable, like I don't belong here. All these people probably go to Harvard or MIT, or went there at some point in their lives. And here I am, a bipolar girl with suicidal tendencies who goes to community college. Crush and I are from totally different worlds.

The elevator doors slide open and it takes me a moment to realize I should step inside. He presses the button for the fifth floor then turns to me.

'Are you all right?'

'What do you think your parents will think when they find out about me? Because my parents were obviously very happy to finally meet the person who saved my life, and they don't even know how many times you've saved me. Will you tell your parents what happened to me? I'm not sure I could handle them knowing.'

'Don't let what my parents may or may not think about you worry you. If you never want to meet them, that's fine with me. Or, if you want, we can pretend to be roommates.' He winks at me and my stomach flips. 'Bottom line is, my parents opinions have no bearing on how I feel about you or anyone else for that matter. And they never will. The only person who ever really knew me, other than Jordan, was Grandpa Hugh. And believe me when I say that both of them would have loved you.'

The doors slide open and he places his hand on the small of my back to guide me forward. A guy in jeans and a thick, gray parka glances at me before he nods at Crush, then pulls a navy-blue knit cap over his head. He's getting ready to brave the storm. Crush nods back at the guy and I smile, in case he glances at me again, but he doesn't.

We reach the door for apartment 522 and my entire body is buzzing with nervous energy. I'm excited to get inside and see where he lives, but I'm also anxious about what's going to happen in there.

He pushes the door open and the first thought that comes to my mind also comes out of my mouth. 'Hey, this is pretty normal.'

He laughs as I walk farther inside, taking in the modern but not spectacularly sleek open kitchen with the two swivel bar stools. I try not to imagine that he's sat there before and had breakfast with some other girl.

As this thought crosses my mind, he comes up behind me and whispers in my ear. 'Can I take your coat?'

I unbutton my wool coat and let him slip it off me, then I unzip my black hoodie and pull it off as he hangs up my coat in a closet. I hand him the hoodie and he hangs that up too, then he puts his own coat away.

'I have to say, I really like your apartment. I was sort

of expecting some penthouse or something really outrageous with a floating staircase and servants' quarter.'

He smiles as he heads into the kitchen and opens the refrigerator. 'You should know by now that I'm a bit more low-key than that. Do you want water, beer, or orange juice? That's all I have.'

I consider this for a moment, thinking that the beer will probably make this easier. But just as it will dull the anxiety, it will also dull the pleasure.

'Water.'

He hands me the water and I take a seat on the bar stool to drink my beverage.

'Do you want a tour?'

'Oh, I didn't realize your apartment was an attraction. Sure. I'll take a tour. How much—'

I almost ask how much the tour is going to cost, but I stop myself. That's unintended sexual innuendo. After the attack, I had to train myself to avoid these, especially when alone with a male in an enclosed space. I read a study that said men who are sexually excited lose a great deal of their reasoning ability. What I took away from that is that I had to be careful never to get a guy sexually excited. Which is why I never went beyond first-base with a guy and there were times where I even pretended to be a bad kisser.

He stands a few feet away from the bar stool where I sit and holds out his hand. I jump off the stool and grab his hand, letting him lead me through the living-room area toward a dimly lit corridor. He flips a couple of switches on the wall and the hallway blazes with warm light. His bedroom door is wide open, so I walk ahead of him and my hand instantly finds the light switch just inside the doorframe.

The bedroom is a bit nicer than the rest of the apartment. This space seems to have the most personal touch. Everything from the guitars hanging on the wall, the upright piano and mixing equipment in the corner, and the soft gray decor, feels like Crush.

I turn around to face him as he stands in the doorway, awaiting my assessment, and I hold out my hand to him. He takes my hand and I pull him toward the far wall with the large almost floor-to-ceiling windows.

'The balcony is off the living room. Come on, I'll show it to you.'

I squeeze his hand tighter to stop him. 'I don't want to see the balcony. I want you to sing for me.' I glance at the piano in the corner and he smiles. 'I've been dying to hear you play piano. I was going to ask you to sing "Black Box" for me, but, now that I see that piano, can you sing something else? Something I haven't heard before?'

He chuckles then plants a soft kiss on my lips. 'Of course I'll play for you. What do you want to hear?'

I laugh at this. 'What are you, a jukebox? You know every song there is?'

'Not every song, but I know a lot of them. And if I don't know it, I can at least try.'

I think about this for a while, then I think of a song I heard last week, which filled me with so much sadness because I was certain I would never find that kind of love.

Chapter Forty-one

January 7th
Mikki

'It's an Elvis Presley song. "I Can't Help Falling In Love."'

I don't know why I'm so nervous about asking him to sing this song. He's the one who should be nervous. But he just flashes me that confident smile and leads me toward the piano in the corner as if he takes song requests all day long.

'Sit.' He pats the wooden piano bench for me to sit next to him. 'I do know this song. I know just about every Elvis song there is. And it just so happens that this is an easy song to play. So I'm going to play it once, then I'm going to teach you how to play it.'

I laugh pretty hard at this and he waits patiently for me to finish. 'I have no musical talent. We'll be here all night if you try to teach me this song.'

'I wouldn't mind being here all night with you.' He

kisses my jaw and I close my eyes, wishing I understood the science of how he can make me feel this way with such a simple gesture. 'I'll teach you the first verse and I can teach you the rest later. Deal?'

I open my eyes and nod. 'Deal.'

The first chords he plays are soft and lulling. Then he looks me straight in the eye as he sings the first line about fools rushing into love and I bite my lip against the surge of emotion his voice brings. But the second line is all it takes to make me cry. He looks back and forth between the black and white keys and, through the tears, I keep my gaze locked on his beautiful face. When he sings the part about some things being meant to be, there is no question in my mind that everything in my life has led to this one moment. As he arrives at the last verse, I do as the song says and I take his hand. He stops playing and looks into my eyes as he sings the last two lines to me a cappella.

I rise slowly from the bench and he rises with me. Leading him to the bed, I stop next to it and stand there for a moment.

'I don't want to think about anything.' I reach for his face and trail the backs of my fingers over his jaw. 'I just want to feel you.'

Grabbing the hem of his shirt, I slowly pull it over his head, then I reach for the bottom of my shirt. He places his hand over mine to stop me and I realize it's because he wants to do it. I let go of the fabric and raise my arms in the air so he can remove my shirt. He gazes as my breasts for a moment and I find myself anticipating the moment he will put his mouth on them. He must also be anticipating this as he grabs my hips and gently turns me around so he can undo the clasp on my bra.

I let the bra fall to the floor next to the shirts and his hands are on my waist, this time pulling me backwards until his chest is flush with my back. He drapes my hair over my shoulder and lays a soft trail of kisses from my shoulder to my neck and up to my earlobe. The moment he takes my earlobe into his mouth, and I can feel his breath in my ear, a powerful surge of pleasure rushes through me, pulsing between my legs. He lightly drags his teeth over my earlobe, then he tortures me a little more, tracing his tongue inside the rim of my ear before he turns me around again.

'I want you.' There's a definite note of desperation in my words, but I don't care.

His gaze roams over every inch of my torso until it lands back on my face. 'I've never wanted anything more than I want you right now.'

I reach for the waistband of his jeans and he presses his lips together as I undo the button and pull his zipper down. He's wearing black boxer briefs today. Something about this makes me smile. I slowly push his jeans down and he helps me out a little, kicking them aside once they're at his feet. I reach for his boxers, but he stops me as he reaches for my jeans. Once we've both removed our pants and underwear, I know this is it.

'I should get some protection before we go any further.'

'Will it hurt more with or without it?'

He tilts his head, appearing almost apologetic. 'It will probably hurt more with.'

'Without. I want to do it without.'

He nods and plants a kiss on my forehead. 'I'll never hurt you.'

I tilt my head to the side to kiss his scratchy jaw and once again he pulls my body against his. I lick his skin to taste him and I'm surprised it tastes a bit like snow and salt.

'You taste like a storm.'

I clasp my hand on the back of his neck and pull him down a little so I can taste his earlobe, the way he did mine. As soon as my tongue touches his ear, his erection springs up, pressing against my thigh. His grip on my waist slackens and I wrap my arms around his neck so he doesn't pull away like he did in the shower yesterday.

'I'm not pulling away,' he murmurs in my ear.

I loosen my hold on him and tilt my head back to look in his eyes. Then he cradles my face in his hands and kisses me. This is a movie kiss. The angle of his head; the firm grip on my face; the slow, but assertive, stroke of his tongue; the way he sucks on my top lip every so often. Yes, I could definitely do this every day for the rest of my life.

Without noticing, his erection has found its way

between my legs. I can feel my moisture on him and it feels good. The accidental movements caused by our kissing result in a warm friction between my legs that builds with each second.

I run my hand down his washboard abs until my fingers find the place where his hair melts until sheer solidity. He pulls his head back to look at me, and there's a sly look in his eyes that makes me feel as if I did something very wrong or very right. Then he scoops me up in his arms.

I yelp as my feet leave the ground and he chuckles as he slowly sets me down on the bed. 'You could have asked me to lie down.'

'Not quite as fun that way.' He lies next to me on the bed, propping himself up on one elbow so he can look at me as he traces his finger lightly down the center of my chest all the way to my navel. 'Do you want me to keep the lights on?'

'Yes.'

'Good.'

He kisses me again, but this time his hand slowly moves from my waist up to my breast. I whimper as he gently rolls my nipple between his fingers.

'Does that feel good?' He looks me in the eye as he asks this question and something about this drives me crazy.

'Yes.'

He kisses his way down my neck and chest and I hold my breath, waiting for the moment his mouth is on me. I moan as he gently sucks and licks my flesh until I feel as if I might orgasm just from this simple, yet sensual, act.

He looks up at me as he moves down to my belly and I nod to let him know it's okay. He lifts my knee a little as he carefully positions himself between my legs. The soft kiss he plants on the inside of my thigh leaves a lingering burn, which tingles as he kisses his way up my thigh until his mouth is on me.

I draw in a deep breath and hold it, afraid of the sounds I'll make if I let myself breathe. His lips close around my sensitive flesh as his tongue stimulates my center. He alternates between light strokes and an out-of-this-world swirling pattern. My entire body is warm with pleasure, as if I've been dipped in a warm oil bath. But the sensation soon becomes irrelevant as all my muscles, especially those in my legs, begin spasming. He hooks his arms around my thighs to steady me as he gently sucks on my flesh as if I were a ripe fruit.

I cry out loudly, unable to contain myself. He keeps his mouth on me, comforting me, as the orgasm continues to roll through me. When my body finally stops twitching, he pulls his head back and looks up at me.

'A billion times better than pizza.' His smile is to die for, but I shake my head at his comment.

'Not a quadrillion?' I reply as his chest slides over mine and he settles himself between my legs.

'I have to leave us something to strive for.'

He places his hands on the pillow on either side of my head and leans down to kiss me. I can taste myself all over his mouth and I don't mind. I'm part of him now. And soon he'll be a part of me.

'Are you ready?' His eyes are locked on mine.

I nod as I open my legs a little wider. 'I'm ready.'

'Just keep your eyes open and locked on me so I know whether I'm hurting you.'

He lowers himself down onto his elbows so our noses are almost touching, then his hand reaches down between us to guide himself in. He only makes it in an inch or so before he meets heavy resistance.

'Are you okay?' I nod and he nods back. 'I'm going to go very slow, okay?'

I nod again, unable to speak. He kisses my forehead and I reach up to hold his face as he looks into my eyes. He moves slowly in and out of me, just a sliver of an inch farther with each stroke.

'I love you.'

He smiles and kisses my nose. 'I love you.'

'Kiss me.' He looks hesitant about not being able to see my face, to know if he's hurting me, but that's exactly what I want. 'Please.'

He leans in to kiss me and it doesn't take long for the whole world to fall away. I coil my arms tightly around his neck as I wrap my legs around his hips, coaxing him farther into me. I gasp into his mouth, but I hold onto him firmly so he can't pull away.

'Don't stop.' I whisper this plea into his mouth, then I kiss him hard.

The pain is bearable.

'Just breathe in,' he whispers, sliding a few inches into me, 'and breathe out.' He slides out and my muscles relax. I grip his arms, amazed at how solid they feel. 'Keep your eyes on mine. Don't look anywhere else. Just look at me.'

I take a deeper breath as he slides in a bit further and I groan.

He freezes. 'Are you okay?'

I nod and he leans forward to lay a soft kiss on my eyebrow. 'Please tell me if I hurt you.'

'I will.'

He brushes his lips across my brow and down my temple, then he kisses my cheekbone. Tilting his head back, he looks me in the eye again as he eases himself a little farther inside and I dig my nails into his shoulders.

'Is that okay?'

'Yes.' I slide my hands over his shoulders and up his neck until I have his face in my grasp. 'You could never hurt me.'

He groans, fighting to keep his eyes open as he gets closer to orgasm. His arms begin to tremble and I can see it's taking quite a bit of effort for him to continue to move so slowly. But he never breaks eye contact as his hips thrust into me, stretching me ever so gently. I find myself already thinking of the next time we get to have sex. This is the way it's supposed to feel; the closeness and the primal connection of skin on skin; pleasure for pleasure.

He grunts softly as he lets go inside of me and I smile, through my panting.

The pain is bearable.

Chapter Forty-two

January 8th
Crush

My first indication that something is very wrong is the smell. I can smell Mikki's hair, but it's mixed with something else. Fabric softener. I open my eyes and panic sets in when I see the guitars hanging on the wall on my right. The smell is coming from my freshly laundered sheets.

'Fuck,' I whisper this, but it's enough to wake Mikki.

'What's going on?' She lifts her head off my chest and squints at her surroundings. 'Oh my God! What time is it?'

'We have to get up now or we're going to miss the flight.' I glance at the clock on my nightstand. 'It's seven twenty-six. We have an hour and forty-five minutes to get to the hotel and pack our suitcases and head to the airport. Then we'll have to hope that we make it through security in time for the nine-fifteen flight.'

'Then we'd better hurry up. You can't miss that flight!' She throws the covers off, but I grab her hand before she can hop out of bed.

'Hey. How are you feeling?'

She stares at me for a moment and I hope she's not trying to think of a lie. 'A little sore.'

'I'm sorry.'

'Don't apologize.' Her eyes begin to tear up and she takes a breath to compose herself. 'I'm not sure I'll ever be able to describe what you did for me last night. Please don't ever think you have to be sorry for that. The pain is just a subtle reminder of how alive you made me feel.'

My chest swells with warmth. 'God, I fuckin' love you.'

By the time we're dressed and we've made it down to the curb, my heart is hammering against my chest. Kane has agreed to move my appointment from three o'clock to five o'clock today. But I won't make it if I don't catch this flight. Mikki and I should have brought our luggage to my apartment, but I was certain we'd go back to the hotel room. I didn't think we were going to get completely lost in each other last night.

She's still trying to pull on her gloves as we wait for the car. I reach over to help her. It's freezing out here; negative fifty-two, factoring in wind-chill.

'I hope they don't cancel the flight again.' She says this through chattering teeth.

I pull the strings on her hood a bit tighter and plant

a soft kiss on her lips. 'If they cancel our flight, then we'll charter a plane.'

Her eyes light up at this suggestion. 'And we won't have to sit in separate cabins.'

'When we get on the flight, we can trade seats.'

She shakes her head adamantly. 'Nope. I'd like to enjoy my final flight in coach, cause I know we're flying first class from here on out, right?'

'We'll buy a plane if that will make you happy.'

'You know how to fly a plane?'

'No, but I can learn. And I didn't mean that kind of plane. I meant a jet. Someone else would fly the plane while we enjoy the flight.' She rolls her eyes and I kiss her temple as the black town car rounds the corner. 'Watch your step.'

I open the door for her to get in, then I round the back of the car to the other side. Slamming the door shut, I reach across and grab Mikki's gloved hand.

'Forget the seatbelt. Come here.'

She looks relieved that I've invited her to cuddle with me. It's too cold, even with the heater on in this car, to sit two feet away from the one you love. I reach into my pocket and pull out my crushed penny guitar pick. Rubbing it between my fingers, I think of how proud Grandpa Hugh would be if he could see me making my own way instead of depending on my father.

Mikki reaches up and grabs the penny from my fingers. 'The copper's all green from your sweaty fingers. I'm going to get you some new guitar picks –

custom-engraved with "Crush picked me". Then you can throw them out into the crowd at concerts and all the girls will swoon.'

'This is my lucky pick.' I take the pick back from her and tuck it into my pocket. 'And I don't care about driving the girls wild.'

'But that's what makes you successful,' she insists. 'You don't have to sleep with them to make them think you want to. You have to appear totally into your music while you're performing, but flash a little smile here and there. It tells them you're enjoying their presence.'

'Since when do you know so much about performing for a crowd?'

'I don't. I just watch a lot of live performances on YouTube.'

I tilt her head up and I can see a bit of sadness and embarrassment at this admission. 'You've never been to a concert?' She shakes her head. 'I'm taking you to a concert in L.A.'

She smiles. 'You're going to be pretty busy making up for all the things I haven't done.'

'Spring semester doesn't start for more than two weeks. We've got time.'

Her smile disappears and she pulls back a little. 'What's going to happen when we're both back in school?'

'I don't know. I can make it down to Brockton to see you at least a couple of times a week. And definitely every weekend, except some Sundays when I'm performing.'

'Where do you perform? Wally's?'

'I go to Wally's a lot, but I don't perform there all the time. I'll probably take you there pretty often so you can get comfortable with those guys. Is that okay?'

'Yes, but where do you perform?'

'I'm in the Sunday Band. It's one of two jazz bands at Harvard. We do local jazz festivals and university events. Sometimes we only perform once a month and sometimes it's every weekend for a few weeks in a row. Just depends on what's going on.'

'Sunday? That means you have Saturdays free. So . . .' Her eyes are focused on her lap as she takes a beat. 'Will I be able to spend the night at your apartment on Fridays?'

'You can spend the night at my apartment every night.'

She looks up at me, a tiny smile forming on her gorgeous lips, but she doesn't say anything. She just needed to hear me say the words aloud, whether or not she'll actually take me up on the offer. Sometimes, you just have to reassure the ones you love in precise language that you'll always be there. Sometimes words are enough.

We manage to pack our suitcases in less than ten minutes and the bellman drags them across the path they've cleared in front of the hotel so we're back in the car by 8:06 a.m. The driver stuffs everything into the trunk and we head for the airport. The first thought that hits me as the car drives away from the hotel is how much has changed since Mikki and I got into a cab outside Terminal B on Monday morning.

She drops her purse onto the floor then lies back with her head in my lap. 'I can see inside your nostrils from here.'

'See anything that interests you?'

'Ew.' She tries to act disgusted, but she's still smiling. 'I'm hungry, but we don't have time to stop for anything. I guess I'll have to eat airplane food.'

'Looking inside my nostrils made you hungry?'

She smacks my chest. 'I'm serious.'

'I'll ask the flight attendant to donate my food to the little people in coach.'

'Ooh, so generous. You're like Brad Pitt. You're hot and you love poor people.'

'If we get to the gate in time, I'll grab you something to eat on the concourse.' I trace my fingertip over her bottom lip and she puckers up. 'I can't let you go hungry.'

She grabs my hand and lays it on the side of her face, then she closes her eyes for the last five minutes of the ride to the airport. I wish I knew what she's thinking. What I do know is that she loves me. The girl who was planning to kill herself five days ago. The girl who saved my life. The girl I killed for. The girl I'd give my life for. She loves me and all the blackness inside me.

Chapter Forty-three

January 8th
Mikki

The driver unloads our luggage while Crush gets a Smarte Carte so we can zip through the terminal. We already checked in for our flight online. All we have to do is get our bags checked and head straight to security. But as soon as we enter the terminal and see the line of people waiting at the check-in counter, we realize it's not going to be so simple.

'Holy shit. It looks worse than when we were here Monday.'

Crush pushes our luggage cart to the back of the line as I crane my neck to view the length at the first-class check-in counter.

'There are only a few people at the first-class counter. You can check your bag and go ahead of me. You're the one who needs to make the flight, not me.'

Just saying this aloud makes me want to cry for two

reasons. First, because I don't want to think about how much it will hurt to know the flight, and Crush, took off without me. And second, because I'm not the same person I was five days ago when I was desperate to make that flight.

'I'm not leaving without you, so just get that thought out of your head. But I'm going to go stand in the first-class line and see if they'll allow me to check your bags at the same time. I'll be right back.'

It's painful watching him walk away, even with the knowledge that he will be back soon. I don't know if it's dangerous to need someone this much. Did I just swap one drug for another? I don't think I even want to know the answer to that question. I don't want it to taint my mind with doubts. If love is a drug, then it's the kind that should be prescribed.

I drag my suitcase a few inches forward every minute or so until Crush rushes toward me with a smile on his face. 'Come on. They're gonna check your bag.'

Once my suitcase is checked, we race to the security line, which is about a hundred feet away. A stern TSA officer checks our boarding passes to make sure we're at the right checkpoint, then he waves me toward the long line of harried travelers.

'You're pre-check. You can go to the front of the line,' the officer says to Crush and he instantly turns to me, a guilty look washing over his face.

I turn away from him to look at the line of approximately fifty people waiting to be screened. This line splits off into four lines of passengers dumping their belongings onto conveyor belts.

'Go ahead,' I say, pushing him ahead of me.

'Other side,' the officer says to Crush, pointing at the other side of the line with absolutely no people on the other side of the cordon.

I push him toward the other line. 'Maybe you can make them stop the plane for me. Go!'

He kisses my forehead then ducks under the cordon. 'If they can't wait for you, I'm not leaving. See you soon.'

I sigh as I watch him leave, ignoring the angry looks from the six or seven passengers queuing behind me. Then I trudge toward the back of the line and wait. It takes about twenty minutes to get to the front of the line. The whole time I'm placing my purse, shoes, and coat on the conveyor, I keep hoping that the ring in my lip won't earn me a pat-down.

When I make it through the body scanner, the woman holds up her blue-gloved hand for me to wait. My heart pounds, looking on anxiously as she stares at the screen to my left.

She glances at my lips then waves me past. 'Go ahead.'

I quickly gather my belongings off the conveyor and dump them onto a small table where I can shakily put on my boots without the annoyed looks of the other travelers. I drape my coat over my arm, sling my purse across my body, and take one last glance at the gate number on my boarding pass before I race to gate thirty-four.

The smell of food instantly makes me hungrier as I pass a seafood restaurant at the end of the corridor. Then I turn left and find another short corridor with a gift shop and frozen yogurt shop. Racing past them, I follow the sign to take another left toward gate thirty-four and I nearly bump right into Crush as I take the turn.

'What happened? Did you miss the flight?'

'It's been pushed back an hour.' I throw my arms around his neck and he laughs. 'Don't get too excited. This weather is shit and they're hoping there won't be any more delays, but they're not sure.'

I let go of his neck and shrug. 'I'm not happy because of the flight. I'm happy because now I have time to eat.'

Crush gets us both a breakfast sandwich and an orange juice at the Dunkin Donuts kiosk. We sit in gate thirty-four eating our breakfast while I try desperately not to appear too nervous. But it doesn't take long for Crush to notice something is wrong.

'I can't believe I never asked you this before. Is this your first time flying.'

I shake my head. 'No. I went to Mexico on a family vacation when I was thirteen.'

'Are you afraid of flying?' He places his hand on my knee to stop my leg from bouncing up and down nervously.

'A little. I read a lot and I was reading about the probability of getting in a plane crash.' He shakes his head in dismay. 'I know it's almost impossible. What I'm trying to say is that I ended up stumbling upon all these investigation reports on various plane crashes and I found a few where the cause of the crash was never determined.'

'What are you trying to say?'

He glances at the person seated on my other side, probably to see if she can hear what we're talking about. It's probably an unspoken rule that it's bad luck to talk about plane crashes while sitting in an airport. I'm not a superstitious person, so if she doesn't like it, she can move.

'I'm trying to say that the odds of being in a plane crash are low, but . . . apparently, there is no way to know if you'll be in a plane crash. Even if conditions are perfect. Great weather. New airplane. Plenty of fuel. Experienced flight staff. There are just some plane crashes that can't be avoided or explained.'

Shit. I probably sound like a crazy person right now. I wrap the paper around my half-eaten breakfast sandwich, my fingers shaking profusely. Crush takes the sandwich from my hands and gets up to throw it away for me. When he sits back down, he grabs my hand and brings it to his lips.

'At least if we go down, we go down together.'

Moments later, they begin calling people by groups to board the plane. Crush is in group one, but he insists on waiting to board with me and the rest of the cattle in group four. When they call my group, I'm surprised to find that I'm not really anxious any more. I pull out my boarding pass and hand it to the lady at the counter. She scans it and hands it back and I wait for Crush to get his pass scanned before we head through the jet bridge.

The bridge is enclosed, but the air inside the bridge is cold enough for my breath to steam and my nose to start aching as we wait in line for people to board ahead of us. I rub my hands together, almost contemplating pulling the gloves out of my purse, but we're only about four bodies away from entering the plane. Once we're inside, Crush asks the flight attendant if he can give me his first-class seat and I smack his arm.

'I don't want it.' I turn to the woman who looks confused. 'He's just trying to be nice.'

She smiles at me. 'If any seats open up near you, you two are welcome to move around so you can sit next to each other. Just make sure you do it quickly.'

I set off toward my seat: 25B. I'm relieved to find I'm next to the window and there's no one seated in the aisle. I take the aisle-seat and grab my phone out of my purse before I sit down. I'm about to text Crush when I see he's already texted me.

Crush: Seat next to the guy behind me was canceled this morning. I just switched rows. Come on up to first class, baby.

Oh, how I love that man. I wait until everyone is seated, then I grab my purse and head quickly toward the first-class cabin. When I get there, the blonde flight attendant smiles at me as I take the aisle-seat next to Crush.

'What did you do, hand her a thousand-dollar bill or something?' I whisper to him as I fasten my seatbelt.

'She couldn't resist my smile.'

I don't bother asking for the real story. I pull my phone out of my purse and text Meaghan.

> **Me:** Taking off soon to L.A. I'll call you when we get there. Love you.
>
> **Meaghan:** I've been rereading AGAIN. Is it possible for a book to get better on the hundredth read? Tell your boyfriend I said thanks. Ttyl. Love ya.

I tuck the phone in my pocket and the pilot soon comes over the speaker to make an announcement.

'Ladies and gentlemen, thank you for your patience. We apologize for the slight delay this morning. It's going to be another fifteen minutes or so as the maintenance crew does one last check on the oil levels, then we will be set to go. Thank you for flying with us.'

Crush laces his fingers through mine and I turn to him. 'If this plane crashes, thank you for saving me and for killing someone for me.'

He laughs nervously as a male flight attendant walks by at this very moment. 'You're welcome.'

The flight attendant turns on a safety video and I give it my full attention. *This aircraft is equipped with two safety slides, which can also be used as life rafts . . . Pull the strap to tighten the belt and pull down on the tab to inflate the vest . . . Put on your mask before helping others.*

The pilot's voice comes on again after the video and I squeeze Crush's hand. 'Flight attendants, cross-check and prepare for takeoff.'

Chapter Forty-four

January 8th
Mikki

The plane bumps along as it taxis to the runway and it's almost lulling me to sleep. I close my eyes and lean my head back on the headrest. Crush squeezes my hand gently and I squeeze back, but I keep my eyes shut. He squeezes my hand again and my eyelids flash open.

'What?'

'Thank you for saving me, too.'

A rush of euphoria sweeps through me as I realize this is what it's like to be normal. Going outside and doing stuff like catching a flight with your boyfriend to L.A. so he can record a demo for a hot record producer. Is that normal? Now that I think of it, it does not sound normal. And I can't even ask myself if it feels normal because I'm not sure I know what normal feels like. Well, if this *isn't* normal, then I don't want to know what *is*.

Suddenly, I'm pushed back into my seat by a powerful unseen force as the plane speeds down the runway. I close my eyes, thinking it has to end soon. Please let it end soon. And it does. I get a strange whooping sensation in my belly and I open my eyes to see the airport and the rest of Boston falling away like a jagged, gray dream.

After a couple of minutes of steady climb in altitude, the plane begins to bank to the right and I quickly look away from the window, as the movement is making me want to vomit.

'Are you okay?'

Before I can answer Crush's question, two loud banging noises, almost like gunshots, come from somewhere near the left wing. The aircraft dips sharply and the collective gasp of more than one hundred passengers is almost as unsettling.

'What was that?' I shriek as the plane begins to climb altitude again.

'It's fine.' Crush's thumb rubs the top of my hand as he attempts to reassure me. 'Takeoff is always a little rough.'

'Just a little turbulence, folks.' The flight attendant sounds bored as she makes her announcement. 'Nothing to be alarmed about, but please do remain seated with your seatbelts fastened until the pilot has turned off the seatbelt sign.'

How can anyone endure this level of anxiety on a daily basis?

The plane begins to bank to the right again, steeper this time. I turn to Crush to see his reaction, but he's staring out the window with a worried look on his face.

I squeeze his hand to get his attention. 'What's going on?'

'I don't know. It looks like we're heading back to the airport.'

But the steepness of the turn is interrupted by another loud bang, then stillness. I'm no expert in airline safety or aerodynamics, but it sounds as if the engine has stalled. Then the lights go out.

The eerie gray light of the storm clouds that pierces through the oval windows is not enough. Panic sets in throughout the cabin and this time the pilot attempts to ease our anxiety.

'We're experiencing some electrical trouble, which has caused an engine stall. We're pulling back for an emergency landing. Please remain seated with your seatbelts fastened.'

Just when I'm beginning to think everything is fine, they're getting us off this rickshaw, I begin to feel light-headed. Then the engine that seemed to stall earlier is suddenly screaming back to life as the pilot attempts to get the plane horizontal.

Crush turns to me and says something I can barely hear. 'I didn't hear the landing gear deploy. Did you?'

I don't even know what it's supposed to sound like when the landing gear is deployed. Or maybe I'm just feeling too sick to think right now. The deafening whine of the engine combined with the turbulence is making my insides crawl. Then my ears pop and everything sounds even louder.

The lights flicker again and the cabin temperature begins to plummet as a majority of the overhead bins open, their contents tumbling into the aisle. Something is wrong, but, suddenly, everything feels right. We're going to die and I'm . . . euphoric.

The moment you realize you're going to die is nothing like I imagined it would be. I imagined a deep internal struggle coupled with a visceral, physical response – fight or flight. But there's no fighting this. I'm going to die.

It's possible that everyone on this plane is going to die. I wonder if they feel this overwhelming sense of peace, or if the squeal of the plane engine has drowned out all their thoughts.

He grabs the oxygen mask as it drops from the compartment and he's yelling something as he puts the elastic band over my head. He pulls his own mask over his head then he grabs my hand and looks me in the eye. There's no panic in his eyes. Maybe he feels this same calm I'm feeling. Or maybe he just wants me to know that he loves me.

He loves me.

Or maybe the look in his eyes is his way of telling me he trusts that whatever happens to us in the next few seconds is just one of those things that was meant to be.

Fate.

I used to think fate was for religious nuts and people who were too afraid to take their fate into their own hands. Now I know the truth.

Fate is death. No one escapes it. But if you stick around long enough, you might find someone to help you cheat fate for a while. And when you can't cheat any more, and fate finally catches up to you, maybe it won't seem so scary with that someone by your side.

The voice that comes over the speaker is largely drowned out by the noise in the plane, but I recognize it as the pilot. 'Ladies and gentleman, this is your captain . . . your oxygen masks tightly secured. The landing gear . . . Repeat: . . . without full deployment of the landing gear. We will attempt to circle . . . dump fuel then . . . come in on our belly. Emergency crews are standing by.'

A flash of white light engulfs the forward cabin as something explodes in the center of the floor, right next to the bulkhead. A large silver cylinder shoots up, hits the ceiling of the plane and drops back down through the new hole in the floor. The bulkhead wall on the other side of the aisle has splintered and is coming down on top of the two passengers in the first row.

All I hear is screaming. All I feel is freezing-cold air rushing into the cabin through the gaping hole in the floor. And Crush's hand. I feel Crush's hand gripping mine. And it's as if all my senses return to me at once. I don't want to die on this plane.

Then, the impact.

The force of the belly landing jolts me upward and my mask slides off as my head hits the bottom of the compartment above me. I hear a brief flash of screeching metal on asphalt as the plane skids down the runway on its belly before I lose consciousness.

My brain claws its way back to reality and I can hear the screaming wail of sirens approaching – and the panic. Passengers are fighting to get off the plane as quickly as possible. The stench of burned metal and some sort of chemical is toxic in the air.

The male flight attendant is looking down at me. 'Ma'am? Can you hear me?'

I can taste blood in my mouth.

'Your head is bleeding.' I don't know who said this.

Instinctively, I look to my left and I can't breathe. My vision blurs . . . there's blood trickling from Crush's head onto the curved ledge of the window. His head. His beautiful head that holds all the most gorgeous words I've ever heard.

I scream words that even I can't understand as I attempt to tear off my seatbelt, but this simple movement makes the entire plane sway beneath me. I clutch desperately to the armrests to stop the motion, but I can feel my consciousness slipping away, pulsing at the edges of my vision, until the blackness closes in on me.

Voices . . . There are so many voices . . . There's blood all over my right hand . . . *'Wake up!'* . . . *'Ma'am, stop shaking him!'* . . . *'Crush! Look at me!'*

The hands are everywhere . . . grabbing me, pinching my arms, holding my waist, yanking me away . . . I'm floating across the seat and into the aisle, vision pulsing with the beat of my heart . . . bodies press against me, pushing me toward the back of the plane . . . I can't see through the blood and tears.

All I know is that Crush is gone and the darkness is edging toward me again. This is what it must feel like to die.

Chapter Forty-five

January 8th
Mikki

The bumpy movement startles me awake and I'm certain I'm going to open my eyes and find I'm still on that plane and we haven't taken off yet. But I'm not. I'm in the back of some sort of emergency vehicle. I try to turn my head to get a better look at the medic on my left, but my head and chin are strapped to two cushioned blocks positioned on either side of my head.

'What's going on?' My hands struggle against the restraints that cross my chest and abdomen. 'I'm not the one who's hurt.'

The medic leans forward into my field of vision so I can see his face. He has kind eyes that seem to be filled with genuine concern, but his words don't match his eyes.

'Ma'am, a couple of the passengers said you hit your

head upon landing and that may be why you were upset. We're trying to minimize any possible injury to your head and neck. The restraints will be removed as soon as we've verified there is no cervical or cerebral damage.'

'Cerebral damage? You mean, brain damage?'

'Ma'am, please calm down.'

'*Calm down!* I was just in a fucking plane crash!'

The kindness in his eyes disappears and he sits up straight so I can't see his face. I can feel him moving on my left, but I can't see what he's doing.

He leans forward again and this time I can see the corner of a clipboard in his lap. 'Ma'am, I need you to answer a few questions. Can you please state your full name?'

Crush's bloody head flashes in my mind and the tears rush forth, a guttural sob building inside my belly, mangling my insides, until it stops at my throat, choking me.

'Are you in pain?' he asks.

I can't breathe, I want to say, but the words are stuck somewhere between my lips and my broken heart.

The medic lets me grieve in peace for the rest of the ride to the hospital. But as soon as he wheels me through the sliding doors of the emergency room at Mass General, it becomes clear that the hospital staff is not going to let me off so easy. A nurse with ash-blonde curls wheels me into a trauma bay then hovers over me firing off questions. I just keep hoping that the faster I answer, the faster I'll get to see Crush.

'On a scale of one to ten, one being no pain and ten being the worst pain you could imagine, how severe is the pain in your head?'

'One.' She shoots me a skeptical look. 'Two? I swear I'm not in severe pain. I'm fine. Just please get me out of these restraints. *Please.* I need to find my boyfriend. He was hurt on the plane. *Please* let me go.'

The tears slide down my temples and she purses her lips. 'Oh, goodness. Just do me a favor and touch each one of your fingertips to the tip of your thumb, like this.'

I quickly do as she says and she sighs, looking over her shoulder as she begins unbuckling my restraints. She removes the straps over my forehead and chin first and I sit up too suddenly. The room undulates beneath me and I clutch the sides of the gurney to keep from tipping over. Luckily, the nurse is too busy undoing the straps on my neck brace to notice my swaying.

She pulls the brace off my neck and as soon as the cool air hits my neck I can breathe again. 'Thank you.'

She nods. 'Just wait here and I'll find out where he is. What's his name?'

'Crush.'

'Crush?'

I grit my teeth, trying to temper my impatience. 'I don't know. Probably Slayer.'

'Crush Slayer?' She raises her eyebrows. 'Okay.'

Judging by the look she just gave me, she probably thinks she's looking for someone with more piercings and tattoos than me. I need my phone. I had that fucking phone turned off for days and now that it's fully charged, it's probably lying on the floor of that plane. That stupid plane!

I slide off the gurney, keeping one hand on the foam mattress to keep from collapsing in case I have a concussion. My feet hit the floor and I peek around the curtain separating this bay from the one next to me. I don't see the nurse anywhere. She's probably in one of the nurses' stations wishing she hadn't agreed to help me.

My head does hurt, but it's more like a four or five on a scale of one to ten. It's not an unbearable pain. Of course, I'm not sure there's any such thing as unbearable pain. It all depends on the individual and what each of us is equipped to endure. Apparently, I can endure a lot, but I can't endure not knowing what happened to Crush.

I reach up to touch the top of my head and right near the hairline I feel a nasty bump approximately half the size of an egg. My hair is sticky with half-dried blood. What the hell just happened?

I wait a few moments as more patients are brought into the emergency room. One man is moaning as they wheel him past me, and I note the exasperated expression on the nurse's face as she pushes his gurney. Then another woman goes by with no head restraints, but her eyes are closed and her arm is bandaged. Every patient that comes in, every opening and closing of the emergency-room doors, just adds to my anxiety, until I can't take it any more.

Fuck this. I'll find Crush myself.

Chapter Forty-six

January 8th
Mikki

My attempt to sneak past the nurses' station does not go well. Nurse Goldilocks spots me instantly from where she's hunched over a computer screen.

'Nuh-uh,' she says, pointing her finger at me and shaking her head as she approaches me. 'You are not well enough to go gallivanting about this hospital without assistance. You go wait in there and I'll come back with a wheelchair as soon as I find your boyfriend.'

'What's taking so long? How are you going to feel if he dies while you're staring at that fucking computer screen?'

She raises her eyebrows. 'Young lady, you are testing my patience. And that is *not* the way you speak to someone who's trying to help you. Now go lie down and I'll be back when I know more.'

Lie down? Yeah, right.

My stomach is in knots as I turn around to head back to the gurney. Then I feel it. My phone vibrates in my pocket and I frantically dig into my jeans.

Please let it be him. Please let it be him.

It's my mom.

I almost hit reject, but then I wonder if maybe she knows something I don't know. 'Mom?'

'Honey, are you all right?'

'I'm fine. Have you heard anything? Do you know what happened to Crush?'

'Crush? What are you talking about?'

'I have to go.'

I hang up the phone and open up the browser to search the internet for articles about the crash. There has to be something posted already. More than an hour has passed since we landed. I type in the search box *logan airport crash january 8*, then I hit *go.* Two articles come up at the top of the results; one posted two minutes ago. I click on that one and scan the article for words like fatalities, injured, victim, and dead. I learn that twenty-two passengers were transported to Mass General with minor to serious injuries.

Serious injuries? What the fuck does that mean?

I dial Crush's number, but it doesn't even ring. It goes straight to voicemail, but the sound of his voice on the greeting makes me physically sick. I need to see him. I need to know he's all right.

Another two patients are wheeled in and I watched

eagerly to see if either of them is Crush. The first one is pushed back here to a trauma bay across from me. It's an obese woman who appears to be having a panic attack or chest pains. The medic is standing next to the nurses' station, blocking my view of the patient in the gurney next to him. I wait anxiously as two nurses and a woman in a white coat approach the gurney. This patient is different. This must be one of the serious ones.

The doctor and the medic finally take a step back, and that's when I see Crush's jeans and the sleeve of his green hoodie. I race across the emergency room, all sound blocked out by the roaring beat of my heart pounding inside my head. My eyeballs hurt. This is the first thought that comes to mind before the room begins to spin around me. I'm six feet away from him when the vomit streams out of my mouth, burning my throat. Remnants of the breakfast sandwich and coffee Crush bought me splash onto the tile floor.

'Crush,' I choke out, gripping the wall as I attempt to swallow the bits of undigested food in my mouth, but my gag reflex won't allow it.

A nurse arrives with a waste bin just in time to catch the next stream of vomit. I'm sweating and my vision is clouded with dazzling sparks of lights. I spit a few more times before another nurse arrives with a paper cup of water and attempts to direct me toward a sink on the other side of the room to rinse my mouth. But

I take the cup and rinse my mouth out into the waste bin instead, then I squeeze through them to get to Crush.

He's gone.

'Where is he?' I round on the nurses who were helping me. 'He was just right there. Where did they take him?'

'Mikki?' Crush's voice is like a beacon guiding me to shore. 'Mikki, where are you?'

I turn around toward the trauma bays and the nurse points at the middle bay across the aisle. Behind the curtain, I barely glimpse the bottoms of his sneakers. Then they're gone.

I hear struggling and I race toward the sound. It's him. He's struggling against the restraints around his head. With a soft snap and ripping noise, he tears the straps off his bloodstained face and jumps off the bed.

'Fuck! I thought you were dead,' he whispers, taking me into his arms. 'Are you okay?'

'I am now.'

He gazes into my eyes and a tear slides down his chiseled cheek. 'I thought I had lost you. I don't ever want to feel like that again.'

I wipe the moisture from his face, leaving a smear of blood and tears behind. 'I need you to do something for me.'

'I'll do anything for you. What do you need?'

‘I need you to teach me how to breathe when you’re gone.’

I close my eyes as he lays a soft kiss on each of my eyelids, then he wraps his arms around me again and lifts me a few inches off the ground. ‘That’s a lesson I hope you never have to learn.’

Chapter Forty-seven

January 8th
Crush

I was nine years old the first time I saw my dad shoot a deer. I remember being sick with anticipation as we lay on the embankment behind the scrub. The blast of his Ruger barely kicked him back and he burst to his feet. I followed quickly after him and I'll never forget the steam coming out of that buck's mouth or the desperate plea in its glossy eyes. It was the same thing I saw when Jordan died.

I was thirteen the first time Jordan told me he wanted to kill himself. He asked me if I could get him one of my dad's guns out of the safe and I refused. I told my Aunt Deb and Jordan was put on anti-depressants. He became a different person after that. Sometimes he'd want to do crazy shit like ditch class and go to Harvard to hit on chicks three years older than us. Other times, he'd talk to me for hours about wanting to die.

The night he died, he was drunk and high and threatening to pull a gun on a police office to commit suicide-by-cop. I got drunk with him, trying to convince him to let it go, but he wouldn't. Finally, I told him I would give him a loaded shotgun and take him out to the woods behind the house so he could get it over with. I thought I was so fucking clever, loading the wrong size shell into that Ruger .270. I thought the gun would jam and he'd get frustrated and change his mind. I never thought my plan would literally backfire on me.

I wonder now, if I had run into Mikki in that parking lot one year earlier and witnessed the power of fate then, would I have loaded that shotgun for Jordan? Or would I have told him to hold on just a little longer? Of course, if he had never died, I would have never been in that parking lot. And Mikki would be dead.

Fate can save you and it can kill you. Either way, fate binds us through an invisible web of circumstances. Change one undesirable fate and another desirable fate is canceled out.

Do you think saving someone's life cancels out taking another person's life?

In terms of fate and circumstance, yes. In terms of retribution and contrition, no.

The moment doctor's viewed the results of my CAT Scan, they discharged Mikki and me with instructions for how to care for a concussion. The nurses were pretty enamored with us at this point and one of the older nurses sent us off with a picture they printed on a sheet of printer paper. She had taken the picture of Mikki and me hugging with her phone. It's a picture of the moment we found each other in the emergency room.

'Look at your face. You look like Carrie,' Mikki teases me as we wait for our driver to arrive.

We told Mikki's parents not to bother coming down to the hospital, since our injuries were minor. We promised them I'd take her home myself. They don't know that I'm just taking her home so we can tell them that she'll be spending the next two weeks with me.

'Hey, you're just as bloody as I am in that picture. Unless you're just trying to tell me I look like a telekinetic teenage girl.'

'That's exactly what I meant.'

'I'll take that as a compliment.'

'Have you seen today's boy bands? Trust me, teenage girls love guys that look like teenage girls.'

I laugh as I think of how lucky I was to get in a plane crash today. It would have been a great excuse to give if I had called to reschedule the meeting with Kane. But I didn't. The more time I spend with Mikki, the more I realize how happy I am right now. I don't need a record deal and I certainly don't need the money. And Mikki doesn't need the constant traveling or the lack of privacy. All I need is right here in Boston.

She glances through the emergency-room doors

at the curb, then turns to me. 'You should call your parents.'

I shake my head. 'My relationship with my parents is not the same as yours. Your parents have fucked up, but they had good intentions. My parents' intentions are for me to not fuck up their reputation any more. I don't need their pity for being in a plane crash that resulted in a grand total of eight stitches.'

'Are you sure you're not just afraid to introduce me to them?'

'What? Don't even fucking think that. If I'm afraid of anything it's of you getting scared off by their smugness.'

She shrugs as she folds the paper picture and tucks it into her back pocket. 'Maybe you don't need their pity and you don't need them to accept me. But maybe they deserve to know that you survived.'

'They know. I called my sister and I texted my mom while you were getting your cranial X-ray.'

'Well, I guess you took care of that.'

The car pulls up and I grab her arm to stop her before she exits through the sliding doors. 'Being a part of my family means being a part of the phoniness and the deceit. The way they pretend like everything is okay. Like me going to Harvard means that I'm over what happened with Jordan. That my mother's alcoholism isn't a problem or the way she pretends not to know that my father is a cheating bastard. My parents live in their own land of denial and I refuse to live there with them.' I sigh, wishing I didn't have to talk about this now. 'If you want to know that part of me, I'll maintain a relationship with them for you. But, honestly, I hope you'll tell me that I'm enough.'

She smiles. 'You're more than enough. You're my circuit breaker.'

I shake my head as I lace my fingers through hers and pull her outside, back into the snow, where it all began. 'A circuit breaker cuts the power when the circuit is being overloaded.'

'Then I rest my case.' She taps her skull as I open the car door for her. 'I think you've prevented these circuits from overloading on multiple occasions. You're like a superhero for crazy people.'

I pretend to brush something off my shoulder. 'All in a day's work.'

Chapter Forty-eight

January 8th
Mikki

When I call my parents on the way home to tell them that I'll be having a two-week slumber party with Crush at his apartment before Spring semester begins, they flip out for about ten seconds. Before I remind them that Crush is the only reason I'm still talking to them. The moment I enter my home, I'm drawn in by the lingering aroma of pancakes and coffee: Saturday-morning breakfast. I'll have to learn how to make my mom's special pancakes so I can make them for Crush.

Meaghan insists on getting a rundown on exactly what happened on the plane and I try to be as succinct as possible. The adoring looks my mom is directing at Crush and me are making me nervous. She watches Crush and me going back and forth, telling the story, and once we get to the part where we were reunited in the emergency room, her eyes tear up. I smile at her as I try to hold back my tears.

Eventually, I lead Crush upstairs so he can wait while I pack another suitcase with clothes and toiletries for a few days. The airline is allowing us to pick up our carry-ons tomorrow, but they're holding all the checked baggage for a few more days, *for further testing*. I took that to mean they're looking for a way to blame the crash on someone else. Doesn't matter. As long as I get my purse back, I don't care if I ever get the stuff in my suitcase or my carry-on.

I open my bedroom door and let Crush enter ahead of me. He walks to the foot of my bed then looks around at the black comforter, the hot-pink wall behind my headboard, and the opposite wall that's plastered with dozens of papers where I've doodled my favorite quotes from books I've read. In the center of the wall is a purple letter-sized piece of thin tissue paper with the *Black Box* quote he tweeted me four years ago.

'It's the first thing I see when I wake up and the last thing I see before I close my eyes every night.'

His gaze roams over every inch of the wall. Occasionally, his fingers reach up to trace the lines of the curvy letters inked in a simple black ballpoint pen. He comes to a Dante quote on the far right side of the wall near the corner and he stands there for a moment, mesmerized.

He turns around and walks toward me as he recites

the quote. *'Do not be afraid; our fate cannot be taken from us; it is a gift.'*

I smile as I wrap my arms around him. 'I'm glad I met you.'

I hold onto Crush tightly and think to myself, *I agree with Elvis; some things* are *meant to be.* And I do believe in fate, but I don't believe Crush and I are meant to be together until we grow old and gray. I believe we were supposed to die the night we met on Twitter, and in that parking lot a year later, and again on that plane today, but we cheated death three times. I don't know how much longer we can continue to escape our fate, and that scares me.

Fear is crippling. Fear of the future can convince us that there is no way out and nothing is ever going to get better. Fear is blinding; it can make us miss the warning signs flashing right in front of our eyes. It can also make you miss those brilliant flashes of color, when the world isn't so gray. But, if you think about it, being afraid isn't such a bad thing. Because fear is a reminder that you still have something to lose. Something worth holding onto.

Chapter Forty-nine

March 17th – Four years ago
Mikki

Dear Mom and Dad,

I'm sorry that it's come to this. I never wanted to hurt you guys, and especially not Meaghan, but I think you'll all be better off this way. If you don't believe me, keep reading.

I've been thinking a lot about luck and how some people seem to have it and others don't. I think there's a quote from Abraham Lincoln or Benjamin Franklin about how hard work makes us luckier. Well, I've been working hard just trying to stay above water this year and I still have lousy luck.

<u>*Things you don't know about me:*</u>

I have a tattoo you've never seen.

I've been cutting myself since I was nine.

I'm failing four out of six classes right now.

I didn't go to school at all last week.

Mom, you asked me why I started taking lunch to school

three months ago. I try to remember to take lunch every day, but I forgot again this morning. I wouldn't have gone into the cafeteria if it weren't for the fact that I also forgot to eat breakfast this morning. (I forget a lot of stuff lately. I think I'm going crazy. Nope, I know I'm going crazy.) Well, who do you think I saw in the cafeteria? Brad and Nellie were just a few bodies behind me in line. Nellie was talking about me, loud enough so I could hear. Calling me names again. Brad called me a loser and said I should kill myself. I think telling someone to kill themselves has become the new ultimate insult because it really seems to work. It gets you thinking. And you know what I've been thinking for the last four hours?

I feel like I'm living someone else's life. This isn't the life I signed up for. Is this what you imagined for me when you found out you were pregnant with me, Mom? A weak daughter who offers to help a cute guy study and ends up with a bad reputation? A daughter who can't stand up for herself? Or did you imagine a happy kid who's popular and gets straight As? Because that's never going to be me.

I'm not like everyone else. I don't care what Kim Kardashian is wearing and I hate putting on makeup. I just want to lie in bed and forget that I exist.

Dad, you're always telling me to cheer up, but it's not that easy! Don't you think I want to be happy? You tell me to stop wearing black because it sends the wrong message. But I like the color black. Does that mean there's something wrong with me?

I'm not invisible. I'm here and I'm suffering. And I don't know how to stop it.

I don't know if I'm doing the right thing. Part of me is wishing, hoping that someone or something will give me a sign that this isn't it. This is not the way I'm going to feel for the rest of my life.

I love you guys.

Mikki

I set down my pen and swipe my hands over my cheeks to wipe away the tears. My stomach is clenched so tightly, I'd probably break in half if someone walked in on me right now. I glance at the purse on my bed then back to the letter on the top of the desk where I'm sitting. I grab my laptop from the right side of the desk and lay it on top of the letter as I log into Twitter, my fake Twitter account, and I get an idea. I've never actually tweeted from this account. This is the account where I follow celebrities and authors I like. Today, I'll send out my first tweet.

burninbushytail: just finished writing my suicide letter.

I almost don't hit send, but then I realize I don't fucking care. If no one responds, I'll just delete the tweet and kill myself.

crushedeyes: @burninbushytail You can't die today because today's your lucky day.

burninbushytail: @crushedeyes Why is it my lucky day? Did I win a new car?
crushedeyes: @burninbushytail Better. I'm going to share a quote with you from a very special book. Do you like books?
burninbushytail: @crushedeyes I love books.
crushedeyes: @burninbushytail So do I. This is from my favorite book.
burninbushytail: @crushedeyes Waiting . . .
crushedeyes: @burninbushytail This black box is yours to keep, to stash your troubles away. Just lock it up and call my name and I'll be there always.
burninbushytail: @crushedeyes what's a black box?
crushedeyes: @burninbushytail Can't tell you, but I can give you a hint. We all have one, but it breaks easily.

The first thing that comes to mind is a heart and this instantly brings tears to my eyes. *This black box is yours to keep, to stash your troubles away.*

burninbushytail: @crushedeyes What's the book about?
crushedeyes: @burninbushytail Can't tell you that either.
burninbushytail: @crushedeyes Not even a hint? Does it have a happy ending?
crushedeyes: @burninbushytail Someone wise once

told me that not all books have happy endings, but that doesn't mean . . .
crushedeyes: @burninbushytail . . . they're not worth the read. Same person also told me you should never spoil the ending of a great story.

I get a strange feeling he's no longer talking about the ending to the story in a book. And suddenly I'm desperate to know more about this book, as if knowing the ending will give me some clue as to how *my* story ends.

burninbushytail: @crushedeyes Just one hint. Please?
crushedeyes: @burninbushytail OK. . . spoiler alert: Everything is going to be okay.

I open the top drawer of my desk and grab a small packet of tissues from the pile of junk I dumped in there the last time I cleaned out my purse. I take a moment to compose myself before I respond.

burninbushytail: @crushedeyes What's your name?

There's a long pause and I begin to think he's gone.

crushedeyes: @burninbushytail You can call me Jordan.

burninbushytail: @crushedeyes Is that your real name?

crushedeyes: @burninbushytail No, but I used to know a Jordan who was almost as cool as you.

burninbushytail: @crushedeyes Don't you want to know my name?

crushedeyes: @burninbushytail Can we make a deal?

Now I pause for a moment to wipe away more tears as I realize this person who doesn't even know me cared enough to respond to my cry for help.

burninbushytail: @crushedeyes What kind of deal?

crushedeyes: @burninbushytail If we ever meet in person, we'll tell each other our names.

burninbushytail: @crushedeyes How are we going to meet in person if we don't know each other?

crushedeyes: @burninbushytail We met here tonight and you probably didn't think that was possible until five minutes ago. Think about it.

burninbushytail: @crushedeyes But how will we recognize each other?

crushedeyes: @burninbushytail Judging by your profile pic, I'm thinking I'll recognize a girl with a giant bunny head resting on her shoulders.

I glance at his profile pic, which I hadn't noticed until now, and laugh out loud. It's a large glass full of crushed ice.

burninbushytail: @crushedeyes I guess I'll recognize you when

The knock at the door makes me slam my laptop shut. I turn around in my desk chair and shout, 'Who's there?'

'It's me,' my mom calls back to me. 'Can I come in?'

My eyes flit back to my laptop and my heart pounds as I realize I have to delete all those tweets. I yank the suicide letter out from underneath the laptop and crumple it up. Then I stuff it into the bottom of my waste bin before I head for the door. When I open the door, my mom is smiling and her hands are tucked behind her back. But her smile disappears when she sees my face.

'Have you been crying?'

'I'm fine. What do you have behind your back?'

'I brought you something from Aunt Crystal's house.' She brings her hands forward, revealing a plate of Aunt Crystal's homemade chocolate-chip muffins. 'Want one?'

My stomach gurgles at the sight of the muffins. It's past six in the evening and I haven't eaten anything all day. Aunt Crystal always makes these just for me and my mom picks them up on her way home from work.

As I reach for a muffin, I think of the mysterious guy who just saved my life on Twitter. Then I look into my mom's worried eyes and the tears come again.

Once you see the good in someone, it's hard not to notice the good in everyone.

'Mom . . . I'm not okay. I need to talk.'

Epilogue

Fifteen years later
Mikki

Sometimes I wonder if my life is real. How is it possible that I'm married to the most perfect man in the world? How is it that I conceived such a perfect, intelligent, healthy son when I was never supposed to have children of my own?

Other times, I wonder how I could possibly deserve such a charmed life when I've almost thrown away that life so many times? The guilt is worse than the disbelief. In times when I doubt whether I deserve the life Crush and I have built together, he always reminds me of everything we endured to get here. And no one deserves it more than us.

I don't know if I believe that, but just knowing that *he* believes it always makes me feel better.

The hotel in Sydney is nicer than I expected. I don't know if I expected the room to be crawling with poisonous spiders and crocodiles. All I know is that Crush never ceases to impress me. Even when I think I'm bored with the usual routine, he continues to show me that the most amazingly, ridiculously beautiful moments await me on the other side of every lull.

Ty hands me the bottle of pills from the nightstand and a glass of water as he sits on the edge of the hotel bed. He's only eleven, but he has his father's vibrant green eyes and patient temperament. He's my BFF #2, as I like to call him. He pretends to hate it.

I sit up in bed and take the bottle of pills from him first. Dumping out a few supplements, I'm happy to report that I am still off psych meds. There were a few touchy years, while I was finishing college and after Ty was born, where I was on and off the synthetics. But I've been off psych meds for more than eight years now.

And, more importantly, it doesn't look like Ty took after me. He had a pretty high shot at having bipolar disorder, with me as a mom and Crush's family history. But my Ty is perfect. Even if he does develop the demon, I will never let it drown him. And Crush can always be counted on to bring light where the blackness prevails.

'Dad said he's going to be back in two hours. Should you take a shower?'

I sigh as I reach up and brush his hair off his forehead. My Ty is always careful to say 'should you' instead of 'you should.'

'Yep,' I reply, taking the glass of water from him so I can swallow my supplements. 'I'll shower right now, then we'll head out of here. Order us some breakfast.'

'Dad already did.'

'Muffins?' He smiles and I shake my head. 'Go get dressed. I'll be right out.'

'Are you going to tell me *now*?'

I smile at this question he's asked me at least five times since we arrived in Sydney. 'I'll tell you tonight.'

I linger a bit in the shower as I mentally prepare myself to go out into a brand new city and talk to strangers. My baby Ty doesn't know anything about the things Crush and I had to go through to find each other. For some reason, I always think about this in the shower. It's my place to remember.

I dress quickly and pull on a hoodie and jeans. Old habits die hard and Sydney, Australia is pretty cold at the end of July. Besides, if I put on something fancy, Crush will suspect something is up. And today's surprise is all for him.

Crush turns thirty-seven today. I wanted to surprise him two years ago for his thirty-fifth birthday, but Ty wasn't ready. Fifteen and a half years together seemed like a good enough milestone to wait for.

Fifteen and a half years. Just thinking about that brings tears to my eyes. The man deserves a quadrillion medals for putting up with me for that long. For saving me over and over again.

After our stay at the Park Plaza Hotel fifteen years ago, I attempted suicide once more. Ty was two weeks old. I was obsessed with the surrogate mother's post-partum symptoms. Calling her at least three times a day to see how she was feeling. Just to torture myself. To remind myself of the pain and sadness I would never feel. How sick is that? To long for pain and sadness.

Eventually, I stopped calling her altogether. I knew I was behaving like a crazy person. And I wrote a note to Crush about how Ty was still young enough to bond with a new mother. A better mother.

Luckily, my lack of phone calls alerted the surrogate mother and she contacted Crush. He found me in the hotel room where I had charged my one-night-stay on our credit card. Breaking down doors had become a regular thing for Crush at that point.

He hasn't broken down a single door for at least ten years.

I grab Ty's jacket off the sofa and hold it up for him. He slips his arms into the sleeves and I wrap my arms around his shoulders, shaking him a little as I hug him from behind. He chuckles, humoring me for a bit as I get my Ty fix.

'I'm so proud of you,' I murmur in his ear. He smiles that bashful smile that reminds me so much of his father. 'Okay, okay.' I let him go and we head out of the hotel minutes before Crush is due back.

We set off to the hotel lobby to wait for our taxi. The note I left for Crush on the hotel bed says that Ty and I will be waiting for him at the restaurant we planned to go to for lunch. It doesn't say that Crush will actually find another note at that restaurant directing him to go to The Basement, a classic jazz club in Sydney. Ty and I have planned a surprise celebration for Crush for his birthday.

Crush is not big on surprises. His sister Harlow and I threw him a surprise birthday party for his twenty-fifth birthday. The whole night he kept pulling me aside and asking when the party would be over so he could have his real birthday present. It took Crush about three years to tear down my walls brick by brick until, finally, sex became as pleasurable for me as it was for him. Well, maybe more so.

Even now, after fifteen years together, there's no one I'd rather fantasize about than Crush. Not only does he make me feel safe, but he makes me feel like a whole woman. I'm alive and sensual and unburdened when Crush and I make love.

Just last night, as he moved in and out of me, his thrusts in time with the rhythm of my gasps, I had an odd thought. Crush moves his hips the way he plays piano. At times languid and effortless and other times frenzied and feverish, but always methodical and musical. Always with my pleasure and safety in mind.

The taxi pulls up in front of the hotel. Ty and I rush outside to bypass the cold. For many years after Crush and I met for the third time in Terminal B, cab rides in the winter always reminded me of the time we made out in the back of a cab after he sang 'Black Box' for me at Wally's Cafe.

It took me more than a year to convince Crush to record the 'Black Box' demo after that night. But he sent it to a few producers and he released his *Black Box* album almost exactly two years to the day after we met in Terminal B. Crush's need to be near me hurt his musical career – a career he said he never really wanted. So I didn't press him to continue down that path. You have to trust that the people you love know what they need better than you do. Because there's nothing more important in a healthy relationship than trust. And I've learned to trust Crush more than I trust myself.

Fifteen years ago, he promised he'd never hurt me. And he never has.

When we arrive at The Basement, the manager, Lou, shows us how the piano has been set up. Lou takes us on a tour of the club and we meet Jessie, the caterer. Jessie shows us how the banquet has been set up on the second floor, leaving the first floor for everyone to watch the show. By the time my phone rings at two p.m., both Ty and I are looking pretty anxious.

'Hello?' I say as casually as possible.

'Baby, I went to the restaurant and they told me to go to some club called The Basement. Did you change the reservation? Is Ty with you?'

I smile at Ty and squeeze his shoulder so he knows it's his dad and everything is okay. 'Yeah, I changed the reservation. Ty and I thought you might like this place better. It is *your* birthday.'

Ty is staring off into the distance, probably trying to

stay calm as he anticipates tonight's performance. I kiss the top of his head and he flashes me a nervous smile.

'You're planning some kind of surprise. You know I don't like surprises.'

'Just get over here. We're starving.'

He laughs as we say our goodbyes. I end the call and tuck my phone into my back pocket. Then I grab Ty's face and force him to look at me.

'Listen, sweetie. You don't have to do it if you don't want to.'

'I want to,' he replies immediately, then he lowers his gaze. 'I'm just scared. Do you think anyone will laugh?'

'Laugh? Are you kidding me? No one is going to laugh. And if they do, what do you think your dad will do to them?' He laughs at this suggestion. 'Don't you worry about a thing. You're going to do great. You always do.'

He nods and sits down on a chair so he can play a game on his phone. I plant a loud kiss on his cheek then sit in the chair next to him. Looking around the club, I take deep breaths to try to quell my tension. My stomach is a tight ball of anxiety. I think I'm more nervous for Ty than he is.

Ty and I have kept this surprise a secret for almost three years. That's a long time to keep a secret from someone with eyes as dreamy as Crush's. He's suspected we were up to something almost from the start. It's hard to hide something of this magnitude from someone you live with. Someone as smart as Mr Harvard.

But we did it. I worked every bit of preparation around Crush's schedule. It helps that Ty's teachers are very flexible with him. He goes to a new progressive private school that encourages children to excel at what they are naturally good at, rather than pushing the same standards on all children. Ty is in a class with children aged eight to thirteen. All of them excel in the arts. It's like a think tank for young artists. Young *brilliant* artists.

Ty has tested in the top one percentile of his class in language, science, and math. But music is his passion. Naturally.

Crush began teaching in the music department at Harvard when Ty was two years old. He began teaching Ty the piano that same day. His music teachers have used the word *virtuoso* to describe him. Ty knows what that means and he rejects the title. He likes Crush's nickname for him much better: Ty the Piano Slayer.

A few minutes later, Lou comes by to let us know he'll be letting people into the club now. Lou is a skinny gentleman with a pointy nose and fleshy jowls that hang a little too loosely. His silver comb-over is a bit messy and he smells a little of whiskey, but he's been extremely kind and helpful with setting up this surprise since I contacted him five months ago.

Lou sets off toward the entrance to let in the crowd outside who've been promised a special performance. Ty and I decide to hang out near a small side stage where the brass players are setting up. I hold his hand, giving it a squeeze every now and then. He looks around as people enter the club and take seats at the many tables set up on the floor all the way up to the piano.

Normally, the tables are set back a bit so people can stand right next to the stage. But today's concert is going to be a bit different. A bit more intimate. And I didn't want the crowd standing next to the stage with their grabby hands and desperate eyes scaring my baby.

Once almost all the tables are full, I squeeze Ty's shoulder and he looks up. 'Are you ready?'

He nods and I lead him up onto the stage. He sits on the piano bench and I help him adjust it so he can reach the pedals. He sits up straight and hits middle C. The sound is full and vibrant as it echoes through the club. A few people cheer at this single note. This makes Ty smile and I press my lips together to keep from crying.

Blinking back tears, I kiss Ty on the cheek and whisper in his ear, 'Slay 'em.'

I speak briefly with the videographer, then I set off for the small area near the brass players where I'll be just a few feet away if Ty should need me. I don't know what he would need me for. But that doesn't matter. I just want him to know exactly where I am.

I glance at the entrance as a few stragglers make it in. Crush should be here any minute.

As soon as I think this, he walks into the club with

a confused expression on his face. It's the first time I've seen him today. He's wearing a black hoodie and jeans on his birthday. Standard Crush attire. And he looks beautiful.

I wave at him across the sea of tables and people. He squints at me, then his eyes dart to the stage. His jaw drops when he sees Ty at the piano. I look at Ty and he's looking straight at me, waiting for the sign. I nod and he begins.

The first few notes of Chopin's 'Nocturne Op. 9 No. 2' in E-flat major play and my throat closes. The crowd is completely silent as the adagio melody eases into the second bar. And just as the notes come more fortissimo, he transitions so smoothly into 'In a Sentimental Mood' by Art Tatum. The crowd, who've all come to hear a jazz virtuoso, clap loudly. But I'm glad that they reserve any loud cheering. This is Ty's first show for anyone other than the parents who attend the academy recitals. I don't want him to freak out.

Crush appears at my side as the song transitions into 'Black Box.' He laces his fingers through mine and lays a soft kiss on the back of my hand, his eyes locked on his son. As Ty sings the first line, I can see the muscle in Crush's jaw twitching as he tries not to cry.

He shakes his head as he watches Ty sing the song he wrote for me more than fifteen years ago. I turn back to watch my baby, wiping tears as his voice cracks slightly on the chorus. I knew he would do well. I've watched him perform this medley a hundred times, and I've cried a hundred times. He has his father's voice. I've seen videos of little William Slayer singing at recitals as a boy. It's easy to see all the things Ty inherited from Crush. But there's another thing he inherited from Crush that is not entirely obvious.

His heart.

Only a boy with a heart the size of Ty's would work as many long hours as he has to make his father this happy. To make me this happy.

Ty finishes the medley with a bluesy version of Elvis's 'Can't Help Falling in Love' and the crowd goes absolutely ballistic. Crush whistles and shouts at the stage, 'Yeah! That's my boy!' Ty stands from the piano bench and gazes out at the crowd. He seems a bit blinded by the lights and more than a little shocked at the reaction. He looks to his left and finds Crush and me. His face lights up when he sees his dad and Crush pulls me up onto the stage with him.

Ty bends over and says, 'Happy birthday, dad,' into the microphone just as Crush reaches him and lifts him into a monster bear hug. The sound of Ty's laughter is musical. I come behind him and ruffle his hair until his dad sets him down. Then I give him a big hug and a loud kiss on the cheek.

'You did so good, baby,' I whisper in his ear.

'I slayed 'em?'

I nod vigorously. 'Absolutely.'

Another band takes over as Crush and I take Ty up to the second floor to get him some food. Once he's seated at a table with his plate, Crush pulls me aside into a small corridor.

His nose is inches from mine as he holds my waist and presses me against the wall. 'I don't know how you planned this without me knowing, but I fucking love you.'

'I know.' I reach up to caress his scruffy cheek and he nuzzles his face into my hand.

'I had a terrible thought last night while we were lying in bed. I wasn't going to tell you about it, but now I have to.'

'What is it?'

He heaves a deep sigh as he gazes into my eyes. 'Do you think . . . Do you think Jordan died so that we could have Ty?'

I shake my head. 'No. I don't think so.'

'But I probably never would have gone on Twitter that day if it weren't for the trial.'

I grab his face and look him in the eye. 'Jordan died because he wanted to. I've already told you this. He didn't die so you and I could be together. And he certainly didn't die so we could have Ty. Jordan wanted to die and you were not prepared to deal with that at the age of sixteen. When you were older . . . when you met me, you knew better.'

I hold him tightly and he hugs me back so hard I can barely breathe. Over the years, Crush has seen many therapists to deal with his guilt over Jordan's death. But no amount of talking seems to lighten the burden.

I just keep hoping that one day he'll understand what an impossible position he was in the night Jordan died.

'Happy birthday, baby,' I whisper in his ear.

He grunts as he squeezes me even tighter. 'When is this party going to be over so I can get my real present?'

He kisses me slowly; the kind of kiss that gets my heart racing. He pulls his lips away reluctantly, but he softly brushes the tip of his nose over mine as I breathe in each breath he exhales. We stay like this for a while, lost in the intensity of the moment. Then he plants a soft kiss on my lips and tilts his head back.

'This will all be over very soon,' I whisper. 'I just have one more surprise for Ty.'

A few hours later, after Crush has met Lou and some of the regulars and we've all gorged ourselves on cake and ale, the three of us drag ourselves into the back of a taxi. We arrive at Darling Harbour minutes later, where we walk off the food.

Ty gives me the usual '*oh, man*' when I take out my camera. And I capture at least two dozen shots of the sun setting over the harbor. I still write poetry, but I've never published anything. I took a photography class at Boston University my junior year, and I was hooked when I realized a camera could create poetry with light and shadow.

No bleeding onto the page required.

At nine p.m., we find a place to stand where we have a good view of the harbor. Then the music begins. It's dramatic as three glowing balls of fire materialize in the water. Right in the middle of the harbor, the flames dance and the glow sparkles on the water as the dramatic music fades away. Then fireballs shoot out of the flames and into the sky. They explode into dazzling fireworks and Ty gasps.

I stand behind him, my arms wrapped around his shoulders. Crush crouches next to him, answering his pyrotechnical questions in typical Harvard professor fashion. The air is filled with the scent of smoke and seawater. And I don't think I could have imagined a more magical end to our first day in Sydney.

When the show ends, Ty turns around in my arms and looks up at me with a deviously hopeful look in his eyes. 'Can you tell me now, Mom?'

Crush looks at me. 'Tell him what?'

I smile as I grab Ty's hand. 'Ty practiced a very long time for that performance today without knowing how much those songs mean to you.' I look at Crush as we walk and he looks a bit confused. 'He promised he'd keep your birthday surprise a secret, and, in turn, I promised to tell him how we met.'

Crush smiles and shakes his head. 'I wondered how that question hadn't come up yet.'

'Can you tell me, Dad?' Ty asks.

I feel a twinge of guilt for not telling him sooner. But I knew Ty would appreciate the story much more once he saw his father's reaction to his performance. Once he knew how our love grew as much from music as from tragedy.

Crush is silent for a moment, and I begin to wonder if maybe this topic has upset him. Then he nods his head and looks down at Ty as he begins.

'Your mom and I met during a storm that had lasted almost four years.'

Black Box Playlist

Chapter One
'Feels Like the End' by Mikky Ekko

Chapter Two
'Tomorrow Will Be Kinder' by The Secret Sisters
'Take You Higher' by Goodwill & Hook N Sling

Chapter Three
'Boston' by Augustana

Chapter Four
'I'm In Here' by Sia

Chapter Six
'Breathe Me' by Sia

Chapter Eight
'Feel It All' by KT Tunstall

Chapter Twelve
'Nothin' On You' by B.o.B feat. Bruno Mars

Chapter Thirteen
'Nocturne In E Flat Major' by Frederic Chopin

Chapter Nineteen
'Now Is Not The Time' by Chvrches

Chapter Twenty-Three
'Us' by Regina Spektor

Chapter Twenty-Nine
'Silk' by Giselle

Chapter Thirty-Two
'Feeling Good' by Nina Simone

Chapter Thirty-Three
'Hold You In My Arms' by Ray LaMontagne

Chapter Thirty-Four
'The Beacon' by A Fine Frenzy

Chapter Thirty-Five
'Shelter' by Birdy
'In A Sentimental Mood' by Art Tatum

Chapter Thirty-Seven
'Let It Be Me' by Ray LaMontagne

Chapter Forty
'Eye Of Your Storm' by Kyler England

Chapter Forty-One
'Can't Help Falling Love' by Ingrid Michaelson

Chapter Forty-Two
'The Way I Am' by Ingrid Michaelson

Chapter Forty-Three
'Clair De Lune' by Flight Facilities feat. Christine Hoberg

Chapter Forty-Four
'Those Eyes' by Feint

Chapter Forty-Six
'Tourist' by Yuna

Chapter Forty-Nine
'Now My Feet Won't Touch The Ground' by Coldplay

Listen to the playlist on YouTube.
Listen to the playlist on Spotify.

Author's Note

If you or someone you know needs assistance or
information about sexual assault or abuse,
please contact the Rape and Incest National Network
(RAINN) at www.rainn.org or
call 1-800-656-HOPE. Or, if you are in the UK,
contact the Rape Crisis Centre at
www.rapecrisis.org.uk or call 0808 802 9999.

For your local suicide hotline number, please visit
www.suicidehotlines.com or
www.suicidepreventionlifeline.com. If you or
someone you know has contemplated suicide, please
call 1-800-273-TALK.
You can also visit www.samaritans.org.

Acknowledgements

I always feel like I'm writing a Grammy acceptance speech when I write the acknowledgments in a book. I guess in a way a book is a bit like a piece of music. And I have so many collaborators to thank this time around.

My beta readers: Jordana Rodriguez, Kristin Shaw, Paula Jackman, Sam Stettner, Sarah Arndt, Cathy Archer, Carrie Raasch, Jodie Stipetich, Jennifer Mirabelli, Haley Douglas, Vilma Gonzalez, and Deborah Meissner. This is a group of people who endure my mood swings, my doubts, my never-ending typos, and my crazy deadlines, and they do it with such love and commitment to me and to the written word. Words cannot express how much I appreciate every ounce of feedback and laughter you all have provided.

Sarah Hansen. I am so grateful that you didn't chuck me out a window when I told you to throw out the first cover you did for *Black Box* and start over. But aren't you glad you didn't? This is one of my favorite covers of all time for all the small touches you put into it that made it so absolutely perfect for this book and these characters. Thank you from the bottom of my heart.

Thank you to Lauren Abramo for your sage advice.

To my editor, Harriet Bourton. Thank you for your enthusiasm and for working with my original timeline.

Thank you and congratulations to Cassie Hoffman for winning the *Black Box* Character Name Contest. Hope you're enjoying your new claim to fame as Crush's ex-girlfriend.

Thank you to the incomparable Mimi Strong for being one of the most awesome human beings I've ever known and for all the midnight chats about my 'clichéd author feelings.'

Thank you to all the bloggers who shared the *Black Box* cover reveal and preorder links and those who participated in the blog tour and release celebration. I didn't know what the heck a blog tour was a few years ago, and now I see how much work goes into it and I stand in awe of the folks who organize them. I'm looking at you Holly Malgieri. Thank you for being so amazing and for making me feel like I never have to stress. Your hair is pure devil, but your devotion to books is all angel.

To the readers who have reached out to me and not only shared their excitement for the release of *Black Box*, but have shared their personal stories and experiences with mental illness. That's the kind of stuff that keeps me going on the days when I doubt myself. Please never stop sharing your stories with me and I'll never stop sharing my stories with you.

A huge thank-you to the city of Boston for providing a magical backdrop for a heart-rending story. I apologize if I may have twisted the facts to suit my fictional world.

To the people I interviewed while researching *Black Box*, there are really no words to convey my gratitude to you. You shared some of the most painful moments of your lives and I will always cherish the trust you placed in me to bring those experiences to life on the page.

To my mother, who taught me how to care.

To my daughter, who taught me how to listen.

Other books by Cassia Leo

Relentless **(New Adult Romance)**
Shattered Hearts #1

Pieces of You **(New Adult Romance)**
Shattered Hearts #2

Bring Me Home **(New Adult Romance)**
Shattered Hearts #3

Abandon
(a spin-off of the Shattered Hearts Series)

LUKE Series **(Erotic Romance)**
CHASE Series **(Erotic Romance)**

Now you can also read the gritty spin-off of the *Shattered Hearts* series featuring mysterious, sexy Tristan as he attempts to abandon his demons in the name of love . . .

ABANDON

A steady stream of meaningless sex is all Tristan has left when he discovers the grandmother who raised him is dying and his best friend is getting married. He is lost; and the dark secrets in his past keep coming back to remind him of this.

Until Tristan has an idea that will change his life and fulfill his dying grandmother's wishes: Abandon his playboy ways and settle down. And who better to do it with than Senia, the girl who makes him laugh and feel like a kid again.

But when his world begins to crumble around him, the pain Tristan is hiding finds its way to the surface. Will he finally learn to trust again? Or will he abandon his chance at love?

Have you discovered Cassia Leo's addictive *Shattered Hearts* series yet?

RELENTLESS

Claire Nixon is a twenty-year-old college dropout with a secret she'll never tell. Then she meets sexy Adam Parker and suddenly her past seems like a distant memory . . . until the love of her life Chris reappears on her doorstep and she is forced to make the biggest decision of her life.

PIECES OF YOU

Claire's ex, rock star Chris Knight, is back in her life and he is refusing to leave until he has her back. How will she choose between taking a chance on new love with sexy Adam Parker, or a second chance at having a family and a home with Chris?

BRING ME HOME

With Adam's former girlfriend in the picture, Claire finds herself torn between her past love and her present. Both men own a piece of her heart, and one of them will get hurt no matter what she decides . . .

Get Involved!

RATE IT: If you enjoyed this book, please consider leaving a review wherever you purchased it or Goodreads.

DISCUSS IT: Discuss the books with us on Facebook.

JOIN US: Follow Cassia on Facebook and Twitter. Sign up for email updates on Cassia's blog or become part of her street team to get inside information on new releases, exclusive street team giveaways, and more.

Page
TURNERS
• TRANSWORLD •